A GLADIATOR
DIES ONLY
ONCE

ALSO BY STEVEN SAYLOR

A Twist at the End: A Novel of O. Henry

Have You Seen Dawn?

ROMA SUB ROSA

Consisting of

Roman Blood

The House of the Vestals

Arms of Nemesis

Catilina's Riddle

The Venus Throw

A Murder on the Appian Way

Rubicon

Last Seen in Massilia

A Mist of Prophecies

The Judgment of Caesar

STEVEN SAYLOR

A GLADIATOR DIES ONLY ONCE

THE FURTHER INVESTIGATIONS
OF GORDIANUS THE FINDER

ST. MARTIN'S MINOTAUR
NEW YORK

www.minotaurbooks.com

"The White Fawn" first appeared in *Classical Whodunnits*, edited by Mike Ashley, Robinson (London), 1996, and Carroll & Graf (U.S.), 1997; first publication, *EQMM*, December 1996. "Archimedes's Tomb" first appeared in *Crime Through Time*, edited by Miriam Grace Monfredo and Sharan Newman, Berkley, 1997. "Poppy and the Poisoned Cake" first appeared in *EQMM*, December 1998. "Death by Eros" first appeared in *Yesterday's Blood: An Ellis Peters Memorial Anthology*, edited by Maxim Jakubowski, Headline (London), December 1998; first U.S. publication *EQMM*, August 1999. "The Consul's Wife" first appeared in *Crime Through Time III*, edited by Sharan Newman, Berkley, 2000. "If a Cyclops Could Vanish in the Blink of an Eye" first appeared in *Candis* (UK), September 2002; first U.S. publication, *EQMM*, August 2003. "A Gladiator Dies Only Once" first appeared in *The Mammoth Book of Ancient Roman Whodunnits*, edited by Mike Ashley, Constable & Robinson (London), August 2003, and Carroll & Graf (U.S.), November 2003. "Something Fishy in Pompeii" first appeared in *Candis* (UK), July 2003; first U.S. publication, *EQMM*, March/April 2004. "The Cherries of Lucullus" first appeared in *EQMM*, May 2005.

LIBRARY OF CONGRESS CATALOGING-IN-PUBLICATION DATA

Saylor, Steven, 1956–
    A gladiator dies only once : the further investigations of Gordianus the
Finder / Steven Saylor.
        p. cm.
    ISBN-13: 978-0-312-35744-3
    ISBN-10: 0-312-35744-3
    1. Gordianus the Finder (Fictitious character)—Fiction.   2. Rome—
History—Republic, 265–30 B.C.—Fiction.   3. Private investigators—Rome—
Fiction.   4. Detective and mystery stories, American.   5. Historical fiction,
American.   I. Title.

PS3569.A96G57 2005
813'.54—dc22

                                                                            2004065828

First St. Martin's Minotaur Paperback Edition: June 2006

10   9   8   7   6   5   4   3   2   1

To Rick,
who read them first

Contents

Natura inest in mentibus nostris insatiabilis quaedam cupiditas veri videndi.

(Nature has planted in our minds an insatiable longing to see the truth.)

MARCUS TULLIUS CICERO
Tusculan Disputations

PREFACE

Gordianus the Finder, detective of ancient Rome, was introduced in a novel called *Roman Blood*, first published in 1991.

Over the course of the eight subsequent novels and eighteen short stories of the Roma Sub Rosa series, Gordianus has progressed from the age of thirty to the age of sixty-one. His concubine, Bethesda, has become his wife, and his family has expanded to include a daughter, two adopted sons (one born a slave), and four grandchildren ("a typically Roman extended family," as the classicist Mary Beard commented in the *Times Literary Supplement*). He has rubbed elbows with the most famous men and women of his time, including Caesar, Cicero, Marc Antony, Pompey, Crassus, and Cleopatra. He has taken part (usually behind the scenes) in many of the most important events of his era, witnessing the final decades of the Roman Republic as it disintegrates into the civil wars that ultimately will give rise to the empire of the Caesars.

Through it all, Gordianus's adventures and investigations have been followed by readers in fifteen languages, and a fair number of these readers (thanks to the invention of e-mail) have seen fit to contact his creator with comments, questions, words of encouragement, and notification of the occasional typographical error.

The first nine short stories about Gordianus (all of which take place in the eight-year period between the first two novels, *Roman Blood* and *Arms of Nemesis*) were assembled in a collection titled *The House of the Vestals*. Since that book was published, nine more short stories have been written; readers will find them collected in these pages. Like the stories in *The House of the Vestals,* all these tales take place early in Gordianus's career. Often at his side, rapidly growing up, is Eco, the mute boy he met in *Roman Blood*. Also here is Bethesda, Gordianus's Jewish-Egyptian concubine, who eventually becomes his wife. Frequently conferring with Gordianus is his good friend and patron, Lucius Claudius. Cicero, the great lion of the Roman law courts, makes several appearances. Sertorius, the rebel general who set up a rival Roman state in Spain, casts a shadow across the book's beginning and end, and makes an appearance in "The White Fawn." Two towering figures of the late Republic who have figured very little in the novels, Lucullus and Cato, appear in the collection's final story.

One of the joys of writing the Gordianus short stories is the chance to explore various aspects of Roman life and history which simply have not come up in the novels. In these pages, readers will learn about gladiator combats, chariot racing, and the role of the Roman censor, as well as some curious facts regarding food—the making of garum (the fish-pickle sauce essential to Roman cuisine), the origin of Cicero's famous epigram about a piece of cake, and the first appearance of cherries in Rome. (Regarding this last, somewhat touchy subject, see more details in the historical notes at the end of the book.)

The setting of most of the stories is the teeming, beautiful, endlessly fascinating, endlessly wicked city of Rome, but Gordianus's investigations also take him to Spain, Sicily, the Bay of Naples, and across the breadth of Italy.

The stories are presented in chronological order. At the back of the book, readers will find a detailed chronology, which incorporates all the short stories and novels, along with some notes on historical sources.

Why "Roma Sub Rosa" for the collective series title of the Gordianus novels and stories? In ancient Egypt, the rose was the emblem of the god Horus, later regarded by the Greeks and Romans as the god of silence. Customarily, a rose hanging over a council table indicated that all present were sworn to secrecy. "Sub rosa" (literally, "under the rose") has come to mean "that which is carried out in secret." Thus "Roma Sub Rosa": a history of Rome's secrets, or a secret history of Rome, as seen through the eyes of Gordianus.

A GLADIATOR
DIES ONLY
ONCE

THE CONSUL'S WIFE

"Honestly," muttered Lucius Claudius, his nose buried in a scroll, "if you go by these accounts in the *Daily Acts*, you'd think Sertorius was a naughty schoolboy, and his rebellion in Spain a harmless prank. When will the consuls realize the gravity of the situation? When will they take action?"

I cleared my throat.

Lucius Claudius lowered the little scroll and raised his bushy red eyebrows. "Gordianus! By Hercules, you got here in a hurry! Take a seat."

I looked about for a chair, then remembered where I was. In the garden of Lucius Claudius, visitors did not fetch furniture. Visitors sat, and a chair would be slipped beneath them. I stepped into the spot of sunlight where Lucius sat basking, and folded my knees. Sure enough, a chair caught my weight. I never even saw the attendant slave.

"Something to drink, Gordianus? I myself am enjoying a cup of hot broth. Too early in the day for wine, even watered."

"Noon is hardly early, Lucius. Not for those of us who've been up since dawn."

"Since dawn?" Lucius grimaced at such a distasteful notion. "A cup of wine for you, then? And some nibbles?"

I raised my hand to wave away the offer, and found it filled with a silver cup, into which a pretty slavegirl poured a stream of Falernian wine. A little tripod table appeared at my left hand, bearing a silver platter embossed with images of dancing nymphs and strewn with olives, dates, and almonds.

"Care for a bit of the *Daily*? I'm finished with the sporting news." Lucius nodded toward a clutter of little scrolls on the table beside him. "They say the Whites have finally got their act together this season. New chariots, new horses. Should give the Reds a run for the prizes in tomorrow's races."

I laughed out loud. "What a life you lead, Lucius Claudius. Up at noon, then lolling about your garden reading your own private copy of the *Daily Acts*."

Lucius raised an eyebrow. "Merely sensible, if you ask me. Who wants to elbow through a crowd in the Forum, squinting and peering past strangers to read the *Daily* on the posting boards? Or worse, listen to some clown read the items out loud, inserting his own witty comments."

"But that's the whole point of the *Daily*," I argued. "It's a social activity. People take a break from the hustle and bustle of the Forum, gather round the posting boards and discuss whatever items interest them most—war news, marriages and births, chariot races, curious omens. It's the highlight of many a man's day, perusing the *Daily* and arguing politics or horses with fellow citizens. One of the cosmopolitan pleasures of city life."

Lucius shuddered. "No thank you! My way is better. I send a

couple of slaves down to the Forum an hour before posting time. As soon as the *Daily* goes up, one of them reads it aloud from beginning to end and the other takes dictation with a stylus on wax tablets. Then they hurry home, transcribe the words to parchment, and by the time I'm up and about, my private copy of the *Daily* is here waiting for me in the garden, the ink still drying in the sun. A comfy chair, a sunny spot, a hearty cup of broth, and my own copy of the *Daily Acts*—I tell you, Gordianus, there's no more civilized way to start the day."

I popped an almond into my mouth. "It all seems rather antisocial to me, not to mention extravagant. The cost of parchment alone!"

"Squinting at wax tablets gives me eyestrain." Lucius sipped his broth. "Anyway, I didn't ask you here to critique my personal pleasures, Gordianus. There's something in the *Daily* that I want you to see."

"What, the news about that rebellious Roman general terrorizing Spain?"

"Quintus Sertorius!" Lucius shifted his considerable bulk. "He'll soon have the whole Iberian Peninsula under his control. The natives there hate Rome, but they adore Sertorius. What can our two consuls be thinking, failing to bring military assistance to the provincial government? Decimus Brutus, much as I love the old bookworm, is no fighter, I'll grant you; hard to imagine him leading an expedition. But his fellow consul Lepidus is a military veteran; fought for Sulla in the Civil War. How can those two sit idly on their behinds while Sertorius creates a private kingdom for himself in Spain?"

"All that's in the *Daily Acts*?" I asked.

"Of course not!" Lucius snorted. "Nothing but the official government line: situation under control, no cause for alarm. You'll find more details about the obscene earnings of charioteers than you'll

find about Spain. What else can you expect? The *Daily* is a state organ put out by the government. Deci probably dictates every word of
the war news himself."

"Deci?"

"Decimus Brutus, of course; the consul." With his ancient patrician connections, Lucius tended to be on a first-name basis, sometimes on a pet-name basis, with just about everybody in power. "But
you distract me, Gordianus. I didn't ask you here to talk about Sertorius. Decimus Brutus, yes; Sertorius, no. Here, have a look at *this*."
His bejeweled hand flitted over the pile and plucked a scroll for me
to read.

"Society gossip?" I scanned the items. "A's son engaged to B's
daughter . . . C plays host to D at his country villa . . . E shares her
famous family recipe for egg custard dating back to the days when
Romulus suckled the she-wolf." I grunted. "All very interesting, but
I don't see—"

Lucius leaned forward and tapped at the scroll. "Read *that* part.
Aloud."

" 'The bookworm pokes his head outside tomorrow. Easy prey for
the sparrow, but partridges go hungry. Bright-eyed Sappho says: Be
suspicious! A dagger strikes faster than lightning. Better yet: an arrow. Let Venus conquer all!' "

Lucius sat back and crossed his fleshy arms. "What do you make
of it?"

"I believe it's called a blind item; a bit of gossip conveyed in code.
No proper names, only clues that are meaningless to the uninitiated.
Given the mention of Venus, I imagine this particular item is about
some illicit love affair. I doubt I'd know the names involved even if
they were clearly spelled out. You'd be more likely than I to know
what all this means, Lucius."

"Indeed. I'm afraid I do know, at least in part. That's why I called you here today, Gordianus. I have a dear friend who needs your help."

I raised an eyebrow. Lucius's rich and powerful connections had yielded me lucrative work before; they had also put me in great danger. "What friend would that be, Lucius?"

He raised a finger. The slaves around us silently withdrew into the house. "Discretion, Gordianus. Discretion! Read the item again."

" 'The bookworm—' "

"And whom did I call a bookworm only a moment ago?"

I blinked. "Decimus Brutus, the consul."

Lucius nodded. "Read on."

" 'The bookworm pokes his head outside tomorrow . . .' "

"Deci will venture to the Circus Maximus tomorrow, to watch the races from the consular box."

" 'Easy prey for the sparrow . . .' "

"Draw your own conclusion from that—especially with the mention of daggers and arrows later on!"

I raised an eyebrow. "You think there's a plot against the consul's life, based on a blind item in the *Daily Acts*? It seems far-fetched, Lucius."

"It's not what *I* think. It's what Deci himself thinks. The poor fellow's in a state; came to my house and roused me out of bed an hour ago, desperate for advice. He needs someone to get to the bottom of this, quietly and quickly. I told him I knew just the man: Gordianus the Finder."

"Me?" I scowled at an olive pit between my forefinger and thumb. "Since the *Daily* is a state organ, surely Decimus Brutus himself, as consul, is in the best position to determine where this item came from and what it really means. To start, who wrote it?"

"That's precisely the problem."

"I don't understand."

"Do you see the part about 'Sappho' and her advice?"

"Yes."

"Gordianus, who do you think writes and edits the *Daily Acts*?"

I shrugged. "I never thought about it."

"Then I shall tell you. The consuls themselves dictate the items about politics and foreign policy, giving their own official viewpoint. The drier parts—trade figures, livestock counts and such—are compiled by clerks in the censor's office. Sporting news comes from the magistrates in charge of the Circus Maximus. Augurs edit the stories that come in about weird lightning flashes, comets, curiously shaped vegetables, and other omens. But who do you think oversees the society news—weddings and birth announcements, social engagements, 'blind items,' as you call them?"

"A woman named Sappho?"

"A reference to the poet of ancient Lesbos. The consul's wife is something of a poet herself."

"The wife of Decimus Brutus?"

"She wrote that item." Lucius leaned forward and lowered his voice. "Deci thinks she means to kill him, Gordianus."

"My wife . . ." The consul cleared his throat noisily. He brushed a hand nervously through his silvery hair and paced back and forth across the large study, from one pigeon-hole bookcase to another, his fingers idly brushing the little title tags that hung from the scrolls. Outside the library at Alexandria, I had never seen so many books in one place, not even in Cicero's house.

The consul's house was near the Forum, only a short walk from that of Lucius Claudius. I had been admitted at once; thanks to Lucius, my visit was expected. Decimus Brutus dismissed a cadre of secretaries and ushered me into his private study. He dispensed with formalities. His agitation was obvious.

"My wife . . ." He cleared his throat again. Decimus Brutus, highest magistrate in the land, used to giving campaign speeches in the Forum and orations in the courts, seemed unable to begin.

"She's certainly beautiful," I said, gazing at the portrait that graced one of the few spaces on the wall not covered by bookcases. It was a small picture, done in encaustic wax on wood, yet it dominated the room. A young woman of remarkable beauty gazed out from the picture. Strings of pearls adorned the masses of auburn hair done up with pearl-capped pins atop her head. More pearls hung from her ears and around her throat. The chaste simplicity of her jewelry contrasted with a glint in her green eyes that was challenging, aloof, almost predatory.

Decimus Brutus stepped closer to the painting. He lifted his chin and squinted, drawing so close that his nose practically brushed the wax.

"Beautiful, yes," he murmured. "The artist didn't capture even a fraction of her beauty. I married her for it; for that, and to have a son. Sempronia gave me both, her beauty and a baby boy. And do you know why *she* married *me?*" The consul stepped disconcertingly close and peered at me. With another man, I would have taken such proximate scrutiny as an intimidation, but the myopic consul was merely straining to read my expression.

He sighed. "Sempronia married me for my books. I know, it sounds absurd—a woman who reads!—but there it is: she didn't assent to the marriage until she saw this room, and that made up her mind. She's read every volume here—more than I have! She even writes a bit herself—poetry and such. Her verses are too . . . passionate . . . for my taste."

He cleared his throat again. "Sempronia, you see, is not like other women. Sometimes I think the gods gave her the soul of a man. She reads like a man. She converses like a man. She has her own motley circle of friends—poets, playwrights, dubious women. When Sempronia has them over, the witticisms roll off her tongue. She even appears to think. She has opinions, anyway. Opinions on everything—art, racing, architecture, even politics! And she has no shame. In the company of her little circle, she plays the lute—better than our best-trained slave, I have to admit. And she dances for them." He grimaced. "I told her such behavior was indecent, completely unsuitable for a consul's wife. She says that when she dances, the gods and goddesses speak through her body, and her friends understand what they see, even if I don't. We've had so many rows, I've almost given up rowing about it."

He sighed. "I'll give her this: she's not a bad mother. Sempronia has done a good job raising little Decimus. And despite her youth, her performance of official duties as consul's wife has been impeccable. Nor has she shamed me publicly. She's kept her . . . eccentricities . . . confined to this house. But . . ."

He seemed to run dry. His chin dropped to his chest.

"One of her duties," I prompted him, "is to oversee society news in the *Daily Acts,* is it not?"

He nodded. He squinted for a moment at Sempronia's portrait, then turned his back to it. "Lucius explained to you the cause for my concern?"

"Only in the most discreet fashion."

"Then I shall be explicit. Understand, Finder, the subject is . . . acutely embarrassing. Lucius tells me you can keep your mouth shut. If I'm wrong, if my suspicions are unfounded, I can't have news of my foolishness spread all over the Forum. And if I'm right—if what I suspect is true—I can afford the scandal even less."

"I understand, Consul."

He stepped very close, peered at my face, and seemed satisfied.

"Well, then . . . where to begin? With that damned charioteer, I suppose."

"A charioteer?"

"Diocles. You've heard of him?"

I nodded. "He races for the Reds."

"I wouldn't know. I don't follow the sport. But I'm told that Diocles is quite famous. And rich, richer even than Roscius the actor. Scandalous, that racers and actors should be wealthier than senators nowadays. Our ancestors would be appalled!"

I doubted that my own ancestors would be quite as upset as those of Decimus Brutus, but I nodded and tried to bring him back to the subject. "This Diocles . . ."

"One of my wife's circle of friends. Only . . . closer than a friend."

"A suspicion, Consul? Or do you have sure knowledge?"

"I have eyes in my head!" He seemed to realize the irony of claiming his feeble eyesight as reliable witness, and sighed. "I never caught them in the act, if that's what you mean. I have no proof. But every time she had her circle in this house, lolling about on couches and reciting to each other, the two of them seemed always to end up in a corner by themselves. Whispering . . . laughing . . ." He ground his jaw. "I won't be made a fool of, allowing my wife to sport with her lover under my own roof! I grew so furious the last time he was here, I . . . I made a scene. I chased them all out, and I told Sempronia that Diocles was never again to enter this house. When she protested, I commanded her never to speak with him again. I'm her husband. It's my right to say with whom she can and cannot consort! Sempronia knows that. Why could she not simply defer to my will? Instead she had to argue. She badgered me like a harpy—I never heard such language from a woman! All the more evidence, if I needed any, that her relationship with that man was beyond decency. In the end, I banned her entire circle of friends, and I ordered Sempronia not to leave the house, even for official obligations. When her duties call, she simply has to say, 'The consul's wife regrets that illness prevents her.' It's been like that for almost a month now. The tension in this house . . .'"

"But she does have one official duty left."

"Yes, her dictation of society items for the *Daily Acts*. She needn't leave the house for that. Senators' wives come calling—*respectable* visitors are still welcome—and they give her all the tidbits she needs. If you ask me, the society section is terribly tedious, even more so than the sporting news. I give it no more than a quick glance to see if family are mentioned, and their names spelled correctly. Sempronia knows that. That's why she thought she could send her little message to Diocles through the *Daily Acts*, undetected."

He glanced at the portrait and worked his jaw back and forth. "It was the word 'bookworm' that caught my eye. When we were first married, that was the pet name she gave me: 'My old bookworm.' I suppose she calls me that behind my back now, laughing and joking with the likes of that charioteer!"

"And 'Sappho'?"

"Her friends call her that sometimes."

"Why do you assume the blind item is addressed to Diocles?"

"Despite my lack of interest in racing, I do know a thing or two about that particular charioteer—more than I care to! The name of his lead horse is Sparrow. How does the message start? 'The bookworm pokes his head outside tomorrow. Easy prey for the sparrow . . .' Tomorrow I'll be at the Circus Maximus, to make a public appearance at the races."

"And your wife?"

"Sempronia will remain confined to this house. I have no intention of allowing her to publicly ogle Diocles in his chariot!"

"Won't you be surrounded by bodyguards?"

"In the midst of such a throng, who knows what opportunities might arise for some 'accident' to befall me? In the Forum or the Senate House I feel safe, but the Circus Maximus is Diocles's territory. He must know every blind corner, every hiding place. And . . . there's the matter of my eyesight. I'm more vulnerable than other men, and I know it. So does Sempronia. So must Diocles."

"Let me be sure I understand, Consul: You take this item to be a communication between your wife and Diocles, and the subject is a plot on your life . . . but you have no other evidence, and you want me to determine the truth of the matter?"

"I'll make it worth your while."

"Why turn to me, Consul? Surely a man like yourself has agents of his own, a finder he trusts to ferret out the truth about his allies and enemies."

Decimus Brutus nodded haltingly.

"Then why not give this mission to your own finder?"

"I had such a fellow, yes. Called Scorpus. Not long after I banned Diocles from the house, I set Scorpus to find the truth about the charioteer and my wife."

"What did he discover?"

"I don't know. Some days ago, Scorpus went missing."

"Missing?"

"Until yesterday. His body was fished out of the Tiber, downriver from Rome. Not a mark on him. They say he must have fallen in and drowned. Very strange."

"How so?"

"Scorpus was an excellent swimmer."

I left the consul's house with a list of everyone Decimus Brutus could name from his wife's inner circle, and a pouch full of silver. The pouch contained half my fee, the remainder to be paid upon the consul's satisfaction. If his suspicions were correct, and if I failed him, I would never collect. Dead men pay no debts.

For the rest of the day and long into the night, I learned all I could about the consul's wife and the charioteer. My friend Lucius Claudius might move among the rich and powerful, but I had contacts of my own. The best informants on Sempronia's circle of intimates, I decided, would be found at the Senian Baths. Such a close-knit group would visit the baths socially, in couples or groups, the men going to their facility and the women to theirs. Massage and a hot soak loosen the tongue; the absence of the opposite gender engenders even greater candor. What masseurs, masseuses, water bearers, and towel boys fail to overhear is hardly worth knowing.

Were Diocles and Sempronia lovers? Maybe, maybe not. According to my informants at the baths, reporting secondhand the gossip of Sempronia's circle, Diocles was notorious for his sharp tongue, and Sempronia had an ear for cutting remarks; there might be nothing more to their relationship than whispering and laughing in corners. Sempronia chose her friends, male and female alike, because they amused her or pleased her eye or stimulated her intellect. No one considered her a slave to passion; the abandon with which she danced or declaimed her verses was only part of her persona, one small facet of the steel-willed girl who had made herself a consul's wife and had read every volume in the consul's study.

Regarding a plot against the consul, I heard not a whisper. Sempronia's circle resented her confinement and their banishment from the consul's house, but the impression passed on by the bathing attendants was more of amusement than of outrage. Sempronia's friends considered Decimus Brutus a doddering, harmless fool. They playfully wagered among themselves how long it would take Sempronia to bend the old bookworm to her will and resume her social life.

One discovery surprised me. If I were to believe the bathing attendants, Sertorius, the renegade general in Spain, was a far hotter topic of conversation among Sempronia's circle than was the consul, his wife, and the charioteer. Like my friend Lucius Claudius, they believed that Sertorius intended to wrest the Spanish provinces from Rome and make himself a king. Unlike Lucius, Sempronia's friends, within the whispered hush of their own circle, applauded Sertorius and his rebellion.

Decimus Brutus had dismissed his wife's friends as frivolous people, careless of appearances, naive about politics. I tried to imagine the appeal a rebel like Sertorius might hold for such dilettantes. Were they merely infatuated by the bittersweet glamour that emanates from a desperate cause?

From the baths, I moved on to the Circus Maximus, or, more precisely, to the several taverns, brothels, and gambling dens in the vicinity of the racetrack. I paid bribes when I had to, but often I had only to drop the name of Diocles to get an earful. The consensus among the circus crowd was that the charioteer's tastes ran to young athletes, and always had. His current fascination was a Nubian acrobat who performed publicly during the intervals between races, and was thought to perform privately, after the races, in Diocles's bedchamber. Of course, the Nubian might have been only a cover for another, more illicit affair; or Diocles, when it came to his lovers, might have been something of a juggler himself.

If Sempronia's circle was abuzz about Sertorius, the circus crowd, disdainful of politics, was abuzz about the next day's races. I had a nagging sense that some of my informants were hiding something. Amid the horse talk and the rattle of dice, the raucous laughter and the cries of "Venus!" for luck, I sensed an edge of uneasiness, even foreboding. Perhaps it was only a general outbreak of nerves on the night before a racing day. Or perhaps, by then, I had shared too much wine with too many wagging tongues to see things clearly.

Still, it seemed to me that something untoward was afoot at the Circus Maximus.

Cocks were crowing when I left the neighborhood of the circus, trudged across Rome, and dragged myself up the Esquiline Hill. Bethesda was waiting up for me. Her eyes lit up at the sight of the pouch of silver, somewhat depleted by expenditures, which she eagerly snatched from my hands and deposited in the empty household coffer.

A few hours later, my head aching from too much wine and too little sleep, I found myself back in the consul's study. I had agreed to arrive at his house an hour before the first race to deliver my report, such as it was.

I told him all I had learned. The secondhand gossip of bathing attendants and tavern drunks seemed trivial as I recounted it, but Decimus Brutus listened in silence and nodded gravely when I was done. He squinted at the portrait of his wife.

"Nothing, then! Scorpus is drowned, and the Finder finds nothing. Have you outsmarted me after all, Sempronia?"

The portrait made no reply.

"I'm not done yet, Consul," I told him. "I shall attend the races today. I'll keep my eyes and ears open. I may yet—"

"Yes, yes, as you wish." Decimus Brutus vaguely waved his hand to dismiss me, never taking his furiously squinting eyes from the image of Sempronia.

A slave escorted me from the consul's study. In the atrium, a small retinue crossed our path. We paused as the train of women flitted past, escorting their mistress from one part of the house to another. I peered into their midst and glimpsed a wealth of auburn hair set with pearls. Green eyes met mine and stared back. Hands clapped, and the retinue came to a halt.

Sempronia stepped forward. Decimus Brutus had been correct: the picture did not do her beauty justice. She was taller than I expected. Even through the bulky drapery of her stola, her figure suggested a lithesome elegance that carried through to the delicacy of her long hands and graceful neck. She flashed the aloof, challenging smile which her portraitist had captured so well.

"You're new. One of my husband's men?" she said.

"I . . . had business with the consul," I said.

She looked me up and down. "There are circles under your eyes. You look as if you were out all night. Sometimes men get into trouble, staying up late . . . poking their noses where they shouldn't."

There was a glint in her eye. Was she baiting me? I should have kept my mouth shut, but I didn't. "Like Scorpus? I hear he got into trouble."

She pretended to look puzzled. "Scorpus? Oh, yes, my husband's all-purpose sneak. Scorpus drowned."

"I know."

"Odd. He could swim like a dolphin."

"So I heard."

"It could happen to anyone." She sighed. Her smile faded. I saw a glimmer of sympathy in her eyes, and a look that chilled my blood. *Such a pleasant fellow,* her look seemed to say. *What a pity it would be if one had to kill you!*

Sempronia rejoined her retinue, and I was shown to the door.

By the time I reached the Circus Maximus, all Rome seemed to have poured into the long, narrow valley between the Palatine and Aventine Hills. I pushed through the crowds lined up at the food and beverage shops tucked under the stands, stepping on toes and dodging elbows until I came to the entrance I was looking for. Inside the stadium, the seats were already thronged with spectators. Many wore

red or white, or waved little red or white banners to show their affil-
iation. I swept my eyes over the elongated inner oval of the stadium,
dazzled by the crazy patchwork of red and white, like blood spattered
on snow.

Restless and eager for the races to begin, spectators clapped,
stamped their feet, and took up chants and ditties. Cries of "Diocles
in red! Quicker done than said!" competed with "White! White!
Fast as spite!"

A high-pitched voice pierced the din—"Gordianus! Over
here!"—and I located Lucius Claudius. He sat by the aisle, patting
an empty cushion beside him. "Here, Gordianus! I received your
message this morning, and dutifully saved you a seat. Better than last
time, don't you think? Not too high, not too low, with a splendid
view of the finish line."

More important, the consular box was nearby, a little below us
and to our right. As I took my seat, I saw a silvery head emerge from
the box's private entrance. Decimus Brutus and his fellow consul
Lepidus were arriving along with their entourages. He had made it
safely to the circus, at least. Partisan chants were drowned out by
cheers. The two consuls turned and waved to the crowd.

"Poor Deci," said Lucius. "He thinks they're cheering him. The
fact is, they're cheering his arrival, because now the races can begin!"

There was a blare of trumpets and then more cheering as the
grand procession commenced. Statues of the gods and goddesses
were paraded around the racetrack on carts, led by Victory with
wings outspread. As Venus passed—favorite of gamblers as well as
lovers—coins showered down from the crowd and were scooped up
by her priests. The procession of gods ended with an enormous
gilded statue of Jupiter on his throne, borne upon a cart so large it
took twenty men to pull it.

Next came the charioteers who would be racing that day, slowly circling the track in chariots festooned with the color of their team, red or white. To many in the stands, they were heroes larger than life. There was a chant for every racer, and chants for the lead horses as well. The noise of all the competing chants ringing out at once was deafening.

Never having been a gambler or a racing aficionado, I recognized few of the charioteers, but even I knew Diocles, the most renowned of the Reds. He was easy to spot by the extraordinary width of his shoulders, his bristling beard, and his flowing mane of jet-black hair. As he passed before us, grinning and waving to the crowd, I tried to see the reaction of Decimus Brutus, but I was able to see only the back of the consul's head. Did Diocles's smile turn sarcastic as he passed the consular box, or did I only imagine it?

The procession ended. The track was cleared. The first four chariots took their places in the starting traps at the north end of the circus. Two White chariots, a principal along with a second-stringer to regulate the pace and run interference, would race against two Red chariots.

"Did you get a racing card?" Lucius held up a wooden tablet. Many in the stands were using them to fan themselves; all around the red-and-white checkered stadium, I saw the flutter of racing cards.

"No?" said Lucius. "Never mind, you can refer to mine. Let's see, first race of the day . . ." The cards listed each charioteer, his color, and the name of the lead horse in his team of four. "Principal Red: Musclosus, racing Ajax—a hero of a horse, to be sure! Second-string Red: Epaphroditus, racing a five-year-old called Spots—a new horse to me. For the Whites: Thallus, racing Suspicion, and his colleague Teres, racing Snowy. Now there's a silly name for a horse, don't you think, even if it is pure white. More suitable for a puppy, I should think—by Hercules, is that the starting trumpet?"

The four chariots leaped out of their traps and onto the track. Once past the white line, they furiously vied for the inner position alongside the spine that ran down the middle. Clouds of dust billowed behind them. Whips slithered and cracked as they made the first tight turn around the post at the end of the spine and headed back. The Reds were in the lead, with Epaphroditus the second-stringer successfully blocking the principal White to give his colleague a clear field, while the second-string White trailed badly, unable to assist. But in seven laps, a great deal could happen.

Lucius jumped up and down on his pillow. All around us, spectators began to place wagers with one another on the outcome.

"I'm for Snowy!" shouted the man across the aisle from Lucius.

A man several rows down turned and shouted back. "The second-string White? Are you mad? I'll wager you ten to one against Snowy winning. How much?"

Such is the Roman way of gambling at the races: inspired by a flash of intuition and done on the spur of the moment, usually with a stranger sitting nearby. I smiled at Lucius, whose susceptibility to such spontaneous wagering was a running joke between us. "Care to join that wager, Lucius?"

"Uh . . . no," he answered, peering down at the track. Under his breath, I heard him mutter, "Come on, Ajax! Come on!"

But Ajax did not win. Nor did the long-shot Snowy. By the final lap, it was Suspicion, the principal White, who had pulled into the lead, with no help from the second-string White, who remained far in the rear. It was a stunning upset. Even the Red partisans in the crowd cheered such a marvelous display of Fortune's favor.

"A good thing you didn't bet on Ajax," I said to Lucius. He only grunted in reply and peered at his racing card.

As race followed race, it seemed to me that I had never seen Lucius so horse-mad, jumping up in excitement at each starting trumpet, cheering jubilantly when his favored horse won, but more often sulking when his horse lost, and yet never once placing a bet with anyone around us. He repeatedly turned his racing card over and scribbled figures on the back with a piece of chalk, muttering and shaking his head.

I was distracted by my friend's fidgeting, and even more by the statuelike demeanor of Decimus Brutus, who sat stiffly beside his colleague in the consular box. He was so still that I wondered if he had gone to sleep; with such poor eyesight, it was no wonder he had no interest in watching the races. Surely, I thought, no assassin would be so bold as to make an attempt on the life of a consul in broad daylight, with dozens of bodyguards and thousands of witnesses all around. Still, I was uneasy, and kept scanning the crowd for any signs of something untoward.

With so much on my mind, along with a persistent headache from the previous night's wine, I paid only passing attention to the races. As each winner was announced, the names of the horses barely registered in my ears: Lightning, Straight Arrow, Bright Eyes . . .

At last, it was time for the final race, in which Diocles would compete. A cheer went up as he drove his chariot toward the starting traps.

His horses were arrayed in splendid red trappings. A gold-plumed crest atop her head marked his lead horse, Sparrow, a tawny beauty with magnificent flanks. Diocles himself was outfitted entirely in red, except for a necklace of white. I squinted. "Lucius, why should Diocles be wearing a scrap of anything white?"

"Is he?"

"Look, around his neck. Your eyes are as sharp as mine . . ."

"Pearls," declared Lucius. "Looks like a string of pearls. Rather precious for a charioteer."

I nodded. Diocles had not been wearing them in the opening procession. It was the sort of thing a charioteer might put on for luck just before his race—a token from his lover . . .

Down in his box, Decimus Brutus sat as stiffly as ever, displaying no reaction. With his eyesight, there was little chance that he had noticed the necklace.

The trumpet blared. The chariots sprang forward. Diocles took the lead at once. The crowd roared. Diocles was their favorite; even the Whites loved him. I could see why. He was magnificent to watch. He never once used his whip, which stayed tucked into his belt the whole time, alongside his emergency dagger. There was magic in Diocles that day. Man and horses seemed to share a single will; his chariot was not a contraption but a creature, a synthesis of human control and equine speed. As he held and lengthened his lead lap after lap, the crowd's excitement grew to an almost intolerable pitch. When he thundered across the finish line there was not a spectator sitting. Women wept. Men screamed without sound, hoarse from so much shouting.

"Extraordinary!" declared Lucius.

"Yes," I said, and felt a sudden flash of intuition, a moment of god-sent insight such as gamblers crave. "Diocles is a magnificent racer. What a pity he should have fallen into such a scheme."

"What? What's that you say?" Lucius cupped his ear against the roar of the crowd.

"Diocles has everything: skill, riches, the love of the crowd. He has no need to cheat." I shook my head. "Only love could have drawn him into such a plot."

"A plot? What are you saying, Gordianus? What is it you see?"

"I see the pearls around his neck—look, he reaches up to touch them while he makes his victory lap. How he must love her. What man can blame him for that! But to be used by her in such a way . . ."

"The plot? Deci! Is Deci in danger?" Lucius peered down at the consular box. Even Decimus Brutus, ever the ingratiating politician, had risen to his feet to applaud Diocles along with the rest of the crowd.

"I think your friend Decimus Brutus need not fear for his life. Unless the humiliation might kill him."

"Gordianus, what are you talking about?"

"Tell me, Lucius, why have you not wagered even once today? And what are those numbers you keep figuring on the back of your racing card?"

His florid face blushed even redder. "Well, if you must know, Gordianus, I . . . I'm afraid I . . . I've lost rather a lot of money today."

"How?"

"Something . . . something new. A betting circle . . . set up by perfectly respectable people."

"You wagered ahead of time?"

"I put a little something on each race. Well, it makes sense, doesn't it? If you know the horses, and you place your bet on the best team ahead of time, with a cool head, rather than during the heat of the race . . ."

"Yet you've lost over and over today, far more often than you've won."

"Fortune is fickle."

I shook my head. "How many others are in this 'betting circle'?"

He shrugged. "Everyone I know. Well, everyone who is anyone. Only the best people—you know what I mean."

"Only the *richest* people. How much money did the organizers of this betting scheme take in today, I wonder? And how much will they actually have to pay out?"

"Gordianus, what are you getting at?"

"Lucius, consult your racing card. You've noted all the winners with a chalk mark. Read them off to me—not the color or the driver, just the horses' names."

"Suspicion—that was the first race. Then Lightning . . . Straight Arrow . . . Bright Eyes . . . Golden Dagger . . . Partridge . . . Oh! By Hercules! Gordianus, you don't think—that item in the *Daily* . . ."

I quoted from memory. " 'The bookworm pokes his head outside tomorrow. Easy prey for the sparrow, but partridges go hungry. Bright-eyed Sappho says: Be suspicious! A dagger strikes faster than lightning. Better yet: an arrow. Let Venus conquer all!' From 'Sappho' to 'Sparrow,' a list of horses—*and every one a winner.*"

"But how could that be?"

"I know this much: Fortune had nothing to do with it."

I left the crowded stadium and hurried through the empty streets. Decimus Brutus would be detained by the closing ceremonies. I had perhaps an hour before he would arrive home.

The slave at the door recognized me. He frowned. "The master—"

"—is still at the Circus Maximus. I'll wait for him. In the meantime . . . please tell your mistress she has a visitor."

The slave raised an eyebrow but showed me into a reception room off the central garden. Lowering sunlight on the fountain splashing in the courtyard outside sent reflected lozenges of light dancing across the ceiling.

I did not have long to wait. Sempronia stepped into the room alone, without even a handmaiden. She was not smiling.

"The door slave announced you as Gordianus the Finder."

"Yes. We met . . . briefly . . . this morning."

"I remember. You're the fellow who went snooping for Deci last night, poking about at the Senian Baths and those awful places around the circus. Oh yes, word got back to me. I have my own informants. What are you doing here?"

"I'm trying to decide what I should tell your husband."

She gave me an appraising look. "What is it, exactly, that you think you know?"

"Decimus Brutus thinks that you and the charioteer Diocles are lovers."

"And what do you think, Finder?"

"I think he's right. But I have no proof."

She nodded. "Is that all?"

"You husband thinks you and Diocles were plotting to kill him today."

Sempronia laughed out loud. "Dear old bookworm!" She sighed. "Marrying Deci was the best thing that ever happened to me. I'm the consul's wife! Why in Hades would I want to kill him?"

I shrugged. "He misunderstood that blind item you put into the *Daily Acts*."

"Which . . . blind item?"

"There's been more than one? Of course. That makes sense. What better way to communicate with Diocles, since you've been confined here and he's been banned from your house. What I don't understand is how you ever convinced Diocles to fix today's races."

She crossed her arms and gave me a long, calculating look. "Diocles loves me; more than I love him, I'm afraid, but when was Venus ever fair? He did it for love, I suppose; and for money. Diocles stands to make a tremendous amount of money today, as do all the racers who took part in the fix. You can't imagine how much money. Millions. We worked on the scheme for months. Setting up the betting circle, bribing the racers . . ."

" 'We'? Do you mean your whole circle was in on it?"

"Some of them. But mostly it was Diocles and myself." She frowned. "And then Deci had to throw his jealous fit. It couldn't have happened at a worse time, with the races less than a month

away. I had to have some way to communicate with Diocles. The
Daily was the answer."

"You must have extraordinary powers of . . ."

"Persuasion?"

"Organization, I was going to say."

"Like a man?" She laughed.

"One thing puzzles me still. What will you do with millions of
sesterces, Sempronia? You can't possibly hide that much money from
your husband. He'd want to know where such a windfall came from."

She peered at me keenly. "What do *you* think I intend to do with
the money?"

"I think you intend to . . . get rid of it."

"How?"

"I think you mean to . . . send it abroad."

"Where?"

"To Spain. To Quintus Sertorius, the rebel general."

Her face became as pale as the pearls in her hair. "How much do
you want, Gordianus?"

I shook my head. "I didn't come here to blackmail you."

"No? That's what Scorpus wanted."

"Your husband's man? Did he discover the truth?"

"Only about the racing scheme. He seemed to think that entitled
him to a portion of the takings."

"There must be plenty to go around."

She shook her head. "Scorpus would never have stopped wanting
more."

"So he was drowned."

"Diocles arranged it. There are men around the circus who'll do
that sort of job for next to nothing, especially for a fellow like Diocles. Blackmailers deserve nothing better."

"Is that a threat, Sempronia?"

"That depends. What do you want, Finder?"

I shrugged. "The truth. It's the only thing that ever seems to satisfy me. Why Sertorius? Why risk so much—everything—to help his rebellion in Spain? Do you have a family tie? A loved one who's thrown his lot with the rebels? Or is it that you and Sertorius are . . ."

"Lovers?" She laughed without mirth. "Is that all you can think, that being a woman, I must be driven by passion? Can you not imagine that a woman might have her own politics, her own convictions, her own agenda, quite separate from a husband or a lover? I don't have to justify myself to you, Gordianus."

I nodded. Feeling her eyes on me, I paced the room. The sun was sinking. Flashes of warm sunlight reflected from the fountain outside caressed my face. Decimus Brutus would return home at any moment. What would I tell him?

I made up my mind. "You asked me what I want from you, Sempronia. Actually, there is the matter of a refund, which I think you must admit is only proper, given the circumstances . . ."

At noon the next day, I sat beside Lucius Claudius in his garden, sharing the sunlight and a cup of wine. His interest in that morning's *Daily Acts* had been eclipsed by the bags of coins I brought with me. Scooping the little scrolls off the table, he emptied the bags and collected the sesterces into heaping piles, gleefully counting and recounting them.

"All here!" he announced, clapping his hands. "Every single sesterce I lost yesterday on the races. But Gordianus, how did you get my money back?"

"That, Lucius, must forever remain a secret."

"If you insist. But this has something to do with Sempronia and that charioteer, doesn't it?"

"A secret is a secret, Lucius."

He sighed. "Your discretion is exasperating, Gordianus. But I've learned my lesson. I shall never again be drawn into a betting scheme like that!"

"I only wish I could have arranged for every person who was cheated yesterday to get his money back," I said. "Alas, their lessons shall be more costly than yours. I don't think this particular set of plotters will attempt to pull off such a scheme a second time. Hopefully, Roman racing can return to its pristine innocence."

Lucius nodded. "The important thing is, Deci is safe and out of danger."

"He was always safe; never in danger."

"Rude of him, though, not to pay you the balance of your fee."

I shrugged. "When I saw him at his house yesterday evening, after the races, I had nothing more to report to him. He hired me to uncover a plot against his life. I failed to do so."

And what, I thought, if I had reported everything to the consul—Sempronia's adultery, the racing fix, the betting scheme, Scorpus's attempted blackmail and his murder, Sempronia's seditious support of Sertorius? Terrified of scandal, Decimus Brutus would merely have hushed it all up. Sempronia would have been no more faithful to him than before, and no one's wagers would have been returned. No, I had been hired to save the consul's life, discreetly; and as far as I was concerned, my duty to Decimus Brutus ended when I discovered there was no plot against his life after all. My discretion would continue.

"Still, Gordianus, it was niggardly of Deci not to pay you . . ."

Discretion forbade me from telling Lucius that the other half of my fee had indeed been paid—by Sempronia. It was the only way I could see to save my own neck. I had convinced her that by paying the fee for my investigation she purchased my discretion. Thus I avoided the same fate as Scorpus.

At the same time, I had requested a refund of Lucius's wagers, which seemed only fair.

Lucius cupped his hands around a pile of coins, as if they emitted a warming glow. He smiled ruefully. "I tell you what, Gordianus—as commission for recouping my gambling losses, what if I give you . . . five percent of the total?"

I sucked in a breath and eyed the coins on the table. Bethesda would be greatly pleased to see the household coffer filled to overflowing. I smiled at Lucius and raised an eyebrow.

"Gordianus, don't give me that look!"

"What look?"

"Oh, very well! I shall give you ten percent. But not a sesterce more!"

IF A CYCLOPS COULD VANISH
IN THE BLINK OF AN EYE

Eco was incensed. That was all I could tell at first—that he was angry and frustrated almost to the point of tears. At such a time, I felt acutely aware of his muteness. He was usually quite skilled at expressing himself with gestures and signals, but not when he was flustered.

"Calm down," I said quietly, placing my hands on his shoulders. He was at that age when boys shoot up like beanstalks. It seemed to me that not long ago, placing my hands at the same height, I would have been patting his head. "Now," I said, "what is the problem?"

My adopted son took a deep breath and composed himself, then seized my hand and led me across the overgrown garden at the center of the house, under the portico, through a curtained doorway and into his room. By the bright morning light from the small window I surveyed the few furnishings—a narrow sleeping cot, a wooden folding chair, and a small trunk.

It was not to these that Eco directed my attention, but to a long niche about knee-high in the plastered wall across from his bed. The last time I had ventured into the room, a hodgepodge of toys had been shoved into the niche—little boats made of wood, a leather ball for playing trigon, pebbles of colored glass for Egyptian board games. Now the space had been neatly cleared—the cast-off toys put away in the trunk along with his spare tunic, I presumed—and occupying the shelf were a number of tiny figurines made of fired clay, each representing some monster of legend with a horrible visage. There was a Medusa with snakes for hair, a Cyclops with one eye, a Nemean lion, and numerous others.

They were crudely made but tinted with bright colors, and I knew that Eco treasured them. A potter with a shop down by the Tiber made them in his spare time out of bits of leftover clay; Eco had been doing occasional odd jobs for the man and accepting the figurines as payment. He insisted on showing them off to me and to Bethesda whenever he brought a new one home. I always made a point of admiring them, but my beloved concubine made no secret of her disdain for them. Her upbringing in Egypt had given her attitudes different—dare I say more superstitious?—than those of a Roman, and where I found the figurines to be harmless and charming, she saw in them something distasteful, even sinister.

I had not realized how large Eco's collection had grown. I counted fifteen figurines, all lined up in a row.

"Why do you show me these?" I asked.

He pointed to three gaps in the evenly spaced row.

"Are you telling me that three of your monsters are missing?"

Eco nodded vigorously.

"But where have they gone?"

He shrugged and his lower lip began to tremble. He looked so desolate.

"Which ones are missing? When were they taken?"

Eco pointed to the first gap, then performed a very complicated

mime, snarling and gnashing his teeth, until I grasped that the missing figurine was of three-headed Cerberus, the watchdog of Pluto.
He passed an open palm behind a horizontal forearm—his gesture
for sundown—and held up two fingers.

"The day before yesterday your Cerberus went missing?"

He nodded.

"But why didn't you tell me then?"

Eco shrugged and made a long face. I gathered that he presumed
he might have mislaid the figurine himself.

Our exchange continued—me, asking questions; Eco, answering
with gestures—until I learned that yesterday his Minotaur had disappeared, and that very morning his many-headed Hydra had vanished. The first disappearance had merely puzzled him; the second
had alarmed him; the third had thrown him into utter confusion.

I gazed at the gaps in the row of monsters and stroked my chin.
"Well, well, this *is* serious. Tell me, has anything else gone missing?"

Eco shook his head.

"Are you sure?"

He rolled his eyes at me and gestured to his cot, his chair, and his
trunk, as if to say, *With so little to call my own, don't you think I'd notice
if anything else was gone?*

Eco's figurines were of little intrinsic value; any serious burglar
would surely have been more likely to snatch one of Bethesda's
bracelets or a scroll from my bookcase. But as far as I knew, nothing
else in the house had gone missing in the last few days.

At that time, I was without a slave—other than Bethesda, whom
I could hardly justify calling my slave anymore, considering that she
tended to prevail in any contest of wills between us—so the only oc-
cupants of the house were Bethesda, Eco, and myself. In the last
three days, no tradesmen had come calling; nor, sadly for my purse,
had any client come to seek the services of Gordianus the Finder.

I raised an eyebrow. "Fortunately for you, Eco, I happen to be between cases at the moment, so I can bend all my efforts toward solving this mystery. But the truth can never be hurried. Let me ponder this for a while—sleep on it, perhaps—and I'll see if I can come up with a solution."

Bethesda was out most of the day, shopping at the food markets and taking a pair of my shoes to be resoled by a cobbler. I had business to attend to in the Forum, as well as a special errand to take care of on the Street of the Plastermakers. Not until that night, after Eco had retired to his room and the two of us reclined on our dining couches after the evening meal—a simple repast of lentil soup and stuffed dates—did I find time to have a quiet word with Bethesda about Eco's problem.

"Disappearing? One at a time?" she said. By the warm glow of the nearby brazier, I thought I saw a subtle smile on her lips. The same light captured wine-colored highlights in her dark, henna-treated hair. Bethesda was beautiful at all hours of the day, but perhaps most beautiful by firelight. The black female cat she called Bast lay beside her, submitting to her gentle stroking. Watching Bethesda caress the beast, I felt a stab of envy. Cats were still a novelty in Rome at that time, and keeping one as a house pet, as others might keep a dog, was one of the peculiar habits Bethesda had imported with her from Egypt. Her last cat, also called Bast, had expired some time ago; this one she had recently acquired from a sailing merchant in Ostia. The beast and I got along passably well, as long as I didn't attempt to interpose myself between Bast and her mistress when it was the cat's turn to receive Bethesda's caresses.

"Yes, the little monsters seem to be vanishing, one by one," I said, clearing my throat. "I don't suppose you know anything about it?"

"I? What makes you think *I* might have anything to do with it?" Bethesda raised an eyebrow. For an uncanny moment, her expression and the cat's expression were identical—mysterious, aloof, utterly self-contained. I shifted uneasily on my couch.

"Perhaps . . ." I shrugged. "Perhaps you were cleaning his room. Perhaps one of the figurines fell and broke—"

"Do you think I'm blind as well as clumsy? I think I should know if I had broken one of Eco's figurines," she said coolly, "especially if I did such a thing three days in a row."

"Of course. Still, considering the way you feel about those figurines—"

"And *do* you know how I feel about them, Master?" Bethesda fixed me with her catlike stare.

I cleared my throat. "Well, I know you don't like them—"

"I respect them for what they are. You think they're just lumps of lifeless clay, a child's toys made by a clumsy potter. You Romans! You've put so much of your faith in the handful of gods who made you great that you can no longer see the tiny gods who populate your own households. There's a spark of life in every one of the figurines that Eco has brought into the house. It's unwise to bring so many into the house at once, when there's so little we know about any of them. Do you know what I think? I think the three who've gone missing may have left of their own volition."

"What? You think they jumped from the shelf and scampered off?"

"You scoff, Master, but it may be that the three who left were unhappy with the company in which they found themselves. Or perhaps the others ganged up on them and drove them off!" As her voice rose, so did Bethesda, sitting upright on the couch. Bast, disliking the change in her mistress's disposition, jumped from her lap and ran off.

"Bethesda, this is preposterous. They're only bits of painted clay!"

She recovered her composure and leaned back. "So you say, Master. So you say."

"The point is, those figurines are of great value to Eco. He's very proud of them. They're his possessions. He earned them by his own labor."

"If you say so, Master. Being a mere slave, I wouldn't know much about *earning* and *owning*."

Her tone expressed no empathy for Eco at all, and certainly no remorse. I became more determined than ever to make good on my pledge to Eco to solve the mystery of his disappearing monsters.

That night, after Bethesda was asleep, I slipped out of bed and stole to the garden at the center of the house, which was lit by a full moon. In an inconspicuous spot beside one of the columns of the portico, I located the purchase I had made earlier that day on the Street of the Plastermakers. It was a tightly woven linen bag containing a handful or so of plaster dust. Carrying the bag, I slipped through the curtained doorway into Eco's room. The moonlight that poured in through the small window showed Eco soundly asleep on his cot. Reaching into the bag, I scattered a very fine layer of plaster dust onto the floor in front of the niche that contained his figurines. The dust was so fine that a tiny cloud rose from my hand and seemed to sparkle in the moonlight.

My eyes watered and my nose twitched. I slipped out of Eco's room, put away the bag of plaster dust, and stole back to my bed. I slipped under the covers beside Bethesda. Only then did I release a sneeze that broke the silence like thunder.

Bethesda murmured and rolled onto her side, but did not wake.

The next morning I woke to the sound of birds in the garden—not pleasant singing, but the shrill cawing of two magpies squabbling in the trees. I covered my ears with my pillow, but it was no good. I was up for the day.

Stepping out of bed, I inadvertently kicked a shoe—one of the pair that Bethesda had brought home from the cobbler the previous day—and sent it skittering under the bed. Dropping to my hands and knees to retrieve it, I was stopped short by the sight of four objects on the floor beneath the bed, directly underneath the space where Bethesda slept, against the wall. They were clustered in a little group, lying on their sides. Joining the missing figurines of Cerberus, the Minotaur, and the Hydra was a fourth, Eco's one-eyed Cyclops.

Well, well, I thought, getting to my feet. Sprinkling the plaster dust had been superfluous, after all. Or had it? If Bethesda wouldn't own up to pilfering Eco's figurines, the evidence of her footsteps in the dust, and of the dust adhering to soles of her shoes, would compel her to do so. I couldn't help but smile, anticipating her chagrin. Or would she maintain her fiction that the figurines had walked off by themselves, with the curious goal, as it turned out, of congregating beneath our bed?

Whistling an old Etruscan nursery tune and looking forward to a hearty breakfast, I strolled across the garden toward the dining room at the back of the house. Above my head, the magpies squawked in dissonant counterpoint to my whistling. Bast sat in a patch of sunlight, apparently oblivious of the birds, cleaning a forepaw with her tongue.

No sooner had I settled myself on the dining couch than Eco came running out of his room, a look of confusion and alarm on his face. He ran up to me and waved his arms, making inchoate gestures.

"I know, I know," I said, raising one hand to calm him and gently restraining him with the other. "Don't tell me—your Cyclops has gone missing."

Eco was briefly taken aback, then frowned and peered at me inquiringly.

"How do I know? Well . . ."

At that moment, Bethesda appeared from the kitchen, bearing a bowl of steaming porridge. I cleared my throat.

"Bethesda," I said, "it seems that another of Eco's figurines has vanished. What do you say to that?"

She put the bowl on a small tripod table and began to ladle porridge into three smaller bowls. "What would you have me say, Master?" She kept her eyes on her work. Her face was utterly expressionless, betraying not the least trace of guilt or guile.

I sighed, almost regretting that she had forced me to expose her little charade. "Perhaps you could begin . . ." *By apologizing to Eco,* I was about to say—when I was abruptly interrupted by a sneeze.

It was not Bethesda who sneezed. Nor was it Eco.

It was the cat.

Bethesda looked up. "Yes, Master? I could begin by saying . . . what?"

My face turned hot. I cleared my throat. I pursed my lips.

I stood up. "Eco, the first thing you must remember, if you ever wish to become a Finder like your father, is always to keep a cool head and never to jump to conclusions. Last night I laid a trap for our culprit. If we now examine the scene of the crime, I suspect we shall discover that she has left a clue behind."

Or several clues, as it turned out, if one wished to call each tiny, padded paw print in the fine plaster dust an individual clue. The paw prints led up to the niche; the paw prints led away. Following a barely discernible trail of dusted prints, Eco and I tracked the thief's progress out of his room, around the colonnaded portico, and into the room I shared with Bethesda. The trail disappeared under the bed.

I left it to Eco to discover the pilfered figurines for himself. He let out a grunt, scampered under the bed, and reemerged clutching the clay treasures in both hands, a look of mingled relief and triumph on his face.

Greatly excited, he put down the figurines so that he could com-municate. He pinched his forefingers and thumbs beneath his nose and drew them outward, making his sign for Bast by miming the cat's long whiskers.

"Yes," I said. "It was Bast who took your figurines."

Eco made an exaggerated shrug with his palms held upright.

"Why? That I can't tell you. We Romans don't yet know that much about cats. Not like the Egyptians, who've been living with them—and worshipping them—since the dawn of time. I suppose, like dogs and ferrets—and like magpies, for that matter—some cats display a tendency to pilfer small objects and hide them. One of those figurines would fit quite neatly between Bast's jaws. I'm sure she meant no harm, as none of them seems to have been damaged. She obviously treated them with great respect."

I glanced at the cat. She stood in the doorway beside Bethesda and peered back at me with a bland expression that admitted no guilt. She rubbed herself against Bethesda's ankles, whipped her tail in the air, and sauntered back toward the garden. Bethesda raised an eyebrow and looked at me steadily, but said nothing.

That night, after a very busy day, I slipped into bed beside Bethesda. Her mood seemed a bit cool, but she said nothing.

The silence stretched. "I suppose I owe you an apology," I finally said.

"For what?"

The best course, I decided, was to make light of my mistake. "It was foolish of me, really. Do you know, I almost suspected *you* of tak-ing Eco's figurines."

"Really?" By the pale moonlight, I couldn't quite decipher the expression on her face. Was she angry? Amused? Unconcerned?

"Yes, I actually suspected you, Bethesda. But of course it wasn't you. It was the cat, all along." The creature abruptly jumped onto the bed and crawled over both of us to settle between Bethesda and the wall, purring loudly.

"Yes, it was Bast who took the figurines," said Bethesda. She rolled away from me and laid her hand upon the cat, who responded with a purring that was almost a roar. "But how do you know that it wasn't *I* who put her up to it?"

For that, I had no answer.

THE WHITE FAWN

The old senator was a distant cousin of my friend Lucius Claudius, and the two had once been close. That was the only reason I agreed to see the man, as a favor to Lucius. When Lucius let it slip, on the way to the senator's house, that the affair had something to do with Sertorius, I clucked my tongue and almost turned back. I had a feeling even then that it would lead to no good. Call it a premonition, if you will; if you believe that such things as premonitions exist.

Senator Gaius Claudius's house was on the Aventine Hill, not the most fashionable district in Rome. Still, there are plenty of old patrician households tucked amid the cramped little shops and ugly new tenements that sprawl over the hill. The facade of the senator's house was humble, but that meant nothing; the houses of the Roman nobility are often unassuming, at least on the outside.

The doddering doorkeeper recognized Lucius (could there be two men in Rome with his beaming round face, untidy red hair, and dancing green eyes?) and escorted us at once to the atrium, where a fountain gurgled and splashed but did little to relieve the heat of a cloudless midsummer day. While we waited for our host to appear, Lucius and I strolled from corner to corner of the little square garden. On such a warm day, the various rooms facing the atrium all had their shutters thrown open.

"I take it that your cousin has fallen on hard times," I said to Lucius.

He pursed his lips. "Why do you assume that, Gordianus? I don't recall mentioning it."

"Observe the state of his house."

"It's a fine house. Gaius had it built when he was a young man and has lived here ever since."

"It seems rather sparsely decorated."

"You saw the busts of his noble ancestors lined up in their niches in the foyer," said Lucius, his nose tilting up. "What more ornamentation does the house of a patrician require?" Despite his genial temperament, Lucius sometimes could not help being a bit of a snob.

"But I think your cousin is a great lover of art, or used to be."

"Now why do you say that?"

"Observe the mosaic floor beneath our feet, with its intricate acanthus-leaf pattern. The workmanship is very fine. And note the wall paintings in some of the rooms around us. The various scenes are from the *Iliad*, I believe. Even from here I can see that they're works of very high quality."

Lucius raised an eyebrow. "Cousin Gaius does have good taste, I'll grant you that. But why do you assume he's fallen on hard times?"

"Because of the things that I don't see."

"Now, Gordianus, really! How can you walk into a house you've never entered before and declare that things are missing? I can see into the surrounding rooms as well as you, and they all look adequately furnished."

"Precisely; the furnishings are adequate. I should expect something more than that from the man who built this house and commissioned those wall paintings and mosaics. Where is the finely wrought furniture? Everything I see looks like the common stuff that anyone can buy ready-made down in the Street of the Woodworkers. Where are the paintings, the portable ones in frames, the portraits and bucolic scenes that are so fashionable nowadays?"

"What makes you think that cousin Gaius ever collected such works?"

"Because I can see the discolored rectangles on the wall where they used to hang! And surely a rather substantial statue once filled that empty spot atop the pedestal in the middle of the fountain. Let me guess: Diana with her bow, or perhaps a discus-thrower?"

"A rather good drunken Hercules, actually."

"Such valuables don't vanish from a patrician household without good reason. This house is like a bare cupboard, or a fine Roman matron without her jewelry. Where are the urns, the vases, the precious little things one expects to see in the house of a wealthy old senator? Auctioned off to pay the bill-collector, I presume. When did your cousin sell them?"

"Over the last few years," admitted Lucius with a sigh, "bit by bit. I suppose the mosaics and wall paintings would be gone by now as well, except that they're part of the house and can't be disposed of piecemeal. The Civil War was very hard on cousin Gaius."

"He backed the wrong side?"

"Quite the opposite! Gaius was a staunch supporter of Sulla. But his only son, who was my age, had married into a family that sided with Marius, and was contaminated by his wife's connections; he was beheaded when Sulla became dictator. He did leave an heir, however—Gaius's grandson, a boy named Mamercus, who is now not quite twenty. Gaius took custody of his grandson, but also had to assume his dead son's debts, which were crushing. Poor cousin

Gaius! The Civil War tore his family apart, took his only son, and left him virtually bankrupt."

I looked around. "The house itself looks valuable enough."

"I'm sure it is, but it's all that Gaius has left. The wealth has all fled. And so has young Mamercus, I fear."

"The grandson?"

"Gone to Spain! It's broken his grandfather's heart."

"Spain? Ah, so that's why you mentioned Sertorius on the walk here . . ."

The Civil War had been over for six years. Marius had lost. Sulla had won, and had made himself dictator. He disposed of his enemies, reordered the state, and then retired, leaving his chosen successors in firm control of the senate and the magistracies. The Marians—those who had survived the proscriptions and still had their heads—were lying low. But in Spain, the last embers of resistance still smoldered in the person of Quintus Sertorius. The renegade general not only refused to surrender, but had declared himself to be the head of the legitimate Roman state. Disgruntled Marian military men and desperate anti-Sullan senators had fled from Rome to join Sertorius's government-in-exile. In addition to his own legions, Sertorius had succeeded in rallying the native population to his side. Altogether, Sertorius and his forces in Spain constituted a considerable power that the Roman Senate could not ignore and had not yet been able to stamp out.

"Are you saying that young Mamercus has run off to join Sertorius?"

"So it appears," said Lucius, shaking his head. He leaned over to sniff a rose. "This smells very sweet!"

"So young Mamercus rejected his grandfather's Sullan politics and remained loyal to his mother's side of the family?"

"So it appears. Gaius is quite distraught. The folly of youth! There's no future for anyone who sides with Sertorius."

"But what future would the young man have if he'd stayed here in Rome with his grandfather? You say that Gaius is bankrupt."

"It's a question of loyalty, Gordianus, and family dignity." Lucius spoke carefully. I could see he was doing his patrician best not to sound condescending.

I shrugged. "Perhaps the boy feels he's being loyal to his dead father, by joining the last resistance to Sulla's faction. But I take your point, Lucius; it's a family tragedy, of a sort all too common these days. But what can your cousin want of me?"

"I should think that was obvious. He wants someone to—ah, but here is Gaius himself . . ."

"Cousin Lucius! Embrace me!" A frail-looking old man in a senatorial toga stepped into the atrium with wide-open arms. "Let me feel another of my own flesh and blood pressed against me!"

The two men could hardly have been more different. Gaius was older, of course, but also tall and narrow, where Lucius was short and round. And where Lucius was florid and flushed, there was a grayness about the old senator, not only in his hair and wrinkled hands, but also in his expression and manner, a kind of drawn, sere austerity. Like his house, the man seemed to have been stripped bare of all vain adornments and winnowed to his essence.

After a moment, the two drew apart. "I knew you wouldn't disappoint me, Lucius. Is this the fellow?"

"Yes, this is Gordianus, called the Finder."

"Let us hope he lives up to his name." Gaius Claudius regarded me not with the patronizing gaze I was used to receiving from patricians, but steadily and deeply, as if to judge whether I should be a cause of hope to him or not. "He looks reliable enough," he finally pronounced. "Ah, but what judge of character am I, who let my only son marry into a Marian family, and then could not foresee my grandson's intentions to follow the same course to disaster?"

"Yes, I was just informing Gordianus of your situation," said Lucius.

"And is he willing?"

"Actually, we were just coming to that . . ."

There must indeed have been a last, thin veil of vanity over the old senator's demeanor, for now I saw it fall away. He looked at me imploringly. "The boy is all I have left! I must at least know for certain what's become of him, and why he's done this mad thing, and if he can't be persuaded to see reason! Will you do this for me, Gordianus?"

"Do what, Gaius Claudius?" I said, though I was beginning to see all too clearly.

"Find him! Go to Spain for me. Take my message. Bring him back to me!"

I cleared my throat. "Let me understand you, Gaius Claudius. You wish for me to venture into Sertorius's territory? You must realize that the whole of the Spanish peninsula is wracked with warfare. The danger—"

"You will demand a large fee, I suppose . . ." Gaius averted his eyes and wrung his hands.

"The fee is not an issue," said Lucius.

"I'm afraid that it most certainly is," I said, not following his meaning. Then I saw the look that passed between Lucius and his cousin, and understood. Gaius Claudius had no money; it was Lucius who would be paying my fee, and Lucius, as I well knew, could afford to be generous. The commission would be coming just as much from my dear friend as from his cousin, then. That made me feel all the more obliged to accept it.

Thus I came to find myself, some days later, on the eastern coast of Spain, near the village of Sucro, which is situated not far from the mouth of the river of the same name.

I was not alone. After a great deal of internal debate and

hesitation, I had decided to bring Eco with me. On the one hand, I was likely to encounter danger, quite possibly a great deal of danger; who knows what may happen in a foreign land torn by warfare? On the other hand, a nimble, quick-witted fourteen-year-old boy who had survived the harsh streets of Rome from his earliest years (despite the handicap of his muteness) is not a bad companion to have around in unpredictable surroundings. And for his own benefit, I thought it a good thing that Eco should learn the lessons of travel while he was still young, especially since Lucius Claudius was paying the expenses.

First had come the sea voyage, on a trading ship out of Puteoli bound for Mauretania. For a reasonable sum, the captain agreed to put us ashore at New Carthage, in Spain. That had gone well enough. Pirates had pursued us only once, and our experienced captain had managed to outrun them easily; and Eco had suffered from seasickness only for the first day or two. Once ashore, we sought for news of Sertorius's whereabouts, and made our way north until we caught up with him at Sucro, where we arrived only two days after a tremendous battle on the banks of the river.

According to the locals, Sertorius had suffered heavy casualties, perhaps as many as ten thousand men; but so had the opposing Roman general, the Sullan boy-wonder Pompey (not quite such a boy any longer at thirty), who had been wounded himself, though not gravely. The two sides appeared to be regrouping their forces, and a fresh rumor had it that Pompey's colleague Metellus was soon to arrive with reinforcements from the north. The townspeople of Sucro were bracing themselves for another great battle.

Getting into Sertorius's camp proved to be easier than I anticipated. The traditional rigid discipline of a Roman army camp was missing; perhaps, given Sertorius's mix of Spanish tribesmen and ragtag Romans, such discipline was impossible. In its place, there

seemed to be a great sense of camaraderie, and of welcome to the local camp followers who came to offer food and wares (and, in not a
few cases, themselves) for sale to the soldiers. The air of the camp
was open and almost festive, despite the great slaughter of two days
before. Morale, clearly, was very high.

I inquired after the whereabouts of Mamercus Claudius, using
the description his grandfather had given me—a young patrician of
nineteen, tall, slender, with a pleasant face and a shock of jet-black
hair, a newcomer to the ranks. Among the grizzled Roman veterans
and their Spanish allies, such a fellow was likely to stand out, I
thought, and sure enough, it took only a little asking (and a pittance
of bribes) before Eco and I were pointed to his tent.

The location surprised me, for it was very near the heart of the
camp, and thus not far, I presumed, from Sertorius's own quarters.
Despite his youth and inexperience, Mamercus Claudius was probably quite a catch for Sertorius, evidence to his fellow Romans that
the renegade general could still attract a youth from one of Rome's
best families, that his cause looked toward the future, not just the
past.

This presumption turned out to be more astute than I realized.
When I asked the centurion outside the tent to inform Mamercus
that he had a visitor, I was told that Mamercus was elsewhere. When
I asked where he might be, the centurion suggested that I try the
commander's tent.

So Eco and I made our way to the tent of Quintus Sertorius himself, which was quite conspicuous, thanks to the phalanx of guards
around it. There was also a great crowd of petitioners of the usual
sort, lined up to seek audience—locals who hoped to sell provisions
to the army, or had suffered property damage and wanted restitution,
or had other pressing business with the commander and his staff.

Eco tapped the edge of one hand against the flattened palm of the other, to suggest that we had run into a solid wall: *We shall never get inside that tent*, he seemed to say.

"Ah, but we don't need to get inside," I said to him. "We want someone who's already in there to come out, and that's a different matter."

I walked to the head of the long line. Some in the queue glared at us, but I ignored them. I came to the man who was next to be admitted and cleared my throat to get his attention. He turned and gave me a nasty look and said something in his native tongue. When he saw that I didn't understand, he repeated himself in passable Latin. "What do you think you're doing? I'm next. Get away!"

"You're here to see Quintus Sertorius?" I said.

"Like everyone else. Wait your turn."

"Ah, but I don't want to see the general himself. I only want someone to give a message to a young fellow who's probably in there with him. Could you do me the favor?" I patted my hand against the coin purse inside my tunic, which clinked suggestively. "Ask after a young Roman named Mamercus Claudius. Tell him that someone has come a very long way to talk to him."

"I suppose . . ." The man seemed dubious, but then his face abruptly brightened, as if reflecting the glitter of sunlight on the coins I dropped into his hand.

Just then a guard approached, searched the fellow for weapons, and told him to step into the tent.

We did not have long to wait. Soon a lanky young man stepped out of the tent. His armored leather fittings seemed to have been tailored for a shorter, stockier man; I had noticed that many of Sertorius's junior officers were outfitted in similarly haphazard fashion. The young man pulled uncomfortably at the armholes of his leather shirt and peered into the crowd, looking rather put out. I caught his eye and beckoned for him to meet me at one side of the tent.

"Mamercus Claudius?" I said. "I come with a message from—"

"What do you think you're doing, you idiot, summoning me from the commander's tent like that?" He was angry but kept his voice low.

"I suppose I could have lined up with the rest for an audience with the general—"

"Who are you?"

"My name is Gordianus, called the Finder. This is my son, Eco. We've come all the way from Rome. Your grandfather sent me."

Mamercus seemed taken aback at first, then smiled ruefully. "I see. Poor grandfather!"

"Poor indeed," I said, "and poorer still for lack of your company."

"Is he well?"

"In body, yes. But his spirit is eaten away by fear for you. I've brought a message from him."

I produced the little folded tablet that I had faithfully brought all the way from Rome. The two thin plates of wood were bound together with a ribbon and sealed with a daub of red wax, upon which Gaius Claudius had pressed his signet ring. Mamercus broke the seal, pulled the tablets apart, and gazed at the wax surfaces inside, upon which his grandfather had scratched his plea by his own hand, no longer having even a secretary to write his letters for him.

Had Mamercus's reaction been callous and uncaring, I would not have been surprised. Many an impatient, bitter, dispossessed young man in his situation might have scorned a doting grandparent's concern, especially if that grandparent had always supported the very establishment against which he was rebelling. But Mamercus's reaction was quite different. I watched the swift movement of his eyes as they perused the words and saw them glisten with tears. He clamped his jaw tightly to stop his lips from quivering. His evident distress made him look almost as boyish as Eco.

Gaius Claudius had not kept the contents of his letter secret from me. On the contrary, he had insisted that I read it:

My dearest grandson, blood of my blood, what has induced you to take this foolish course? Do you think to please the shade of your father by joining a hopeless struggle against those who destroyed him? If this were the only course open to you—if your own name and future had been ruined along with your father's and mother's—then honor might demand such a desperate course. But in Rome you still have my protection, despite your father's downfall, and you can still make a career for yourself. We are woefully impoverished, to be sure, but together we will find a way out of our misfortune! Surely the best revenge for your father would be for you to restore our family's fortunes and to make a place for yourself in the state, so that when you are my age you can look back upon a long career and a world you have had a hand in shaping to your liking. Do not throw your life away! Please, I beg you, calm your passions and let reason guide you. Come back to me! The man who bears this message has funds sufficient for your passage home. Mamercus, son of my son, I pray to the gods that I shall see you soon!

After a while, Mamercus pressed the tablets together and retied the ribbon. He averted his eyes in a way that reminded me of his grandfather. "Thank you for bringing the letter. Is that all?"

"*Is it all?*" I said. "I know what's in the letter. Will you honor his request?"

"No. Leave me now."

"Are you sure, Mamercus? Will you think on it? Shall I come back later?"

"No!"

My commission from Gaius Claudius was specific: I was to locate Mamercus, to deliver the message, and to help Mamercus, if he chose, to escape unscathed from Sertorius's service. It was not incumbent on me to persuade him to leave. But I had come a long way, and now I had seen both the old senator's distress and his grandson's response to it. If Mamercus had reacted with derision, if he had betrayed no love for his grandfather, that would have been the end of it. But his reaction had been quite the opposite. Even now, from the way he gently held the tablets, almost caressing them, and reached up to wipe his eyes, I could see that he was feeling a great flood of affection for the old man, and consequently, perhaps, considerable confusion over the choice he had made.

I thought it wise to change the subject for a moment. "You seem to have done well for yourself, here in Sertorius's army," I said.

"Better than I expected, in so short a time," admitted Mamercus. He tucked the tablets under his arm and smiled crookedly. "The commander was very glad to take me in. He gave me a position on his staff at once, despite my lack of experience. 'Look,' he said to everyone, 'a young Claudius, come all the way from Rome to join us! But don't worry, son, we'll be back in Rome before you know it, and it's the blasted Sullans who'll be searching for their heads!'"

"And do you believe that? Is that why you choose to stay?"

Mamercus bristled. "The question is, what's keeping *you* here, Gordianus? I've given you my answer. Now go!"

At that moment, the crowd before the commander's tent broke into a cheer. I heard the name of Sertorius shouted aloud in acclamation, and saw that the great man himself had emerged from the tent. He was a tall, robust-looking man with a strong jaw and a smile that radiated confidence. Years ago, he had lost an eye in battle. Other men might have been embarrassed by the defect, but Sertorius was said to consider his leather eye-patch to be a badge of honor. The many battle scars scattered over his arms and legs he considered to be his medals.

Some mortals possess a charismatic allure that is almost divine, that anyone can see at a glance, and Quintus Sertorius was such a mortal. This was a man whom other men would trust implicitly and follow without question, to glory or death. The cheers that greeted

his appearance, from both his own soldiers and from the local petitioners, were absolutely genuine and spontaneous.

Then the cries died away to a whispered hush. Eco and I looked
at one another, puzzled. The cheering was understandable, but what
was this? It was the hush of religious awe such as one hears in Rome
at certain ancient rites performed in the temples in the Forum, a
barely audible welter of whispers and murmurs and muttered prayers.

Then I saw the remarkable creature that had followed Sertorius
out of the tent.

It was a young fawn. Her soft pelt was utterly white, without a
single spot of color. She gamboled after Sertorius like a loyal hound,
and when he paused, she nuzzled against his thigh and lifted her
snout for him to stroke. I had never seen anything like it.

The hush grew louder, and amid the strange dialects I heard
snatches of Latin:

"The white fawn! The white fawn!"

"They both look happy—that must mean good news!"

"Diana! Bless us, goddess! Bless Quintus Sertorius!"

Sertorius smiled and laughed and bent down to take the fawn's
head in his hands. He kissed her right on the snout.

This evoked an even louder murmur from the crowd—and from
one onlooker, a loud, barking laugh. My dear mute son has a very
strange laugh, alas, rather like the braying of a mule. The fawn's ears
shot straight up and she cowered behind Sertorius, tripping awkwardly over her spindly legs. Heads turned toward us, casting suspicious looks. Eco clamped his hands over his mouth. Sertorius peered
in our direction, frowning. He saw Mamercus, then appraised me
with a curious eye.

"Mamercus Claudius!" he called. "I wondered where you'd got to.
Come!"

Sertorius pressed on through the worshipful crowd, with the
white fawn and a cordon of guards following behind. Included in the

retinue, I was surprised to see, was a girl who could hardly have been older than Eco. She was a beautiful child, with dark eyes and cheeks like white rose petals. Dressed all in white, with her black hair bound up in a scarf, she looked and carried herself like a priestess, keeping her eyes straight ahead and striding between the soldiers with a grace and self-assurance beyond her years.

"A white fawn!" I said. "And that girl! Who is she, Mamercus?"

But Mamercus only glowered at me and went to join Sertorius. I ran after him and clutched his arm.

"Mamercus, I shall try to find lodgings in Sucro tonight. If you should change your mind—"

He yanked his arm from my grasp and strode off without looking back.

Lodgings were not hard to find in Sucro. There was only one tavern with accommodations, and the place was deserted. The battle between Pompey and Sertorius had driven travelers far away, and the likelihood of another battle was keeping them away.

The tavern keeper was a strong-looking Celt with a shaggy black beard, named Lacro. He seemed to be in high spirits despite the hardships of war, and was glad to have two paying guests to share wine and conversation in the common room that night. Lacro's family had lived on the banks of the Sucro for generations. He boasted proudly of the bounty of the river and the beauty of the coast. His favorite recreation was to go trapping and hunting in the marshes near the river's mouth, where birds flocked in great numbers and crustacean delicacies could be plucked from the mud. Lacro had apparently been spending a lot of time in the marshes lately, if only to stay clear of the fighting.

But he did not complain about the war, except to excoriate

Pompey and Metellus. Lacro was very much a partisan of Sertorius, and praised him for unifying the various Celtic and Iberian tribes of Spain. He had no quarrel with Romans, he said, so long as they were like Sertorius; if it took a Roman to give his people leadership, then so be it. When I told him that Eco and I had come that very day from the great commander's camp, and indeed had caught a glimpse of Sertorius himself, Lacro was quite impressed.

"And did you see the white fawn?" he asked.

"Yes, we did. A strange creature to keep as a pet."

"The white fawn is not a pet!" Lacro was appalled at the idea. "The white fawn was sent to Sertorius as a gift, by Diana. The goddess speaks to him through the fawn. The fawn tells Sertorius the future."

"Really?"

"How else do you think he's gone undefeated for so long, no matter how many armies Rome sends against him? Did you think that Sertorius was merely lucky? No, he has divine protection! The white fawn is a holy creature."

"I see," I said, but apparently without sufficient conviction.

"Bah! You Romans, you've conquered the world but you've lost sight of the gods. You saw the white fawn with your own eyes, and thought it was a mere pet! But not Sertorius; that's what makes him different."

"How did Sertorius acquire this amazing creature?"

"They say some hunters came upon the fawn in a wood. She walked right up to them, and told them to take her to the great leader. The hunters brought her to Sertorius. When he bent down to nuzzle the fawn's face, she spoke to him, in his own tongue, and he recognized the voice of Diana. The two have never parted since. The fawn follows Sertorius everywhere, or strictly speaking, he follows the fawn, since it's she who tells him where his enemies are and what routes to take. Ah, so you saw her with your own eyes. I envy you! I've never seen her, only heard of her."

"This white fawn is quite famous then?"

"Everyone knows of her. I keep a tavern, don't I? I know what people talk about, and every man from the Pyrenees to the Pillars of Hercules loves the white fawn!"

Since there was only one tavern in Sucro, Mamercus Claudius had no trouble finding us the next morning. He stepped into the common room just as Eco and I were finishing our breakfast of bread and dates. So, I thought, the young man has decided to return to his grandfather after all. I smiled at him. He did not smile back.

I realized that he was still in his military garb, and that he was not alone. A small band of soldiers entered the room behind him, all wearing the same grim look.

His visit was official, then. My breakfast turned heavy in my stomach. My mouth went dry. I remembered the evil premonition I had felt about this mission from the very first, even before I met Gaius Claudius . . .

Mamercus marched up to us. His manner was soldierly and impersonal. "Gordianus! Quintus Sertorius has sent me to fetch you."

Then it *was* the worst, I thought. Mamercus had betrayed me to Sertorius, and now Sertorius was having me arrested for trying to engineer the defection of an officer. I had known the mission would be dangerous; I should have been more cautious. Mamercus had made it clear the previous day that he had no intention of returning to Rome with me; why I had lingered in Sucro? I had tarried too long, a victim of my own sentimental sympathy for the old senator. And I had made Eco a victim, as well. He was only a boy—surely Sertorius would not lop his head off along with mine. But what would become of him after I was gone? Sertorius would probably conscript him as a foot soldier, I thought. Was that to be Eco's fate, to end his days on a battlefield, fighting for a lost cause in a foreign land? If only I had left him behind in Rome!

I stood as bravely as I could and gestured for Eco to do the same. Mamercus and his men escorted us out of the tavern and marched us up the river road, back to the camp. The men's faces looked even grimmer under the bright morning sun. Not one of them said a word.

The same grimness presided in the camp. Every face we saw was glum and silent. Where were the high spirits of the day before?

We came to Sertorius's tent. Mamercus pulled back the flap and announced my name. He gestured for Eco and me to enter. He himself remained outside, as did the other soldiers.

The commander was alone; more alone, in fact, than I realized at first. He rose from his chair eagerly, as if he had been waiting impatiently, and strode toward us. This was not the reception I had expected.

"Gordianus the Finder!" he said, grasping my hand. "What good fortune that you should happen to be here, on such a day! Do you know why I've summoned you?"

"I'm beginning to think that I don't." The look on Sertorius's face was grim but not hostile. My head started to feel noticeably more secure on my shoulders.

"Then you haven't heard the news yet?"

"What news?"

"Excellent! That means that word hasn't yet spread to the town. One tries to keep down the gossip and rumors when something like this happens, but it's like putting out fires in a hayfield—"

I looked about the crowded tent, at the general's sleeping cot, the portable cabinets with maps and scrolls stacked on top, the little lamps on tripods. Something was missing . . .

"Where is the white fawn?" I said.

The color drained from his face. "Then you *have* heard the news?"

"No. But if there is some crisis at hand, shouldn't your divine counselor be with you?"

Sertorius swallowed hard. "Someone has stolen her, in the night. Someone has kidnapped the white fawn!"

"I see. But why have you sent for me, Quintus Sertorius?"

"Don't be coy, Finder. I know your reputation."

"You've heard of me?"

Sertorius managed a wry smile. "I do have some idea of what goes on in Rome, even if I haven't been there in years. I have my spies and informants there—just as Pompey and the senate no doubt have their spies in my camp. I try to keep abreast of who's taking whom to court, who's up and who's down. You might be surprised how often your name comes up. Yes, I know who you are."

"And do you know what brought me here?" I wanted to be absolutely certain that we understood each other.

"Yes, yes. I asked Mamercus about you yesterday. He showed me the letter. What a silly hen his grandfather is! The Sullans can have the old fellow—I have the grandson, and he's turned out to be worth any three of Pompey's officers, I'll wager! Bright, curious, clever, and wholly committed to the cause. If the powers-that-be in Rome had any sense, they'd have restored his family's estates and tried to win Mamercus over to their side, once his father was out of the way. But the Sullans always were a greedy lot of shortsighted bastards. They've driven all the best young men to Spain; all the better for me!" For just a moment he flashed the dazzling smile which had no doubt won the hearts of those bright young men. Then the smile faded. "But back to the business at hand. They call you the Finder, don't they? Well, I am a man who has lost something, and I must find it again!"

At night, Sertorius explained, the fawn was kept in a little tent of her own, near the general's quarters. For religious reasons, the opening of the fawn's tent was situated to face the rising moon; it had so happened, in this particular camp, that the front of the fawn's tent faced away from most of the others, and so was not visible to Sertorius's own night watch. The tent had its own guards, however, a pair of Celts who had vied for the religious honor of protecting Diana's emissary. These two had apparently been given a powerful drug and had slept the night through. Sertorius was convinced of their tearful remorse at having failed the white fawn, but otherwise had not been able to get any useful information from them.

I asked to see the tent. Sertorius led me there himself. Before we entered, he glanced at Eco.

"The boy has seen death before?" he said.

"Yes. Why do you ask?"

"It's not a gory sight—believe me, I've seen gore! Still, it's not pretty to look at."

He gave no further explanation, but led us into the tent. A little pen had been erected inside, with straw scattered on the ground along with pails of water and fresh grass. There was also, outside the pen, a little sleeping cot, upon which lay the girl we had seen in the general's entourage the previous day. She was dressed in the same white gown, but the white scarf was no longer around her head, so that her hair lay in a shimmering black pool around her white face. Her legs were straight and her hands were folded on her chest. She might almost have been sleeping, except for the unnatural, waxy paleness of her flesh, and the circle of bruised, chafed skin around her throat.

"Is this how you found her?" I asked.

"No," said Sertorius. "She was there in front of the pen, lying crumpled on the ground."

"Who was she?"

"Just a girl from one of the Celtic tribes. Their priests said that only a virgin should be allowed to feed and groom the white fawn. This girl volunteered. It brought great honor to her family. Her name was Liria."

"Where is her white scarf, the one she wore around her hair?"

"You *are* observant, Finder. The scarf is missing."

"Do you think . . . ?" I reached toward the marks on her throat. "A scarf would be one way of strangling someone."

Sertorius nodded gravely. "She must have tried to stop them. The guards were drugged, which means that Liria should have been drugged as well; she always ate the same food. But last night she may have fasted. She did that sometimes; she claimed that the white fawn would order her to fast, to keep herself pure. When they came to take the fawn, she must have woken up, and they strangled her to keep her from crying out."

"But why didn't they simply kill the fawn, instead of kidnapping her?"

Sertorius sighed. "This land is crawling with superstition, Gordianus. Omens and portents are in every breath, and a man can't take a piss without some god or other looking over his shoulder. I suspect that whoever did this had no intention of murdering anyone. What they wanted, what they intended, was that the fawn should simply disappear, don't you see? As if she had fled on her own. As if Diana had abruptly deserted me to my fate. What would my Spanish soldiers make of that? Can you understand what a disaster that would be for me, Gordianus?"

He stared at the dead girl, then tore his gaze away and paced back and forth in the small space before the pen. "The kidnappers added murder to their crime; that was sacrilege enough, though Liria wasn't really a priestess, just a girl from a humble family who happened still to be a virgin. But they would never had killed the fawn. That would have defeated their purpose. To kill the emissary of Diana would be an unforgivable atrocity. That would only strengthen the resolve of the tribes to fend off such an impious enemy. That's why I'm certain the fawn is still alive and unharmed.

"I've tried to keep this quiet, Gordianus, but I think the rumor has already begun to spread among the men that the fawn is missing. The Roman soldiers will suspect the truth, I imagine, that she was kidnapped for political reasons. But the natives—the natives will think that the gods have turned against me."

"Is their faith in the white fawn really so great?"

"Oh, yes! That's why I've used it, as a powerful tool to bind them to me. Powerful, but dangerous; superstition can be turned against the man who uses it, you see. I should have guarded her better!"

"Do you believe in the white fawn yourself, Sertorius? Does she speak to you?"

He looked at me shrewdly. "I'm surprised that you even ask such a question, Gordianus. I'm a Roman general, not a credulous Spaniard. The white fawn is nothing more than a device of statecraft. Must I explain? One day my spies inform me of Pompey's movements; the next day I announce that the white fawn whispered in my ear that Pompey will be seen in a certain place at a certain time, and sure enough, he is. Whenever I learn a secret or see into the future, the knowledge comes to me from the white fawn—officially. Whenever I have to give an order that the natives find hard to stomach—such as burning one of their own villages, or putting a popular man to death— I tell them it must be done because the white fawn says so. It makes things much, much easier. And whenever things look uncertain, and the natives are on the verge of losing heart, I tell them that the white fawn has promised me a victory. They find their courage then; they rally, and they make the victory happen.

"Do you think me blasphemous for resorting to such a device? The best generals have always done such things to shore up their men's morale. Look at Sulla! Before a battle, he always made sure his troops would catch him mumbling to a little image he stole from the oracle at Delphi; the deity invariably promised him victory. And Marius, too—he kept a Syrian wisewoman in his entourage, who could always be counted on to foresee disaster for his enemies. Too bad she failed him in the end.

"Even Alexander pulled such tricks. Do you know the story? Once when things looked bleak before a battle, his priests called for a blood sacrifice. While the sheep was being prepared at the altar, Alexander painted the letters N I backwards on the palms of one hand, and K E on the other. The priest cut open the sheep, pulled out the steaming liver and placed it in Alexander's hands. Alexander turned it over to show his men, and sure enough, there it was, written on the liver in letters no one could mistake—the Greek word for victory!"

"And your device was the white fawn?"

Sertorius stopped his pacing and looked me in the eye. "Here in Spain, the local tribes, especially the Celts, have a special belief in the mystical power of white animals. A good general makes note of such beliefs. When the hunters brought Dianara to me that day—"

"Dianara?"

Did he look slightly embarrassed? "I call the white fawn Dianara, after the goddess. Why not? When they brought her to me, I saw at once what could be done with her. I made her my divine counselor! And the strategy has paid off handsomely. But now—"

Sertorius began to pace again. "My scouts tell me that Metellus has joined Pompey on the other side of the Sucro. If my Spaniards find out that the fawn is missing, and I'm forced into another battle— the result could be an utter disaster. What man will fight for a general whom the gods have deserted? My only chance now is to withdraw west into the highlands, as quickly as I can. But in the meantime, the fawn must be found!" He gave me a look that was at once desperate and demanding.

"I'm a Finder, Quintus Sertorius, not a hunter."

"This is a kidnapping, Gordianus, not a chase. I'll pay you well. Bring Dianara back to me, and I shall reward you handsomely."

I considered. My commission from Gaius Claudius was completed. I had verified young Mamercus's whereabouts, delivered the letter, and given him every chance to accompany me back to Rome. I was a free agent again, in a foreign land, and a powerful man was seeking my help.

On the other hand, to aid a renegade general in the field would surely, in the view of the Roman Senate, constitute an act of treason . . .

I liked Sertorius, because he was honest and brave, and in the long run, the underdog. I liked him even better when he named an actual figure as a reward.

I agreed. If I could not return an errant young man to his grandfather, perhaps I could return a missing fawn to her master.

Sertorius allowed me to question the two guards who had been drugged. I could only agree with his own assessment, that the men were truly remorseful for what had happened and that they had nothing useful to tell. Neither did any of the other watchmen; no one had seen or heard a thing. It was as if the moon herself had reached down to fetch the white fawn home.

By the time Eco and I arrived back in Sucro that afternoon, the tavern was full of locals, all thirsty for wine and hungry for any news they could get of the missing white fawn. The secret was out, and rumors were flying wild. I listened attentively; one never knows when a bit of gossip may be helpful. Some said that the fawn had actually deserted Sertorius long ago (this was patently false, since I had seen the creature myself). Others claimed that the fawn had died, and that Sertorius had buried it and was only pretending that it had disappeared. A few said that the fawn had been stolen, but no one reported the death of the virgin. Perhaps the wildest rumor (and the most ominous) asserted that the fawn had showed up in Pompey's camp, and was now his confidant.

None of this was very helpful. After the local crowd dispersed to their homes for the night, I asked our host what he made of it all.

"Not a one of them knows a blasted thing! All a bunch of windbags." Lacro said this cheerily enough, and why not? He must have turned a nice profit on the sale of wine that day, and quite a few of the crowd had stayed on for dinner. "The only story that rang true to my ears was the one about the fawn being seen in the marshes."

"What's this? I missed that one."

"That's because the fellow who told it wasn't shouting his head off like the fools who had nothing to say. He was here behind the counter, talking to me. An old friend of mine; we sometimes go trapping in the marshes together. He was there early this morning. Says he caught a glimpse of something white off in the distance, in a stand of swamp trees."

"Perhaps he saw a bird."

"Too big for a bird, he said, and it moved like a beast, from here to there along the ground."

"Did he get a closer look?"

"He tried. But by the time he reached the trees, there was nothing to be seen—nothing except fresh hoof prints in the mud. The prints of a young deer, of that he was certain. And footprints, as well."

"Footprints?"

"Two men, he said. One on each side of the fawn."

Eco gripped my arm and shook it. I agreed; this was very interesting. "Did your friend follow these tracks?"

"No, he turned back and went about his business, checking his traps." Lacro raised an eyebrow. "He didn't say as much, but from the look on his face, I think he felt afraid when he saw those tracks. This is a fellow who knows the marshes like his own mother's face; knows what belongs there and what doesn't, and if something's not right. He saw those tracks and felt a bit of awe, standing where Diana's gift had passed. Mark my words, that white fawn is in the marshes."

Eco nudged me and put his hands to his throat, miming strangulation. Lacro looked puzzled.

I translated. "If your friend was afraid to follow those tracks, then his instincts probably *are* good." At least one person had already been murdered by the fawn's abductors.

"I don't quite follow you."

I looked at him steadily. "Yesterday, you spoke well of Sertorius . . ."

"I did."

"And you spoke with reverence about the white fawn . . ."

"Diana's gift."

"Lacro, I want to tell you a secret. Something very important."

"So, what are you waiting for? Who can keep secrets better than an innkeeper?" He hooked his thumb and gestured to the sleeping quarters upstairs, as if alluding to all the trysts which had taken place under his roof that would never be revealed by his telling.

"And do you think this friend of yours could keep a secret, as well?" I said. "And more importantly, do you think he might agree to guide a couple of strangers into the marshes? There's likely to be some danger—but there'll be a fee in it, too. A fee for you both . . ."

Before daybreak the next morning, we set out for the marshes.

Lacro and his friend, who was called Stilensis, led the way. Eco and I followed behind.

We came to the stand of trees where Stilensis had seen the tracks. They were still visible in the mud, picked out sharply by the first slanting rays of sunlight. We followed them. In places where the ground was too hard or too soft, the trail seemed to vanish, at least to my eyes, but our experienced guides were able to discern even the faintest traces. Occasionally even they lost the trail, and when that happened, they would patiently circle about until they found it again. Sometimes I could see how they did it, by spotting a broken twig or a crumpled leaf; at other times, it seemed to me that they were guided by some hidden instinct, or simple luck. Perhaps Lacro would say that Diana showed them the way.

They also seemed to sense, by some unknown faculty, the moment when we came within earshot of our prey. At the same moment, Lacro and Stilensis both turned and gestured for us to be utterly silent.

As for the enemy, there were only two of them, as the tracks had indicated; but the tracks had also indicated, by their size and depth, that the men making them were large fellows, with large shoes and heavy bodies. Fortunately for us, they were still asleep when we came upon them. They had no tent, and had made no fire. They slept on a bed of leaves, with light blankets to cover them.

Lacro and Stilensis had brought their hunting bows. While they notched arrows and took aim, Eco and I yanked away the men's blankets. They woke at once, scrambled to their feet, then froze when they saw the arrows aimed at them. They cursed in some native tongue.

Lacro asked them what they had done with the white fawn. The men grumbled and pointed toward a thick patch of bushes.

In a little clearing, Eco and I came upon the creature. She was tied to a small tree, asleep with her legs folded beneath her. At our approach, she stirred and lifted her head. I expected her to scramble up and try to bolt away. Instead, she stared at us sleepily and blinked several times, then threw back her head and seemed to yawn. She slowly and methodically unfolded her limbs and got to her feet, then sauntered toward us and lifted her face to be nuzzled. Eco let out a gasp of delight as he stroked the back of his hand against the shimmering white fur beneath her eyes.

We marched our prisoners through the marsh and then along the river road, with Eco leading the fawn by her leash, or as often as not being led by her. We stopped short of Sertorius's camp, and while the others waited in a secluded spot by the river, I went to give the general the news.

I arrived just in time. Only a single tent—the general's—was still standing. The troops had already begun the westward march toward the highlands. Sertorius and his staff were busily packing wagons and seeing to the final details of disbanding the camp.

Sertorius was the first to see me. He froze for an instant, then strode toward me. His face seemed to glow in the morning light. "It's good news, isn't it?"

I nodded.

"Is she well?"

"Yes."

"And the scoundrels who took her—did you capture them as well?"

"Two men, both native Spaniards."

"I knew it! I woke up this morning with a feeling that something wonderful would happen. Where is she? Take me to her at once! No, wait." He turned and called to his staff. "Come along, all of you. Wonderful news! Come and see!"

Among the officers, I saw Mamercus, carrying a cabinet out of the general's tent. "Put that down, Mamercus, and come see what the Finder has caught for us!" shouted Sertorius. "Something white! And two black-hearted Spaniards with her!"

Mamercus looked confused for a moment, then put down the cabinet. He nodded and stepped back into the tent.

"Come, Gordianus. Take me to her at once!" said Sertorius, pulling at my arm.

On the banks of the Sucro, the general and his fawn were re-united. I don't think I had ever seen a Roman general weep before. I certainly know that I had never seen one pick up a fawn and carry it about in his arms like a baby. For all his protestations that the white fawn was only a tool of statecraft, a cynical means of exploiting superstitions he did not share, I think that the creature meant much more than that to Sertorius. While she might not have whispered to him in the voice of Diana, or foretold the future, the white fawn was the visible sign of the gods' favor, without which every man is naked before his enemies. What I saw on the banks of the Sucro was the exultation of a man whose luck had deserted him and then had returned in the blink of an eye.

But Sertorius was a Roman general, and not given to undue sentimentality, even about his own destiny. After a while, he put down the fawn and turned to the two Spaniards we had captured. He spoke to them in their own dialect. Lacro whispered a translation in my ear.

They had treated the fawn well, Sertorius said, and had not harmed her; that was wise, and showed a modicum of respect for the goddess. But they had flouted the dignity of a Roman general and had interfered with the will of the goddess; and a young virgin had been murdered. For that they would be punished.

The two men comported themselves with great dignity, considering that they were likely to be slain on the spot. They conferred with each other for a moment, then one of them spoke. They were only hirelings, they explained. They knew nothing of a murdered girl. They had merely agreed to meet a man at the edge of the camp two nights ago. He had brought the fawn to them, wrapped in a blanket. They were to hide with the fawn in the marsh until Sertorius and his army were gone. They would never have harmed the creature, nor would they have harmed the girl who kept her.

Sertorius told them that he had suspected as much, that one of his own men—indeed, someone on his own staff, with adequate knowledge of the general's routine and the workings of the camp— must have been behind the kidnapping. If the two Spaniards were willing to point out this man, the severity of their own punishment might be considerably mitigated.

The two men conferred again. They agreed.

Sertorius stepped back and gestured to the members of his assembled staff. The two Spaniards looked from face to face, then shook their heads. The man was not among them.

Sertorius frowned and surveyed his staff. He stiffened. I saw a flash of pain in his eye. He sighed and turned to me. "One of my men isn't here, Finder."

"Yes, I see. He must have stayed behind."

Sertorius ordered some of his men to stay and guard the fawn. The rest of us hurried back with him to the camp.

"Look there! His horse is still here," said Sertorius.

"Then he hasn't fled," I said. "Perhaps he had no reason to flee. Perhaps he had nothing to do with the kidnapping—"

But I knew this could not be the case, even as Eco and I followed Sertorius into his tent. Amid the clutter of folded cots and chairs, Mamercus lay quivering on the ground, transfixed on his own sword. His right hand still gripped the pommel. In his left hand, he clutched the virgin's white scarf.

He was still alive. We knelt beside him. He began to whisper. We bent our heads close. "I never meant to kill the girl," he said. "She was asleep, and should have stayed that way . . . from the drug . . . but she woke. I couldn't let her scream. I meant to pull the scarf across her mouth . . . but then it was around her throat . . . and she wouldn't stop struggling. She was stronger than you might think . . ."

Sertorius shook his head. "But why, Mamercus? Why kidnap the fawn? You were my man!"

"No, never," said Mamercus. "I was Pompey's man! One of his agents in Rome hired me to be Pompey's spy. They said you would trust me . . . take me into your confidence . . . because of my father. They wanted someone to steal the white fawn from you. Not to kill it, just to steal it. You see, Gordianus, I never betrayed my grandfather. Tell him that."

"But why did you take up with Pompey?" I said.

He grimaced. "For money, of course! We were ruined. How could I ever have a career in Rome, without money? Pompey offered me more than enough."

I shook my head. "You should have come back to Rome with me."

Mamercus managed a rueful smile. "At first, I thought you were a messenger from Pompey. I couldn't believe he could be so stupid, to send a messenger for me into the camp, in broad daylight! Then you said you came from my grandfather . . . dear, beloved grandfather. I suppose the gods were trying to tell me something, but it was too late. My plan was set for that very night. I couldn't turn back." He coughed. A trickle of blood ran from the corner of his mouth. "But I turned your visit to my advantage! I showed Sertorius the letter . . . vowed that I had no intention of leaving him . . . not even to please my grandfather! How could he not trust me after that? Sertorius, forgive me! But Gordianus—"

He released his sword and blindly gripped my arm. With his other hand he still clutched the scarf. "Don't tell grandfather about the girl! Tell him I was a spy, if you want. Tell him I died doing my duty.

Tell him I had the courage to fall on my own sword. But not about the girl . . ."

His grip loosened. The light went out of his eyes. The scarf slipped from his fingers.

I looked at Sertorius. On his face I saw anger, disappointment, grief, confusion. I realized that Mamercus Claudius, like the white fawn, had meant more to him than he would say. Mamercus had been a sort of talisman for him, in the way that a son is a talisman—a sign of the gods' love, a pointer to a brighter future. But Mamercus had been none of those things, and the truth was hard for Sertorius to bear. How had he described Mamercus to me? "Bright, curious, clever, wholly committed to the cause." How painfully ironic those words seemed now!

I think that in that moment, Sertorius saw that the white fawn counted for nothing after all; that his days were numbered; that the might of Rome would never cease hounding him until he was destroyed and all traces of his rival state were obliterated from the earth. He picked up the scarf and pressed it to his face, covering his eye, and for that I was thankful.

The voyage back to Rome seemed long and tedious, yet not nearly long enough; I was not looking forward to meeting with Gaius Claudius and giving him the news.

I had done exactly as he asked: I had found his grandson, delivered the letter, invited Mamercus to flee. I had accepted the task and completed it. When Sertorius asked me to find the white fawn, how could I have known the end?

None of us could have known the outcome of my trip to Spain, least of all Gaius Claudius. And yet, if Gaius had not sent me to find his grandson, Mamercus might still have been alive. Would the old man be able to bear the bitterness of it, that seeking only to bring the boy safely home, he himself had instigated the events that led to the boy's destruction?

And yet, surely Mamercus alone was responsible for his downfall. He had deceived his grandfather, no matter that he loved him; had been a spy for a man and a cause he did not care about; had murdered an innocent girl. And for what? All for money; nothing but that.

I should not waste a single tear on the boy, I told myself, leaning over the rail of the ship that carried me back to Rome. It was night. The sky was black and the moon was full, her face spread upon the dark waters like a great pool of white light. Perhaps I did shed a tear for Mamercus Claudius; but the cold breeze plucked it at once from my cheek and dropped it into the vastness of the salty sea. There it was lost in an instant, and surely never counted for anything in the scales of justice, either as reckoned by mortals or by the gods.

SOMETHING FISHY IN POMPEII

"Taste it," said Lucius Claudius. "Go on—taste it!"

I wrinkled my nose. Strange as it may sound, I was not particularly fond of garum. Never mind that ninety-nine out of a hundred Romans adore it, and add it to ninety-nine out of a hundred dishes, spooning it over everything from sausages to egg custard, from asparagus to honey cakes. "Garum goes with everything," goes the popular saying.

We sat in the garden of Lucius's opulent house on the Palatine Hill. A slave stood before me—a rather beautiful young slave, for in all things Lucius was used to having the best—holding a small silver dish in each hand. In each dish was a dark, glistening dollop of garum.

"Taste it!" insisted Lucius.

I dabbed a finger into the thick, oily sauce in the dish to my left. I smelled it first, breathing in the sharp odor of pickled fish; reluctantly,

I popped my finger into my mouth. The taste was powerful: salty and slightly tangy, the spices playing with remarkable complexity upon my tongue.

I smiled. "Actually, that's not bad. Not bad at all."

"Of course it's not bad!" said Lucius, his fair, chubby cheeks blushing as red as the curls on his head. "That's the finest garum on the market, made exclusively at my manufactory outside Pompeii. The only reason you claim not to be fond of garum, Gordianus, is because you're used to the awful stuff that's passed off as garum— smelly pots of fermented fish entrails with a few crushed olives and a sprig of rosemary thrown in for seasoning. Foul stuff! *This* is the real thing, made from farm-fattened sardines macerated in salt and seasoned with my own secret recipe of spices and herbs, aged for a full month before it's scooped into amphorae for shipment—not the mere twenty days that some of my competitors try to get away with."

I dabbed my finger into the garum and took another taste. "It's really quite delicious. This would be very good on meats. Or vegetables. Or you could simply eat it on a piece of flatbread. Or straight out of the jar! Yes, I could get used to eating this. I suppose it's expensive?"

"Very! But help me with my problem, Gordianus, and you shall have a lifetime supply, free of charge."

"And what would that problem be?"

"Taste the other sample."

I took a sip of wine to cleanse my palate, then dipped my finger into the dollop of garum to my right. I smelled it; popped my finger between my lips; closed my eyes to savor the heady aftertaste that suffused my entire mouth; then dipped my finger to try a second helping.

Lucius leaned toward me. "And?"

"Obviously, I'm no expert on garum, but . . ."

"Yes, yes?"

"I would say that these two samples are . . . identical. The same robust yet subtle taste; the same sublimely slippery texture. No difference whatsoever."

Lucius nodded gravely. "And that's the problem! The first sample you tasted is my own brand of garum. The second is from my competitor, that blasted Marcus Fabricius."

"Fabricius?"

"His little garum manufactory is just a stone's throw from my own, down in Pompeii. I ship all over the world, while Fabricius sells most of his product out of a little shop here in Rome. Every so often I purchase some of his garum, just to remind myself what an inferior recipe tastes like. I bought this batch today. Imagine my shock when I tasted it!"

"It does seems unlikely that garum from different makers could be so completely identical."

"Unlikely? Impossible! Fabricius must have stolen my secret recipe!"

So it happened, for the promise of a lifetime's supply of the world's best garum—and because Lucius Claudius is my good friend and steadfast patron—that I found myself in the vicinity of Pompeii a few days later, taking a tour of Lucius's garum manufactory with the foreman, a tall, wizened slave named Acastus. I carried a letter of introduction from Lucius and posed as a would-be investor.

The impressive compound was situated beside a stream that emptied into the bay at the foot of Mount Vesuvius. Patios surrounded large sunken tanks in which the sardines were fattened; the murky water glistened with masses of darting silver fish. A warehouse held great stores of salt, herbs, and spices. Nearby there was a shed where artisans crafted clay vessels; storage pots for spices, as well as special pots for making the garum and amphorae for transporting it, were made on-site. There was a large stable full of horses and wagons for transporting the finished product overland to various Italian cities, as well as a waterfront facility for loading ships that would take the garum to markets as far away as Alexandria. Among those who could afford it, the garum of Lucius Claudius was a much sought-after, highly valuable commodity, the integrity of which he wished devoutly to safeguard.

At the center of the compound was the large, charmingly rustic house where Lucius stayed when he was in residence. Attached to the house were the guest quarters where I would be staying. The upper story contained Acastus's office, where pigeon-hole shelves were stuffed with correspondence and tables were stacked high with ledgers. From his balcony, beyond the warehouse, I could see the glittering bay dotted with sails. Closer at hand, beyond the wooded cleft by the stream, I could see the roofs and terraces of a neighboring compound.

"What's that place?" I asked.

Acastus squinted. "Oh, that's the manufactory of Marcus Fabricius. They make garum, too, or something they call garum. Of no interest to a serious investor, I assure you. Their product is quite inferior."

"I see. Can you show me exactly how the garum is prepared?"

"What's that you say?"

I repeated my request, more loudly.

"Certainly," wheezed Acastus. He seemed so old and frail that any master but Lucius would likely have replaced him long ago; but Lucius had a kindly streak, despite his patrician snobbery. Acastus, he had assured me, was the most trustworthy of all the foremen on all his farms and manufactories (for garum was only one of Lucius's moneymaking enterprises). Acastus oversaw production, scheduled shipments, billed customers, and kept the books. At all these tasks,

Lucius told me, Acastus excelled. But a foreman must be watchdog as well as overseer; if something odd was going on at the garum manufactory, were Acastus's eyes and ears sharp enough to notice?

With a doddering gait, he led me toward a terrace shaded by olive trees, where various slaves toiled over large clay pots. "Garum was invented by the Greeks, you know," he said. "In the old days it was a luxury that only the wealthiest Romans could afford. Nowadays everyone eats it, every day, on everything—or at least they eat something they call garum, whether it's worthy of the name or not. The best garum is still quite costly. Here, we'll watch this fellow make up a batch. Patro is your name, isn't it?"

"Yes, foreman." A bright-eyed young slave stood before a very large, wide-mouthed, flat-bottomed clay pot that came up to his knees. The bottom of the pot was already covered with a mixture of aromatic dried herbs. I leaned over the pot and breathed in the smells of dill, coriander, celery, fennel, oregano, and mint. No doubt there were other spices my nose was too untrained to discern.

"Who mixes the spices?" I said.

"What's that?"

"I said, who mixes—"

"The master comes down from Rome and does it himself, every other month or so," said Acastus.

This confirmed what Lucius had already told me. "But others must know exactly which spices are stocked in the warehouse. The recipe can't be a secret."

Acastus laughed. "The ingredients aren't the secret. It's the *proportions* that make the difference. The master does the measuring and the mixing himself, with no one else present. He's got a most refined palate, does the master. There are over thirty spices in all. You'd be hard-pressed to reproduce that exact mixture by tasting the finished product, or haphazardly trying this or that amount."

Patro, meanwhile, had fetched another pot, this one filled with sardines. These he spread over the layer of spices. "The fatter the fish, the better," commented Acastus.

Over the sardines, Patro spread a thick layer of salt. "Two fingers high," said Acastus. "More is too salty; less, not salty enough."

Patro repeated these three layers—spices, fish, salt—until the container was full. He then placed a lid on the pot, sealed the rim with pitch, and, with the help of another slave—for the pot must have been quite heavy—carried it to a sunny spot nearby.

"Now we let the mixture sit in the sun for seven days. No more, no less! After that, we'll stir it every day for twenty days. And then . . ." Acastus kissed his fingertips. "The finest garum on earth. I taste each batch myself before it's shipped out." He flashed a gap-toothed smile. "You were wondering, weren't you, why the master has kept me on, long past my prime? Not for my squinting eyes or my half-deaf ears. For *this*." He tapped his nose. "And *this*." He stuck out his tongue.

I heard laughter behind me and turned to see Patro and the other slave cover their mouths and look away. Acastus squinted in their direction. "Did you hear squirrels chattering?" he said. "Terrible pests. Known to open the garum pots during fermentation and scatter it all about. We have to throw the whole batch away when that happens."

"Would it spoil if you simply resealed it?"

"Probably not, but we can't take the chance. The master has a standard to maintain."

"How often does this happen?"

"Perhaps once a month."

"I suppose you note the loss in your ledgers?"

"Of course! I keep strict accounting of all expenditures and losses, including spoilage. It's not a major problem; still, I feed the workers fresh squirrel as often as I can, so as to thin the ranks of those nasty pests!"

That night Acastus and I dined not on squirrel but on herb bread and liver pâté, with generous helpings of garum. Acastus went to bed early. I stayed up for a while, examining the ledgers, with his permission. Eventually I went to bed myself, with instructions to be awakened at the beginning of the workday.

A slave woke me at dawn. I roused myself, went down to the stream to splash my face, and ate a crust of bread on the terrace. Acastus was not yet up, but the rest of the compound was stirring. I strolled over to the fermentation area.

From a distance, I saw young Patro with his hands on his hips, shaking his head. "Can you believe it? They've done it again, those damned squirrels!"

It appeared that the phenomenon Acastus had described had occurred during the night. The lid of the container which Patro had sealed the previous day lay on the grass, salt was scattered about, and a whole layer of sardines was missing.

"Mischievous little pests, aren't they?" I said.

Patro smiled. "More hungry than mischievous, don't you imagine? Either way, they're only as the gods made them. Well, I suppose I should get rid of this batch, then let Acastus know. Here, Motho, come help me carry it down to the stream."

Together, they lifted the open container. Walking slowly and awkwardly, they headed toward the wooded cleft beside the stream.

I headed for the cleft myself, walking fast and taking a different route. I was waiting on the opposite bank when they arrived. Instead of emptying the contents of the pot in the rushing water, they crossed the shallow stream and began to climb the opposite bank, huffing and puffing.

"And where might you fellows be going?" I said.

They froze in their tracks and gazed up at me blankly.

"We . . . that is to say . . ." Patro frantically tried to think of some explanation.

"I think you're headed for Fabricius's place, to sell him that pot of garum. He'll only need to add some sardines and salt to the top, seal it up, and let it ferment. A month from now he can sell it at his little shop in Rome and claim that it's every bit as delicious as the famous garum of Lucius Claudius—since it *is* the garum of Lucius Claudius!"

"Please, this is the first time we've ever—"

"No, Patro. You've been doing this about once a month for almost half a year. That's how often such a loss is noted in Acastus's ledgers."

"But—*we* didn't spoil this batch. I was in my bed all night, and so was Motho—"

"I know you didn't. Nor did a squirrel. I did it myself, to see what would happen. I imagine that the very first time it happened, it *was* the act of a squirrel, or some other nocturnal pest. And you thought: what a pity, to waste all that lovely, valuable garum. Why not sell it to the neighbor? What do you two do with the money Fabricius pays you? Enjoy a night of wine and women down in Pompeii?"

Their faces turned red.

"I thought so. But what was it you said about the squirrels? 'They're only as the gods made them.' Hard to blame you for taking advantage of the occasional accident—except that what began as an accident has become a regular occurrence. If it happens that you two have been damaging batches of garum on purpose—"

"You can't prove that!" said Patro, his voice rising to a desperate pitch.

"No. But I intend to stop it from happening again. What do you say? I'll turn a blind eye to this morning's mischief, in exchange for your promise that you'll never sell garum to Fabricius again."

The two of them looked very relieved and very repentant.

"Very well. Now, let's see you empty that spoiled batch of garum in the stream!"

On the way back to Rome, I pondered the dilemma I had gotten myself into. How could I assure Lucius Claudius that the problem had been taken care of, without getting those two young slaves into trouble? And further, how could I let Lucius know, without getting Acastus into trouble, that the foreman needed an assistant with a sharper pair of eyes and ears and a more suspicious temperament?

I would think of something. After all, a lifetime's supply of the world's best garum was at stake!

ARCHIMEDES'S TOMB

"When I learned that you and your son were here in Syracuse, Gordianus, I sent Tiro to find you at once. You have no idea what a comfort it is, seeing a familiar face out here in the provinces," Cicero smiled and raised his cup.

I returned the gesture. Eco did likewise, and the three of us sipped in unison. The local vintage wasn't bad. "I appreciate the welcome," I said, which was true. Indeed, Tiro's unexpected appearance at the dingy inn down at the harbor where Eco and I were staying had taken me by complete surprise, and the invitation to dine with Cicero and to spend the night at his rented house surprised me even more. In the five years since Cicero had first employed me (to assist him in the defense of Sextus Roscius, accused of parricide), our relationship had been strictly professional. Cicero generally treated me with a cool diffidence: I was merely the Finder, useful for digging up dirt. I regarded him with wary respect; as an advocate and rising

politician, Cicero seemed genuinely interested in justice and truth—
but in the end he was, after all, an advocate and a politician.

In other words, we were on friendly terms, but not exactly friends.
So I found it curious that he should have invited Eco and me to dine
with him purely for pleasure. His twelve months as a government administrator here in Sicily must have been lonely for him indeed if
the sight of my face could bring him much enjoyment. "You're not
exactly at the end of the world here," I felt obliged to point out.
"Sicily isn't all that far from Rome."

"True, true, but far enough to make a man appreciate what Rome
has to offer. And far enough so that all the gossip gets a bit distorted
on the way here. You must tell me everything that's been happening
in the Forum, Gordianus."

"Surely your friends and family keep you informed."

"They write, of course, and some of them have visited. But none
of them have your . . ." He searched for the word. "Your particular
perspective." Looking up at the world, he meant, instead of down.
"Ah, but now that my year of service is up, I shall soon be back in
Rome myself. What a relief it shall be to leave this wretched place
behind me. What's that the boy is saying?"

On the dining couch beside me, my mute son had put down his
cup and was shaping thoughts in the air with his hands. His pictures
were clear enough to me, if not to Cicero: high mountains, broad
beaches, stony cliffs. "Eco likes Sicily, or at least the little we've seen
of it on this trip. He says that the scenery here is beautiful."

"True enough," Cicero agreed, "though not so true of the people."

"The Greek-speaking population? I thought you adored all things
Greek, Cicero."

"All things Greek, perhaps, but not all Greeks." He sighed.
"Greek culture is one thing, Gordianus. The art, the temples, the
plays, the philosophy, the mathematics, the poetry. But—well, since
my other guests haven't yet arrived, I shall speak freely, Roman to

Roman. The Greeks who gave us all that marvelous culture are dust now, and have been for centuries. As for their far-flung progeny, especially in these parts—well, it's sad to see how little they resemble their colonizing ancestors.

"Consider this city: Syracuse, once a beacon of light and learning to the whole of the Mediterranean this side of Italy—the Athens of the west, the rival of Alexandria at its peak. Two hundred years ago, Hiero ruled here, and men like Archimedes walked the beach. Now one finds only the remnants of a proud race, a degraded people, rude and uneducated, without manners or morals. The far-flung colonies of the Greeks have forgotten their forebears. The mantle of civilization has been taken up by us, Gordianus, by Rome. We are the true heir to Greek culture, not the Greeks. Only Romans nowadays have the refinement to truly appreciate, say, a statue by Polyclitus."

"Or is it that only Romans have the money to afford such things?" I suggested. "Or the armies to bring them home by force?"

Cicero wrinkled his nose to show that he found my questions inappropriate, and called for more wine. Beside me, Eco fidgeted on his couch. The early education of my adopted son had been sorely neglected, and despite my best efforts, his progress was still hampered by his inability to speak. At fifteen, he was almost a man, but talk of culture, especially from a snob like Cicero, quickly bored him.

"Your year of foreign service has made you even more of a Roman patriot," I remarked. "But if your term is up, and if you find the company of the Greek Sicilians so lacking, I wonder that you don't leave the place at once."

"Right now I'm playing tourist, actually. I was posted to the other half of the island, you see, over in Lilybaeum on the west coast. Syracuse is a stopover on my way home, a last chance to see the sights before I quit Sicily for good. Don't misunderstand me, Gordianus. This is a beautiful island, as your son says, resplendent with natural wonders. There are many fine buildings and works of art, and many sites of great historical importance. So much has happened in Sicily in the centuries since the Greeks colonized it—the golden reign of Hiero, the great mathematical discoveries of his friend Archimedes, the Carthaginian invasions, the Roman takeover. There's plenty for a visitor to see and do here in Syracuse." He sipped his wine. "But I don't suppose it's pleasure that's brought *you* here, Gordianus."

"Eco and I are here strictly on business. A fellow back in Rome hired me to follow the trail of a business partner who absconded with the profits. I tracked the missing man here to Syracuse, but today I learned that he's sailed on, probably east to Alexandria. My instructions were to go only as far as Sicily, so as soon as I can book passage, I plan to head back to Rome with the bad news and collect my fee."

"Ah, but now that we've found one another here in a strange city, you must stay with me for a while, Gordianus." Cicero sounded sincere, but then, all politicians do. I suspected the invitation for an extended stay was merely a polite gesture. "What a remarkable livelihood you have," he went on, "hunting down murderers and scoundrels. Of course, one hardly meets a better class of people, being in government service, especially in the provinces. Ah, but here's Tiro!"

Cicero's young secretary gave me a smile and mussed Eco's hair as he passed behind our couches. Eco pretended to take offense and put up his fists like a boxer. Tiro indulged him and did likewise. Tiro had an affable, unassuming nature. I had always found him easier to deal with, and to like, than his master.

"What is it, Tiro?" said Cicero.

"Your other three guests have arrived, Master. Shall I show them in?"

"Yes. Tell the kitchen slaves that they can bring out the first course as soon as we're all settled." Cicero turned back to me. "I hardly know these fellows myself. I was told by friends in Lilybaeum that I should meet them while I was here in Syracuse. Dorotheus and Agathinus are important businessmen, partners in a shipping firm. Margero is said to be a poet, or what passes for a poet in Syracuse nowadays."

Despite his disdainful tone, Cicero made a great show of welcoming his guests as they entered the room, springing up from his couch and extending his arms to give them a politician's embrace. He could hardly have been more unctuous had they been a trio of undecided voters back in Rome.

The meal, much of it harvested from the sea, was excellent, and the company more genial than Cicero had led me to expect. Dorotheus was a heavyset, round-faced man with a great black beard and a booming voice. He joked continually during the meal, and his good humor was contagious; Eco particularly succumbed to it, often joining his own odd but charming bray to Dorotheus's pealing laughter. From certain bits of conversation that passed between Dorotheus and his business partner, I gathered that both men had cause to be in high spirits, having recently struck some very lucrative deals. Agathinus, however, was more restrained than his partner; he smiled and laughed quietly at Dorotheus's jokes, but said little. Physically, he was quite the opposite of Dorotheus as well, a tall, slender man with a narrow face, a slit of a mouth, and a long nose. They seemed a perfect example of how a successful partnership can sometimes result from the union of two markedly different natures.

The third Syracusan, Margero, certainly looked and played the part of a pensive Greek poet. He was younger than his wealthy companions and quite handsome, with ringlike curls across his forehead, heavy lips, and a dark-browed, moody countenance. I gathered that his verses were quite fashionable at the moment in Syracusan intellectual circles, and I sensed that he was more an ornament than a friend to the two businessmen. He seldom laughed, and showed no inclination to recite from his poems, which was probably for the best, considering Cicero's snobbishness. For his part, Cicero only occasionally struck a patronizing tone.

There was talk of business regarding the port of Syracuse and the Sicilian grain harvest, talk of the season's dramatic festivals at the old Greek theater in the city, talk of the current fashions among the Syracusan women (who always lagged a few years behind the women of Rome, as Cicero felt obliged to point out). Much of the conversation was in Greek, and Eco, whose Greek was limited, inevitably grew restless; eventually I dismissed him, knowing he would find the conversation much more fascinating if he could eavesdrop from the kitchen with Tiro.

Eventually, over fresh cups of wine after the final course of savory onions stewed in honey with mustard seeds, Cicero steered the conversation to the past. He had spent his year in Sicily making himself an expert on the island's long and tumultuous history, and seemed quite pleased at the chance to demonstrate his knowledge to a native audience. Little by little his voice fell into a speechifying rhythm that invited no interruption. What he had to say was fascinating—I had never heard so many gruesome details of the great slave revolts that wracked Sicily in the previous generation—but after a while I could see that his Syracusan guests were growing as restless as Eco.

Cicero grew especially impassioned when he turned to Hiero, the ruler of Syracuse during its golden age. "Now there was a ruler, an example to all the other Hellenic tyrants who reigned over the Greek cities in his day. But then, you must know all about the glory of Hiero's reign, Margero."

"Must I?" said Margero, blinking and clearing his throat like a man awakening from a nap.

"Being a poet, I mean. Theocritus—his sixteenth idyll," Cicero prompted.

Margero merely blinked again.

"The sixteenth idyll of Theocritus," said Cicero, "the poem in which he extols the virtues of Hiero's reign and looks forward to his ultimate victory over Carthage. Surely you know the poem."

Margero blinked his heavy lashes and shrugged.

Cicero frowned disapprovingly, then forced a smile. "I mean those verses, of course, which begin,

> "This is ever the business of Muses, of poets,
> to sing praise to gods, to sing hymns to heroes . . .

"Surely, Margero . . . ?"

The young poet stirred himself. "It is *vaguely* familiar." Dorotheus laughed softly. Agathinus's thin lips compressed into a smile. I realized that Margero was having Cicero on.

Cicero, oblivious, prompted him with more lines:

> "Bravely the men of Syracuse grip their spears
> and lift up their wickerwork shields.
> Among them Hiero girds himself like a hero of old,
> with a lion's head atop his helmet."

"Horsehair," Margero grunted.

"What's that?"

" 'With a *plume of horsehair* atop his helmet,' " said Margero, indolently raising an eyebrow. "Lion's head, indeed!"

Cicero reddened. "Yes, you're right—'with a plume of horsehair . . . ' Then you *do* know the poem."

"Slightly," allowed Margero. "Of course, Theocritus was just blowing hot air to try to get Hiero's favor. He was a poet without a patron at that particular moment; thought he might enjoy the climate here in Syracuse, so he dashed off an idyll to get Hiero's attention. Figured the tyrant might be shopping for an epic poet to record his victories over Carthage, so he sent some sycophantic scribbles by way of applying for the post. A pity Hiero didn't take him up on the offer—too busy killing Carthaginians, I suppose. So Theocritus dashed off another encomium, to King Ptolemy in Alexandria, and landed a job scribbling on the Nile instead. A pity, how we poets are always at the whim of the rich and powerful."

This was more than Margero had said all evening. Cicero eyed him uncertainly. "Ah, yes. Be that as it may, Hiero did drive back the Carthaginians, whether any poets were there to record it or not, and we remember him as a great ruler, in Rome, anyway. And of course, among educated men, his friend Archimedes is even more famous." Cicero looked for a nod from his guests, but the three of them only stared back at him dumbly.

"Archimedes, the mathematician," he prompted. "Not a philosopher, to be sure, but still among the great minds of his time. He was Hiero's right-hand man. A thinker in the abstract, mostly, consumed with the properties of spheres and cylinders and cubic equations, but quite a hand at engineering catapults and war machines when he set himself to it. They say that Hiero couldn't have driven the Carthaginians from Sicily without him."

"Ah," said Agathinus dryly, "*that* Archimedes. I thought you meant Archimedes the fishmonger, that bald fellow with a stall on the wharves."

"Oh, is the name really that common?" Cicero seemed on the verge of apprehending that he was being mocked, but pressed on, determined to lecture his Syracusan guests about the most famous Syracusan who ever lived. "I refer, of course, to the Archimedes who said, 'Give me a place to stand on, and I will move the earth,' and demonstrated as much to Hiero in miniature by inventing pulleys and levers by which the king was able to move a dry-docked ship by a mere flick of his wrist; the Archimedes who constructed an extraordinary clockwork mechanism of the sun, moon, and five planets in which the miniature spheres all moved together in exact accordance with their celestial models; the Archimedes who is perhaps most famous for the solution he devised to the problem of the golden crown of Hiero."

"Ah, now you are bound to lose me," said Dorotheus. "I've never had a head for logic and mathematics. Remember, Agathinus, how our old tutor used to have weeping fits, trying to get me to understand Pythagoras and all that?"

"Ah, but the principle of the golden crown is quite simple to explain," said Cicero brightly. "Do you know the story?"

"In a vague, general, roundabout way," said Dorotheus, with laughing eyes.

"I'll make the tale brief," promised Cicero. "It seems that Hiero gave a certain weight of gold to an artisan, with a commission to make him a crown. Soon enough, the man returned with a splendid gold crown. But Hiero heard a rumor that the artisan had pilfered some of the gold, and had substituted silver for the core of the crown. It weighed the correct amount, but was the crown made of solid gold or not? The piece was exquisitely crafted, and Hiero hated to damage it, but he could think of no way to determine its composition short of melting it down or cutting into it. So he called on Archimedes, who had helped him with so many problems in the past, and asked if he could find a solution.

"Archimedes thought and thought, but to no avail. Gold was heavier than silver, that much he knew, and a blind man could tell the two apart by weighing them in his hands; but how could one tell if a given object was made of silver covered with gold? They say that Archimedes was sitting in a tub at the baths, noticing how the level of the water rose and fell as the bathers got in and out, when the solution suddenly came to him. He was so excited that he jumped from the tub and ran naked through the streets, shouting, '*Eureka! Eureka!*'—'I have found it! I have found it!'"

Dorotheus laughed. "All the world knows that part of the tale, Cicero. And for better or worse, that's how the world pictures Archimedes—as an absentminded old genius."

"A *naked* absentminded old genius," Agathinus amended tartly.

"Not a pretty picture," said Margero. "A man of a certain age should know better than to subject others to his bony nakedness, even in private." It seemed to me that he shot a caustic look at Agathinus, who stared straight ahead. I realized that the two of them had hardly said a word to each other or exchanged a glance all night.

"Gentlemen, we digress," said Cicero. "The point of the story is the solution that Archimedes devised."

"Ah, now this is the part that I've never been quite able to follow," said Dorotheus, laughing.

"But it's really quite simple," Cicero assured him. "This is what Archimedes did. He took an amount of gold of a certain weight—a single Roman uncia, let's say. He placed the uncia of gold in a vessel of water, and marked how high the waterline rose. Then he took an uncia of silver, placed it in the same vessel, and marked the waterline. Being a lighter substance, the uncia of silver was larger than the uncia of gold, and so displaced more water, and thus caused a higher waterline. Then Archimedes took the crown and, knowing the exact number of uncias of gold that Hiero had given the artisan, calculated how high it should cause the waterline to rise. If the waterline rose higher than expected, then the crown could not be made of solid gold, and must contain some material of greater volume per uncia, such as silver. Sure enough, the crown displaced more water than it should have. The artisan, his deception discovered, confessed to having covered a silver crown with gold."

"I see," said Dorotheus slowly and without irony. A light seemed genuinely to dawn in his eyes. "Do you know, Cicero, I have never before been able to grasp Archimedes's principle."

"Ah, but you should. It can be of great practical use to a man dealing in payments and commodities, as you do."

"Yes, I can see that," said Dorotheus, nodding thoughtfully.

Cicero smiled. "You see, it's really simple, as most basic principles are. But it takes a man like Archimedes to discover such principles in the first place." He gazed at his wine by the lamplight. "But absentminded he certainly was, always drifting into his world of pure geometry. At the baths, they say, he would even use himself as a tablet, drawing geometrical shapes in the massage oil on his belly."

This image pleased Dorotheus, who slapped his own belly and laughed heartily. Even Agathinus grinned. Margero merely raised an eyebrow.

"Thus Archimedes met his death as absentmindedly absorbed in mathematics as ever," said Cicero. "But I'm sure you all know the story of his end already . . ."

"Vaguely," allowed Agathinus.

"Oh, but you must enlighten us," said Dorotheus.

"Very well, if you insist. After Hiero died, the Romans occupied Sicily, to keep it as a bulwark against Carthage. On the day that Syracuse was taken by the general Marcellus, Archimedes was on the beach, working out a theorem by drawing figures with a stick in the sand, when a troop of Roman soldiers came marching up. Archimedes, who didn't even know that the city had been taken, took no notice until the soldiers began to tramp across his drawings. He made a rude remark—"

"He suggested that they all go copulate with their mothers, as I recall," said Margero, smiling languidly.

Cicero cleared his throat. "At any rate, one of the soldiers flew into a rage and killed Archimedes on the spot."

"I had no idea that a preoccupation with mathematics could be so dangerous," quipped Agathinus, straight-faced.

"At least Archimedes knew how to mind his own business," said Margero quietly. Again, I thought I saw him glare at Agathinus, who showed no reaction.

Cicero ignored the interruption. "When the Roman general learned of the tragedy, he was mortified, of course. He ordered a grand funeral procession and the construction of an elaborately ornamented tomb inscribed with the greatest of Archimedes's theorems and decorated with sculptures of the forms whose properties he discovered—the sphere, the cone, the cylinder, and so on. I say—where is the tomb of Archimedes? I should like to see it while I'm here."

Agathinus and Dorotheus looked at each other and shrugged. Margero's face was as unreadable as a cat's.

"Do you mean to say that none of you knows the location of Archimedes's tomb? Is it not general knowledge?"

"Somewhere in the old necropolis outside the city walls, I suppose," said Agathinus vaguely.

"Not everyone is as preoccupied with their dead ancestors as you Romans," said Margero.

"But surely the tomb of a man as great as Archimedes should be regarded as a shrine." Cicero suddenly stiffened. His eyes flashed. His jaw quivered. "Eureka! I have found it!" He was suddenly so animated that we all gave a start, even the heavy-lidded Margero. "Gordianus the Finder, it was the Fates who brought us two Romans together here in Syracuse! I have a purpose here, and so have you."

"What are you talking about, Cicero?"

"What do you say to a bit of employment? You shall locate the lost tomb of Archimedes for me—if it still exists—and I shall restore it to its former glory! It shall be the crowning achievement of my year in Sicily. Brilliant! Who can doubt it was the Fates who engineered this evening and its outcome, who brought us all together, we two Romans and our new Syracusan friends? Eureka! I feel like Archimedes in the bathing tub."

"Just don't go running naked though the streets," quipped Dorotheus, his round body shaking with mirth.

The evening had come to a natural conclusion, and the three Syracusans made ready to leave. Cicero retired, leaving it to Tiro to show them out and to conduct Eco and me to our beds. At the door, Agathinus lingered behind his departing companions and drew me aside.

"I take it that Cicero is serious about hiring you to go looking for Archimedes's tomb tomorrow?"

"So it appears. They call me Finder, after all."

Agathinus pursed his thin lips and studied me with cool, appraising eyes that betrayed a hint of amusement. "You seem to be a decent enough fellow, Gordianus—for a Roman. Ah, yes, don't deny it—I saw you laughing in silence tonight along with us, while your countryman lectured us about Hiero and Archimedes. As if we were schoolboys, indeed! As if he were the native Syracusan, not us! But as I say, you seem decent enough. Shall I do you a favor and tell you where to find the tomb?"

"You know?"

"It's not exactly common knowledge, but yes, I know where it is."

"Yet you didn't tell Cicero."

"Never! I think you know why. The know-it-all! From what I've heard, he's more honest than most of the bureaucrats Rome sends us, but still—the gall of the man! But I like you, Gordianus. And I like your son; I liked the way he laughed at Dorotheus's awful jokes. Shall I show you where to find the tomb of Archimedes? Then you can show it to Cicero, or not, as you please—and charge him a stiff fee for your services, I hope."

I smiled. "I appreciate the favor, Agathinus. Where exactly is the tomb?"

"In the old necropolis outside the Achradina Gate, about a hundred paces north of the road. There are a lot of old monuments there; it's a bit of a maze. My father showed me the tomb when I was a boy. The inscriptions of the theorems had largely worn away, but I remember the geometrical sculptures quite vividly. The necropolis has fallen into neglect, I'm afraid. The monuments are all overgrown." He thought for a moment. "It's hard to give exact directions. It would be easier simply to show you. Can you meet me outside the gate tomorrow morning?"

"You're a busy man, Agathinus. I don't want to impose on you."

"It's no imposition, so long as we do it first thing in the morning. Meet me an hour after dawn."

I nodded, and Agathinus departed.

"How did the dinner go?" asked Tiro as he showed us to our room. "I know that Eco didn't think much of the evening." He mimicked Eco yawning. Meanwhile Eco, yawning for real, tumbled backward onto a sleeping couch that looked infinitely more comfortable than the vermin-ridden mats at the inn where we had been staying.

"An evening is never too dull if it ends with a full stomach, a roof over my head, and the prospect of gainful employment." I said. "As for the company, Dorotheus is likable enough, if a bit loud. And Agathinus appears to be an alright fellow."

"Rather dour-looking."

"I think he just has a very dry sense of humor."

"And the poet?"

"Margero was clearly in no mood to recite poetry. He seemed to be rather preoccupied. There was something going on between him and Agathinus . . ."

"I think I can explain that," offered Tiro.

"You weren't in the room."

"No, but I was in the kitchen, soaking up local gossip from the slaves. Agathinus and Dorotheus are Margero's patrons, you see; every poet needs patrons if he's to eat. But lately there's been a chill between Agathinus and Margero."

"A chill?"

"Jealousy. It seems they're both paying court to the same pretty boy down at the gymnasium."

"I see." The two were rivals in love, then. Margero was younger and more handsome than Agathinus, and could compose love poems; but Agathinus had the attractions of money and power. Clearly, the two of them had not yet fallen out completely—Margero still depended on Agathinus for patronage, Agathinus still used the poet as an ornament—but there was friction between them. "Any other interesting gossip from the kitchen slaves?"

"Only that Agathinus and Dorotheus just received payment for their largest shipment ever of imported goods from the East. Some people say that they're now the richest men in Syracuse."

"No wonder Cicero was advised to make friends with them."

"Do you need anything else before you retire?" asked Tiro, lowering his voice. Eco, not even undressed, was already softly snoring on his couch.

"Something to read, perhaps?"

"There are some scrolls in the room that Cicero uses for an office . . ."

I ended the night curled under a coverlet on my couch, puzzling by lamplight over a musty old scroll of the works of Archimedes, amazed at his genius. Here were such wonders as a method for determining the surface area of a sphere, explained so lucidly that even I could almost understand it. At length I came upon the proposition which had resulted from the problem of the gold crown:

Proposed: A solid heavier than a fluid will, if placed in it, descend to the bottom of the fluid, and the solid will, when weighed in the fluid, be lighter than its true weight by the weight of the fluid.

Yes, well, that much was obvious, of course. I read on.

Let A be a solid heavier than the same volume of fluid, and let $(G + H)$ represent its weight, while G represents the weight of the same volume of the fluid . . .

This was not quite so clear, and I was getting drowsy. Cicero's explanation had been easier to follow. I pressed on.

Take a solid B lighter than the same volume of the fluid, and such that the weight of B is G, while the weight of the same volume of the fluid is $(G + H)$. Let A and B be now combined into one solid and immersed. Then, since $(A + B)$ will be of the same weight as the same volume of fluid, both weights being equal to $(G + H) + G$, it follows that . . .

I gave a great yawn, put aside the scroll, and extinguished the lamp. Alas, it was all Greek to me.

The next morning, at daybreak, I roused Eco, grabbed a handful of bread from the pantry, and the two of us set out for the Achradina Gate.

The stretch of road outside the walls was just as Agathinus had described it, with a great maze of tombs on either side, all overgrown with brambles and vines. It was an unsettling place, even in the pale morning light, with an air of decay and desolation. Some of the stone monuments were as large as small temples. Others were simple stelae set in the earth, and many of these were no longer upright but had been knocked this way and that. Crumbling sculptural reliefs depicted funeral garlands and horses' heads, the traditional symbols of life's brief flowering and the speedy passage toward death. Some of the monuments were decorated with the faces of the dead, worn so smooth by time that they were as bland and featureless as the statues of the Cyclades.

Agathinus was nowhere to be seen. "Perhaps we're early," I said. Eco, full of energy, began nosing about the monuments, peering at the worn reliefs, looking for pathways into the thicket. "Don't go getting lost," I told him, but he might as well have been deaf as well as mute. He was soon out of sight.

I waited, but Agathinus did not appear. It was possible that he had arrived before us and lacked the patience to wait, or that his business had kept him from coming. There was also the chance that he had changed his mind about helping me, decent enough fellow for a Roman though I might be.

I tried to remember his description of the tomb's location. On the north side, he had said, about a hundred paces from the road, and decorated with sculptures of geometrical shapes. Surely it couldn't be that hard to find.

I began nosing about as Eco had done, looking for ways into the thicket. I found his tracks and followed them into a sort of tunnel through the thorns and woody vines that choked the pathways between the monuments. I moved deeper and deeper into a strange world of shadowy foliage and cold, dank stone covered with lichen and moss. Dead leaves rustled underfoot. Whenever the pathway branched I tried to follow Eco's footsteps and called out his name to let him know that I was behind him. I soon realized that finding

Archimedes's tomb would not be such a simple task after all. I considered turning and retracing my steps back to the road. Agathinus might have arrived, and be waiting for me.

Then I heard a strange, twisted cry that was not quite a scream, but rather the noise a mute boy might make if he tried to scream.

Eco!

I rushed toward the noise, but was confounded by the branching maze and the echo of his cry among the stone tombs. "Cry out again, Eco! Cry out until I find you!"

The noise echoed from a different direction. I wheeled about, banged my head against the projecting corner of a monument, and cursed. I reached up to wipe the sweat from my eyes and realized I was bleeding. Eco cried out again. I followed, stumbling over creeping vines and dodging crooked stelae.

Suddenly, above a tangle of thorns, I glimpsed the upper part of what could only be the tomb of Archimedes. Surmounting a tall square column chiseled with faded inscriptions in Greek was a sphere, and surmounting the sphere, balanced on its round edge, was a solid cylinder. These two forms were the concrete representation of one of the principles I had encountered in my reading the night before—but all such thoughts fled from my mind as I found a way through the thicket and stepped into a small clearing before the tomb.

In front of the column there were several other geometrical sculptures. Upon one of them, a cube almost as tall as he was, stood Eco, his eyes wide with alarm. Next to the cube and equally as tall was a slender cone that came to a very sharp point. The point was dark with blood. Impaled on the cone, face-up, long, spindly limbs splayed in agony, was the lifeless body of Agathinus. His upside-down features were frozen in a rictus of pain and shock.

"You found him like this?"

Eco nodded.

How had such a thing happened? Agathinus must have been standing on the cube where Eco now stood, and somehow fallen backward onto the point. I flinched, picturing it. The force of his fall had pushed his body halfway down the cone. But why should he have been standing on the cube at all? The faded inscriptions on the column could as easily be read from the ground. And how could he have been so careless as to fall in such a dangerous spot?

Unless someone had pushed him.

I thought of a triangle, not of the sort which Archimedes studied, but with properties just as predictable—a triangle made not of abstract lines but of the powerful forces that link mortal to mortal.

I told Eco to stop gawking and get down from the cube.

Given the circumstances of our discovery, and the fact that we were strangers in Syracuse, Eco and I might very well fall under suspicion ourselves if it was decided that Agathinus had been murdered. I thought it best to report what I had seen to Cicero, to let him handle reporting the death to the appropriate provincial magistrate, and then to book passage for Rome and have as little to do with the matter as possible.

"But Gordianus," Cicero protested, "this sort of thing is your specialty. And if I understand you correctly, Agathinus was there to meet you, and to do you a favor—though it seems he could as easily have shown the tomb to me instead. Do you feel no obligation to discover the truth?"

Cicero is a master at playing on a man's honor. I resisted. "Are you hiring me to investigate his death?"

"Gordianus—always money! Paying you for such a service would hardly be my responsibility, but I'm sure I can persuade the local Roman magistrate to do so. I might point out that your participation would also remove you from suspicion. Well?" He raised an eyebrow.

There was no debating logic with Cicero. "I'll do it."

"Good! First, someone will have to inform his friends and family. Dealing with a widow takes a certain finesse—I'll handle that. I leave it to you to deliver the sad news to his partner, Dorotheus."

"And Margero?"

"Ah yes, I suppose the poet will want to compose some funeral verses in praise of his dead patron."

Unless, I thought, Margero had been the author of Agathinus's death.

Margero's place was a small but respectable house in the heart of the city. I rapped upon the door politely with my foot and was shown by a slave through a modest atrium into a modest garden. After a long wait, Margero appeared wearing a rumpled robe. The ringlets across his forehead were in disarray and his eyes were puffy with sleep.

"It's close to midday," I said. "Do all poets sleep this late?"

"They do if they've drunk as much as I did last night."

"I didn't notice you drinking any more than the rest of us."

"What makes you think I stopped drinking after I left?"

"You had a late night, then?"

"What business is that of yours, Roman?"

"One of your patrons is dead."

In the span of a heartbeat several emotions crossed his handsome features, beginning with what might have been surprise and a flicker of hope, and ending with a grimace that might have been no more than a symptom of his hangover. "Dorotheus?"

"No."

A definite smile of satisfaction flickered across his lips. "Agathinus—dead? But how?"

"Eco and I found him this morning, outside the Achradina Gate." I described the circumstances.

"Impaled? How gruesome." Margero's disgust slowly turned to amusement. "Yet how appropriate! An ironical turnabout from his usual preference." He laughed out loud. "Agathinus, impaled. Delicious! Poor Nikias will be distraught, no doubt. I shall make a poem to console him."

"Nikias—the boy at the gymnasium?"

Margero darkened. "How do you know about him?"

"I know more than I care to about your affairs, and those of Agathinus—and yet, still not enough . . ."

"What do you think?" I said to Eco as we made our way toward the large building near the docks where Agathinus and Dorotheus kept their offices and warehouse. "Was Margero really surprised by our bad news?"

Eco looked pensive. He rotated his palm up and down inconclusively.

"Let's suppose that Margero overheard Agathinus last night when he arranged to meet us outside the Achradina Gate—"

Eco shook his head.

"Yes, you're right, Margero and Dorotheus had already moved on and were out of earshot. But suppose Agathinus caught up with them and told them of his plan. That's certainly possible."

Eco nodded sagely.

"And suppose that Margero volunteered to meet Agathinus this morning, and the two of them got there ahead of us and began to search for the tomb without us—or perhaps Margero showed up on his own, staying hidden, and secretly followed Agathinus into the maze. One way or the other, the two of them ended up there inside the thicket, safely out of sight, and Margero took the opportunity to get rid of his rival for Nikias once and for all."

Eco shook his head and mimed a poet in the throes of recitation.

"Yes, I know: Margero is a man of words, not actions. And he'd have to be an awfully good actor, too, if he was faking all his reactions when we gave him the news this morning."

Eco put his cheek against folded hands and feigned sleep.

"And yes, he was obviously asleep when we called on him—but that proves nothing. Perhaps he stayed up all night so as to ambush Agathinus, then went to bed after the crime."

Eco clutched an imaginary spike erupting from his chest, then feigned sleep, then shook his head dismissively. How, he asked, could any man sleep after doing such a thing?

"You have a point there," I admitted. Eco winced, catching the pun before I did. "And another thing: Margero is younger than Agathinus, but was he that much stronger—strong enough to force Agathinus up onto the cube, then push him onto the cone?"

Dorotheus kept us waiting for some time in the atrium of his business establishment. At last he appeared, smiling glumly and stroking his bushy beard. "Gordianus and Eco!" he boomed. "Come to say a last farewell before you head back for Rome?"

"I only wish that we were here on such happy business. It's about Agathinus—"

"Ah, yes, I learned of the tragedy earlier this morning—his wife sent a messenger the moment she was given the news by Cicero. I understand that you found his body. Horrible! Shocking!"

"Did you know of his plan to meet me outside the Achradina Gate this morning?"

"What? Of course not."

"I thought he might have mentioned it to you and Margero after you left Cicero's house last night."

"Agathinus caught up with us, yes, and the three of us walked for a while together. But he said nothing of any plans to meet you. I left

the two of them outside my door, so Margero saw him last. Now that
you mention it—"

"Yes?"

"Of late there had been some trouble between them. Perhaps you
noticed Margero's rudeness last night, and Agathinus's aloofness.
Some silly business over a boy. Absurd, isn't it, how people can go
mad over such things? Still, it's hard to believe that Margero
could . . ."

A slave entered the room and spoke to Dorotheus in hushed
tones.

He shrugged apologetically. "Business. Agathinus's death leaves
everything in terrible confusion. You must excuse me. Have a safe
journey home, Gordianus!"

Dorotheus departed with his secretary, leaving us alone in the
atrium.

Or leaving me alone, rather, for when I looked around, Eco had
vanished.

I called his name softly, but this appeared to be another occasion
when he had gone conveniently deaf. There were several doorways
leading out of the atrium into various parts of the building, but my
attention was drawn to a passageway covered by a curtain that had
been straight when we arrived but now hung slightly askew. I pushed
it back and stepped into a dark hallway.

On either side, the hall opened onto a series of small offices clut-
tered with scrolls, bits of papyrus, and wax writing tablets. The offices were deserted, the clerks presumably sent home on account of
Agathinus's death. The records stacked all about appeared to be the
normal stuff of business—invoices, bills, ledgers. I peeked into each
room, softly calling Eco's name.

The hallway ended in a door, which stood ajar. I pushed it open
and stepped into a high, open warehouse filled with crates. The
place appeared to be as deserted as the offices, and the mazelike

aisles between the stacked boxes reminded me uneasily of the maze-like necropolis outside the Achradina Gate.

"Eco!" I called softly. "We've no right to be snooping here. Eco, where are you?" I wandered up and down the aisles, until I discovered another door at the far corner of the room. It opened into yet another office. From small windows set high in the wall came the sounds of ships knocking together in the harbor and the cry of seagulls. There was no sign of Eco inside. I backed out of the room and closed the door behind me. I took several steps before I suddenly realized what I had seen and hurried back.

On a table against one wall I saw a simple scale. Neatly stacked beside it were some sample weights of silver and gold. There was also a small wooden tub on the table. I stepped closer. Sure enough, the tub was half filled with water, and there were several waterline markings made with a piece of chalk along the inner surface.

Behind me, I heard the door close.

"I thought I bade you farewell, Gordianus." There was not the slightest hint of good humor in Dorotheus's voice. Without the beaming smile, his round, bearded face had a stern, almost menacing look; the constant smile had kept me from seeing the cold, predatory gleam in his eyes, so common in successful traders and merchants. I also realized what a large man he was. Fat, yes, but the fellow had arms like a blacksmith's—strong enough, I had no doubt, to drag the smaller, weaker Agathinus onto the stone cube, and then to push him backward onto the cruel spike.

"I'm looking for my son," I said, as innocently as I could. "Eco has a terrible habit of wandering off on his own. I really should be less indulgent . . ."

But Dorotheus wasn't listening. "How much, Finder?"

"For what?"

"How much to shut you up and send you on your way back to Rome?" He might be a murderer, but he was a businessman first.

If accepting his bribe meant getting safely through the door be-hind him, why not? But I thought of Agathinus on the night before—the final night of his life—saying, *I like you, Gordianus . . . and I like your son . . . the way he laughed at Dorotheus's awful jokes . . .* and offering to do me the favor of showing me Archimedes's tomb. I remembered the gaping grimace of horror on his face when we found him, and I shuddered, thinking of the appalling agony he must have suffered at the end, transfixed like an insect on a pin.

"Agathinus did tell you last night about meeting me outside the Achradina Gate?" I said.

Dorotheus, deciding to submit to a bit of conversation, let his face relax. The hint of a smile returned to his lips. "Yes. He was quite looking forward to tramping through the thicket with you. I insisted on coming along for the fun."

"And Margero?"

"I'm afraid I lied to you about that, Finder. Margero excused him-self as soon as Agathinus caught up with us last night. He could hardly stand dining in the same room with him, in case you didn't notice, and he was in no mood to stroll along beside him afterward. Probably Margero was in a great hurry to get home so he could get drunk in solitude and make up new poems for that silly boy at the gymnasium."

"And you?"

"I saw Agathinus home. Then I came here."

"To your offices? In the middle of the night?"

"Don't be coy, Finder. You saw the scale and the tub of water."

"A demonstration of Archimedes's principle?"

"Would you believe, I never quite grasped it, until Cicero ex-plained it last night."

"What could be so important that you had to rush here at once to try it out?"

He sighed. "I've suspected for years that Agathinus must be

cheating me. Why not? He was always smarter than me, ever since we were boys. And the smarter partner always cheats the stupider one—that's the law of business. So I always watched every transaction, always counted every piece of silver and gold we divided between us. Still, I could never catch him cheating me.

"For the last shipment of goods, he talked me into taking my payment in gold vessels—pitchers and bowls and such—while he took his in coin. He needed the ready money to spend on certain investments of his own, he said, and what did it matter anyway, so long as we both received the same weight? Secretly, I thought I must be getting the better deal, because worked gold is more valuable than its weight in coinage. Agathinus was counting on my own greed, you see, and he used it against me. He cheated me. The devious bastard cheated me! Last night, with Archimedes's help, I proved it."

"Proved that your gold vessels weren't made of solid gold?"

"Exactly."

"Perhaps Agathinus didn't know."

"Oh, no, he knew. After we went into the thicket and found the tomb this morning, I confronted him. He denied the deception at first—until I dragged him onto the cube and threatened to throw him on the cone. Then he confessed, and kept on confessing, with the sight of that spike to goad him. It didn't begin with this transaction! He'd been pilfering and corrupting my shares of gold for years, in all sorts of devious ways. I always knew that Agathinus was too clever to be honest!"

"And after he confessed—" I shuddered, picturing it.

Dorotheus swallowed hard. "I could say that it was an accident, that he slipped, but why? I'm not proud of it. I was angry—furious! Anger like that comes from the gods, doesn't it? So the gods will understand. And they'll understand why I had to get rid of you, as well." He reached into the folds of his tunic and pulled out a long dagger.

I coughed. My throat was bone-dry. "I thought you intended to buy my silence."

"I've changed my mind."

"But you said—"

"You never agreed, so there was never a bargain. And now I withdraw that offer."

I looked around the room for something that might equalize the situation, but saw nothing remotely resembling a weapon. The best I could do was to pick up the tub. I threw the water on him, then threw the tub, which he knocked aside. All I managed was to make him furious and dripping wet. All trace of the laughing, genial dinner companion of the previous night had vanished. Seeing his face now, I would not have known him.

It was at that moment that the door behind him gave a rattle and burst open.

Cicero entered first, followed by a troop of well-armed Roman peacekeepers who surrounded Dorotheus at once and took his dagger. Eco trailed behind, leaping in the air in great excitement, the anxious look on his face turning to jubilation when he saw that I was unharmed.

"Eco fetched you?" I said.

"Yes," said Cicero.

"You heard Dorotheus confess?"

"I heard enough."

Eco opened his mouth wide and moved his lips, but managed only to produce a stifled grunt.

"What's the boy trying to say?" asked Cicero.

"I think it must be '*Eureka! Eureka!*'"

"Greed!" I said to Eco the next morning, as we made ready to vacate our room at Cicero's house. "Last night I read that idyll of Theocritus, the poem that Cicero quoted from at dinner the other night. The poet certainly got it right:

> Men no longer aspire to win praise for noble deeds,
> but think only of profit, profit, profit.
> Clutching their coinbags, always looking for more,
> too stingy to give away the tarnish that comes off their coins!

"Thanks to greed, Agathinus is dead, Dorotheus awaits trial for his murder, and Margero the poet has lost both of his patrons in one stroke, which means he'll probably have to leave Syracuse. A disaster for them all. It's very sad; enough to make a man want to leave behind the grubby human cares of this world and lose himself in pure geometry, like Archimedes."

We gathered up our few belongings and went to take our leave of Cicero. There was also the matter of collecting my fees, not only for finding Archimedes's tomb, but for exposing Agathinus's killer.

From the atrium, I could hear Cicero in his office. He was dictating a letter to Tiro, no doubt intending for me to deliver it when I got back to Rome. Eco and I waited outside the door. It was impossible not to overhear.

"Dear brother Quintus," Cicero began, "the fellows I was so strongly advised to cultivate here in Syracuse turned out to be of no account—the unsavory details can wait until we meet again. Nonetheless, my holiday here has not been entirely unproductive. You will be interested to learn that I have rediscovered the lost tomb of one of our boyhood heroes, Archimedes. The locals were entirely ignorant of its location; indeed, denied its very existence. Yesterday afternoon, however, I set out with Tiro for the old necropolis outside the Achradina Gate, and there, sure enough, peeking out above a tangle of brambles and vines, I spied the telltale ornaments of a

sphere and cylinder atop a column. You must recall that bit of dog-
gerel we learned from our old math tutor:

> A cylinder and ball
> atop a column tall
> mark the final stage
> of the Syracusan sage.

"Having spotted the tomb, I gave a cry of '*Eureka!*' and ordered a
group of workers with scythes to clear the thicket all around. Now
the tomb of Archimedes can be seen and approached freely, and has
been restored to its rightful status as a shrine to all educated men."

Cicero did not mention the cube and cone, I noticed. They had
been removed along with the thicket, lest someone else meet Agathinus's fate.

Cicero cleared his throat and resumed dictating. "Ironic, brother
Quintus, is it not, and sadly indicative of the degraded cultural standards of these modern Syracusans, that it took a Roman from
Arpinum to rediscover for them the tomb of the keenest intellect
who ever lived among them?"

Ironic indeed, I thought.

DEATH BY EROS

"The Neapolitans are different from us Romans," I remarked to Eco as we strolled across the central forum of Neapolis. "A man can almost feel that he's left Italy altogether and been magically transported to a seaport in Greece. Greek colonists founded the city hundreds of years ago, taking advantage of the extraordinary bay, which they called the *Krater,* or Cup. The locals still have Greek names, eat Greek food, follow Greek customs. Many of them don't even speak Latin."

Eco pointed to his lips and made a self-deprecating gesture to say, *Neither do I!* At fifteen, he tended to make a joke of everything, including his muteness.

"Ah, but you can *hear* Latin," I said, flicking a finger against one of his ears just hard enough to sting, "and sometimes even understand it."

We had arrived in Neapolis on our way back to Rome, after doing a bit of business for Cicero down in Sicily. Rather than stay at an inn, I was hoping to find accommodations with a wealthy Greek trader named Sosistrides. "The fellow owes me a favor," Cicero had told me. "Look him up and mention my name, and I'm sure he'll put you up for the night."

With a few directions from the locals (who were polite enough not to laugh at my Greek) we found the trader's house. The columns and lintels and decorative details of the facade were stained in various shades of pale red, blue, and yellow that seemed to glow under the warm sunlight. Incongruous amid the play of colors was a black wreath on the door.

"What do you think, Eco? Can we ask a friend of a friend, a total stranger really, to put us up when the household is in mourning? It seems presumptuous."

Eco nodded thoughtfully, then gestured to the wreath and expressed curiosity with a flourish of his wrist. I nodded. "I see your point. If it's Sosistrides who's died, or a member of the family, Cicero would want us to deliver his condolences, wouldn't he? And we must learn the details, so that we can inform him in a letter. I think we must at least rouse the doorkeeper, to see what's happened."

I walked to the door and politely knocked with the side of my foot. There was no answer. I knocked again and waited. I was about to rap on the door with my knuckles, rudely or not, when it swung open.

The man who stared back at us was dressed in mourning black. He was not a slave; I glanced at his hand and saw a citizen's iron ring. His graying hair was disheveled and his face distressed. His eyes were red from weeping.

"What do you want?" he said, in a voice more wary than unkind.

"Forgive me, citizen. My name is Gordianus. This is my son, Eco. Eco hears but is mute, so I shall speak for him. We're travelers, on our way home to Rome. I'm a friend of Marcus Tullius Cicero. It was he who—"

"Cicero? Ah, yes, the Roman administrator down in Sicily, the one who can actually read and write, for a change." The man wrinkled his brow. "Has he sent a message, or . . . ?"

"Nothing urgent; Cicero asked me only to remind you of his friendship. You are, I take it, the master of the house, Sosistrides?"

"Yes. And you? I'm sorry, did you already introduce yourself? My mind wanders . . ." He looked over his shoulder. Beyond him, in the vestibule, I glimpsed a funeral bier strewn with freshly cut flowers and laurel leaves.

"My name is Gordianus. And this is my son—"

"Gordianus, did you say?"

"Yes."

"Cicero mentioned you once. Something about a murder trial up in Rome. You helped him. They call you the Finder."

"Yes."

He looked at me intently for a long moment. "Come in, Finder. I want you to see him."

The bier in the vestibule was propped up and tilted at an angle so that its occupant could be clearly seen. The corpse was that of a youth probably not much older than Eco. His arms were crossed over his chest and he was clothed in a long white gown, so that only his face and hands were exposed. His hair was boyishly long and as yellow as a field of millet in summer, crowned with a laurel wreath of the sort awarded to athletic champions. The flesh of his delicately molded features was waxy and pale, but even in death his beauty was remarkable.

"His eyes were blue," said Sosistrides in a low voice. "They're closed now, you can't see them, but they were blue, like his dear, dead mother's; he got his looks from her. The purest blue you ever saw, like the color of the Cup on a clear day. When we pulled him from the pool, they were all bloodshot . . ."

"This is your son, Sosistrides?"

He stifled a sob. "My only son, Cleon."

"A terrible loss."

He nodded, unable to speak. Eco shifted nervously from foot to foot, studying the dead boy with furtive glances, almost shyly.

"They call you Finder," Sosistrides finally said, in a hoarse voice. "Help me find the monster who killed my son."

I looked at the dead youth and felt a deep empathy for Sosistrides's suffering, and not merely because I myself had a son of similar age. (Eco may be adopted, but I love him as my own flesh.) I was stirred also by the loss of such beauty. Why does the death of a beautiful stranger affect us more deeply than the loss of someone plain? Why should it be so, that if a vase of exquisite workmanship but little practical value should break, we feel the loss more sharply than if we break an ugly vessel we use every day? The gods made men to love beauty above all else, perhaps because they themselves are beautiful, and wish for us to love them, even when they do us harm.

"How did he die, Sosistrides?"

"It was at the gymnasium, yesterday. There was a citywide contest among the boys—discus-throwing, wrestling, racing. I couldn't attend. I was away in Pompeii on business all day . . ." Sosistrides again fought back tears. He reached out and touched the wreath on his son's brow. "Cleon took the laurel crown. He was a splendid athlete. He always won at everything, but they say he outdid himself yesterday. If only I had been there to see it! Afterwards, while the other boys retired to the baths inside, Cleon took a swim in the long pool, alone. There was no one else in the courtyard. No one saw it happen . . ."

"The boy drowned, Sosistrides?" It seemed unlikely, if the boy had been as good at swimming as he was at everything else.

Sosistrides shook his head and shut his eyes tight, squeezing tears from them. "The gymnasiarchus is an old wrestler named Caputorus.

It was he who found Cleon. He heard a splash, he said, but thought nothing of it. Later he went into the courtyard and discovered Cleon. The water was red with blood. Cleon was at the bottom of the pool. Beside him was a broken statue. It must have struck the back of his head; it left a terrible gash."

"A statue?"

"Of Eros—the god you Romans call Cupid. A cherub with bow and arrows, a decoration at the edge of the pool. Not a large statue, but heavy, made of solid marble. It somehow fell from its pedestal as Cleon was passing below . . ." He gazed at the boy's bloodless face, lost in misery.

I sensed the presence of another in the room, and turned to see a young woman in a black gown with a black mantle over her head. She walked to Sosistrides's side. "Who are these visitors, father?"

"Friends of the provincial administrator down in Sicily— Gordianus of Rome, and his son, Eco. This is my daughter, Cleio. Daughter! Cover yourself!" Sosistrides's sudden embarrassment was caused by the fact that Cleio had pushed the mantle from her head, revealing that her dark hair was crudely shorn, cut so short that it didn't reach her shoulders. No longer shadowed by the mantle, her face, too, showed signs of unbridled mourning. Long scratches ran down her cheeks, and there were bruises where she appeared to have struck herself, marring a beauty that rivaled her brother's.

"I mourn for the loss of the one I loved best in all the world," she said in a hollow voice. "I feel no shame in showing it." She cast an icy stare at me and at Eco, then swept from the room.

Extreme displays of grief are disdained in Rome, where excessive public mourning is banned by law, but we were in Neapolis. So-sistrides seemed to read my thoughts. "Cleio has always been more Greek than Roman. She lets her emotions run wild. Just the opposite of her brother. Cleon was always so cool, so detached." He shook his head. "She's taken her brother's death very hard. When I came home from Pompeii yesterday I found his body here in the vestibule; his slaves had carried him home from the gymnasium. Cleio was in her room, crying uncontrollably. She'd already cut her hair. She wept and wailed all night long."

He gazed at his dead son's face and reached out to touch it, his hand looking warm and ruddy against the unnatural pallor of the boy's cold cheek. "Someone murdered my son. You must help me find out who did it, Gordianus—to put the shade of my son to rest, and for my grieving daughter's sake."

"That's right, I heard the splash. I was here behind my counter in the changing room, and the door to the courtyard was standing wide open, just like it is now."

Caputorus the gymnasiarchus was a grizzled old wrestler with enormous shoulders, a perfectly bald head, and a protruding belly. His eyes kept darting past me to follow the comings and goings of the naked youths, and every so often he interrupted me in mid-sentence to yell out a greeting, which usually included some jocular insult or obscenity. The fourth time he reached out to tousle Eco's hair, Eco deftly moved out of range and stayed there.

"And when you heard the splash, did you immediately go and have a look?" I asked.

"Not right away. To tell you the truth, I didn't think much of it. I figured Cleon was out there jumping in and out of the pool, which is against the rules, mind you! It's a long, shallow pool meant for swimming only, and no jumping allowed. But he was always breaking the rules. Thought he could get away with anything."

"So why didn't you go out and tell him to stop? You are the gymnasiarchus, aren't you?"

"Do you think that counted for anything with that spoiled brat? Master of the gym I may be, but nobody was his master. You know what he'd have done? Quoted some fancy lines from some famous play, most likely about old wrestlers with big bellies, flashed his naked behind at me, and then jumped back in the pool! I don't need the grief, thank you very much. Hey, Manius!" Caputorus shouted at a youth behind me. "I saw you and your sweetheart out there wrestling this morning. You been studying your old man's dirty vases to learn those positions? Ha!"

Over my shoulder, I saw a redheaded youth flash a lascivious grin and make an obscene gesture using both hands.

"Back to yesterday," I said. "You heard the splash and didn't think much of it, but eventually you went out to the courtyard."

"Just to get some fresh air. I noticed right away that Cleon wasn't swimming anymore. I figured he'd headed inside to the baths."

"But wouldn't he have passed you on the way?"

"Not necessarily. There are two passageways into the courtyard. The one most people take goes past my counter here. The other is through a little hallway that connects to the outer vestibule. It's a more roundabout route to get inside to the baths, but he could have gone in that way."

"And could someone have gotten into the courtyard the same way?"

"Yes."

"Then you can't say for certain that Cleon was alone out there."

"You are a sharp one, aren't you!" Caputorus said sarcastically. "But you're right. Cleon was out there by himself to start with, of that I'm sure. And after that, nobody walked by me, coming or going. But somebody could have come and gone by the other passageway. Anyway, when I stepped out there, I could tell right away that something was wrong, seriously wrong, though I couldn't quite say what. Only later, I realized what it was: the statue was missing, that little statue of Eros that's been there since before I took over running this place. You know how you can see a thing every day and take it for granted, and when all of a sudden it's not there, you can't even say what's missing, but you *sense* that something's off? That's how it was. Then I saw the color of the water. All pinkish in one spot, and darker toward the bottom. I stepped closer and then I saw him, lying on the bottom, not moving and no air bubbles coming up, and the statue around him in pieces. It was obvious right away what must have happened. Here, I'll show you the spot."

As we were passing out the doorway, a muscular wrestler wearing only a leather headband and wrist-wraps squeezed by on his way in. Caputorus twisted a towel between his fists and snapped it against the youth's bare backside. "Your mother!" yelled the stung athlete.

"No, your shiny red bottom!" Caputorus threw back his head and laughed.

The pool had been drained and scrubbed, leaving no trace of Cleon's blood amid the puddles. The pieces of the statue of Eros had been gathered up and deposited next to the empty pedestal. One of the cherub's tiny feet had broken off, as had the top of Eros's bow, the point of his notched arrow, and the feathery tip of one wing.

"The statue had been here for years, you say?"

"That's right."

"Sitting here on this pedestal?"

"Yes. Never budged, even when we'd get a bit of a rumble from Vesuvius."

"Strange, then, that it should have fallen yesterday, when no one felt any tremors. Even stranger that it should fall directly onto a swimmer . . ."

"It's a mystery, all right."

"I think the word is murder."

Caputorus looked at me shrewdly. "Not necessarily."

"What do you mean?"

"Ask some of the boys. See what they tell you."

"I intend to ask everyone who was here what they saw or heard."

"Then you might start with this little fellow." He indicated the broken Eros.

"Speak plainly, Caputorus."

"Others know more than I do. All I can tell you is what I've picked up from the boys."

"And what's that?"

"Cleon was a heartbreaker. You've only seen him laid out for his funeral. You have no idea how good-looking he was, both above the neck and below. A body like a statue by Phidias, a regular Apollo—he took your breath away! Smart, too, and the best athlete on the Cup. Strutting around here naked every day, challenging all the boys to wrestle him, celebrating his wins by quoting Homer. He had half the boys in this place trailing after him, all wanting to be his special friend. They were awestruck by him."

"And yet, yesterday, after he won the laurel crown, he swam alone."

"Maybe because they'd all finally had enough of him. Maybe they got tired of his bragging. Maybe they realized he wasn't the sort to ever return a shred of love or affection to anybody."

"You sound bitter, Caputorus."

"Do I?"

"Are you sure you're talking just about the boys?"

His face reddened. He worked his jaw back and forth and flexed his massive shoulders. I tried not to flinch.

"I'm no fool, Finder," he finally said, lowering his voice. "I've been around long enough to learn a few things. Lesson one: a boy like Cleon is nothing but trouble. Look, but don't touch." His jaw relaxed into a faint smile. "I've got a tough hide. I tease and joke with the best, but none of these boys get under my skin."

"Not even Cleon?"

His face hardened, then broke into a grin as he looked beyond me. "Calpurnius!" he yelled at a boy across the courtyard. "If you handle the javelin between your legs the way you handle that one, I'm surprised you haven't pulled it off by now! Merciful Zeus, let me show you how!"

Caputorus pushed past me, tousling Eco's hair on his way, leaving us to ponder the broken Eros and the empty pool where Cleon had died.

I managed that day to speak to every boy in the gymnasium. Most of them had been there the previous day, either to take part in the athletic games or to watch. Most of them were cooperative, but only to a point. I had the feeling that they had already talked among themselves and decided as a group to say as little as possible concerning Cleon's death to outsiders like myself, no matter that I came as the representative of Cleon's father.

Nevertheless, from uncomfortable looks, wistful sighs, and unfinished sentences, I gathered that what Caputorus had told me was true: Cleon had broken hearts all over the gymnasium, and in the process had made more than a few enemies. He was by universal consensus the brightest and most beautiful boy in the group, and yesterday's games had proven conclusively that he was the best athlete as well. He was also vain, arrogant, selfish, and aloof; easy to fall in love with and incapable of loving in return. The boys who had not fallen under his spell at one time or another disliked him out of pure envy.

I managed to learn all this as much from what was left unsaid as from what each boy said, but when it came to obtaining more concrete details, I struck a wall of silence. Had anyone ever been heard uttering a serious threat to Cleon? Had anyone ever said anything, even in jest, about the potentially hazardous placement of the statue of Eros beside the pool? Were any of the boys especially upset about Cleon's victories that day? Had any of them slipped away from the baths at the time Cleon was killed? And what of the gymnasiarchus? Had Caputorus's behavior toward Cleon always been above reproach, as he claimed?

To these questions, no matter how directly or indirectly I posed them, I received no clear answers, only a series of equivocations and evasions.

I was beginning to despair of uncovering anything significant, when finally I interviewed Hippolytus, the wrestler whose backside Caputorus had playfully snapped with his towel. He was preparing for a plunge in the hot pool when I came to him. He untied his leather headband, letting a shock of jet-black hair fall into his eyes, and began to unwrap his wrists. Eco seemed a bit awed by the fellow's brawniness; to me, with his babyish face and apple-red cheeks, Hippolytus seemed a hugely overgrown child.

I had gathered from the others that Hippolytus was close, or as close as anyone, to Cleon. I began the conversation by saying as much, hoping to catch him off his guard. He looked at me, unfazed, and nodded.

"I suppose that's right. I liked him. He wasn't as bad as some made out."

"What do you mean?"

"Wasn't Cleon's fault if everybody swooned over him. Wasn't his fault if he didn't swoon back. I don't think he had it in him to feel that way about another boy." He frowned and wrinkled his brow. "Some say that's not natural, but there you are. The gods make us all different."

"I'm told he was arrogant and vain."

"Wasn't his fault he was better than everybody else at wrestling and running and throwing. Wasn't his fault he was smarter than his tutors. But he shouldn't have crowed so much, I suppose. Hubris— you know what that is?"

"Vanity that offends the gods," I said.

"Right, like in the plays. Acquiring a swollen head, becoming too cocksure, until a fellow's just begging to be struck down by a lightning bolt or swallowed by an earthquake. What the gods give they can take away. They gave Cleon everything. Then they took it all away."

"The gods?"

Hippolytus sighed. "Cleon deserved to be brought down a notch, but he didn't deserve that punishment."

"Punishment? From whom? For what?"

I watched his eyes and saw the to and fro of some internal debate. If I prodded too hard, he might shut up tight; if I prodded not at all, he might keep answering in pious generalities. I started to speak, then saw something settle inside him, and held my tongue.

"You've seen the statue that fell on him?" Hippolytus said.

"Yes. Eros with his bow and arrows."

"Do you think that was just a coincidence?"

"I don't understand."

"You've talked to everyone in the gymnasium, and nobody's told you? They're all thinking it; they're just too superstitious to say it aloud. It was Eros that killed Cleon, for spurning him."

"You think the god himself did it? Using his own statue?"

"Love flowed to Cleon from all directions, like rivers to the sea— but he turned back the rivers and lived in his own rocky desert. Eros chose Cleon to be his favorite, but Cleon refused him. He laughed in the god's face once too often."

"How? What had Cleon done to finally push the god too far?"

Again I saw the internal debate behind his eyes. Clearly, he wanted to tell me everything. I had only to be patient. At last, he sighed and spoke. "Lately, some of us thought that Cleon might finally be softening. He had a new tutor, a young philosopher named Mulciber, who came from Alexandria about six months ago. Cleon and his sister Cleio went to Mulciber's little house off the forum every morning to talk about Plato and read poetry."

"Cleio as well?"

"Sosistrides believed in educating both his children, no matter that Cleio's a girl. Anyway, pretty soon word got around that Mulciber was courting Cleon. Why not? He was smitten, like everybody else. The surprise was that Cleon seemed to respond to his advances. Mulciber would send him chaste little love poems, and Cleon would send poems back to him. Cleon actually showed me some of Mulciber's poems, and asked me to read the ones he was sending back. They were beautiful! He was good at that, too, of course." Hippolytus shook his head ruefully.

"But it was all a cruel hoax. Cleon was just leading Mulciber on, making a fool of him. Only the day before yesterday, right in front of some of Mulciber's other students, Cleon made a public show of returning all the poems Mulciber had sent him, and asking for his own poems back. He said he'd written them merely as exercises, to teach his own tutor the proper way to write a love poem. Mulciber was dumbstruck! Everyone in the gymnasium heard about it. People said Cleon had finally gone too far. To have spurned his tutor's advances was one thing, but to do so in such a cruel, deliberately humiliating manner—that was hubris, people said, and the gods would take vengeance. And now they have."

I nodded. "But quite often the gods use human vessels to achieve their ends. Do you really think the statue tumbled into the pool of its own accord, without a hand to push it?"

Hippolytus frowned, and seemed to debate revealing yet another secret. "Yesterday, not long before Cleon drowned, some of us saw a stranger in the gymnasium."

At last, I thought, a concrete bit of evidence, something solid to grapple with! I took a deep breath. "No one else mentioned seeing a stranger."

"I told you, they're all too superstitious. If the boy we saw was some emissary of the god, they don't want to speak of it."

"A boy?"

"Perhaps it was Eros himself, in human form—though you'd think a god would be better groomed and wear clothes that fit!"

"You saw this stranger clearly?"

"Not that clearly; neither did anybody else, as far as I can tell. I only caught a glimpse of him loitering in the outer vestibule, but I could tell he wasn't one of the regular boys."

"How so?"

"By the fact that he was dressed at all. This was just after the games, and everyone was still naked. And most of the gymnasium crowd are pretty well off; this fellow had a wretched haircut and his tunic looked like a patched hand-me-down from a big brother. I figured he was some stranger who wandered in off the street, or maybe a messenger slave too shy to come into the changing room."

"And his face?"

Hippolytus shook his head. "I didn't see his face. He had dark hair, though."

"Did you speak to him, or hear him speak?"

"No. I headed for the hot plunge and forgot all about him. Then Caputorus found Cleon's body, and everything was crazy after that. I didn't make any connection to the stranger until this morning, when I found out that some of the others had seen him, too."

"Did anybody see this young stranger pass through the baths and the changing room?"

"I don't think so. But there's another way to get from the outer vestibule to the inner courtyard, through a little passageway at the far end of the building."

"So Caputorus told me. It seems possible, then, that this stranger could have entered the outer vestibule, sneaked through the empty passage, come upon Cleon alone in the pool, pushed the statue onto him, then fled the way he had come, all without being clearly seen by anyone."

Hippolytus took a deep breath. "That's how I figure it. So you see, it must have been the god, or some agent of the god. Who else could have had such perfect timing, to carry out such an awful deed?"

I shook my head. "I can see you know a bit about poetry and more than a bit about wrestling holds, young man, but has no one tutored you in logic? We may have answered the question of *how*, but that hasn't answered the question of *who*. I respect your religious conviction that the god Eros may have had the motive and the will to kill Cleon in such a cold-blooded fashion—but it seems there were plenty of mortals with abundant motive as well. In my line of work I prefer to suspect the most likely mortal first, and presume divine causation only as a last resort. Chief among such suspects must be this tutor, Mulciber. Could he have been the stranger you saw lurking in the vestibule? Philosophers are notorious for having bad haircuts and shabby clothes."

"No. The stranger was shorter and had darker hair."

"Still, I should like to have a talk with this lovesick tutor."

"You can't," said Hippolytus. "Mulciber hanged himself yesterday."

"No wonder such a superstitious dread surrounds Cleon's death," I remarked to Eco, as we made our way to the house of Mulciber. "The golden boy of the Cup, killed by a statue of Eros; his spurned tutor, hanging himself the same day. This is the dark side of Eros. It casts a shadow that frightens everyone into silence."

Except me, Eco gestured, and let out the stifled, inchoate grunt he sometimes emits simply to declare his existence. I smiled at his self-deprecating humor, but it seemed to me that the things we had learned that morning had disturbed and unsettled Eco. He was at an age to be acutely aware of his place in the scheme of things, and to begin wondering who might ever love him, especially in spite of his handicap. It seemed unfair that a boy like Cleon, who had only scorn for his suitors, should have inspired so much unrequited infatuation and desire, when others faced lives of loneliness. Did the gods engineer the paradox of love's unfairness to amuse themselves, or was it one of the evils that escaped from Pandora's box to plague mankind?

The door of the philosopher's house, like that of Sosistrides, was adorned with a black wreath. Following my knock, an elderly slave opened it to admit us to a little foyer, where a body was laid out upon a bier much less elaborate than that of Cleon. I saw at once why Hippolytus had been certain that the short, dark-haired stranger at the gymnasium had not been the Alexandrian tutor, for Mulciber was quite tall and had fair hair. He had been a reasonably handsome man of thirty-five or so, about my own age. Eco gestured to the scarf that had been clumsily gathered about the dead man's throat, and then clutched his own neck with a strangler's grip: *To hide the rope marks*, he seemed to say.

"Did you know my master?" asked the slave who had shown us in.

"Only by reputation," I said. "We're visitors to Neapolis, but I've heard of your master's devotion to poetry and philosophy. I was shocked to learn of his sudden death." I spoke only the truth, after all.

The slave nodded. "He was a man of learning and talent. Still, few have come to pay their respects. He had no family here. And of course there are many who won't set foot inside the house of a suicide, for fear of bad luck."

"It's certain that he killed himself, then?"

"It was I who found him, hanging from a rope. He tied it to that beam, just above the boy's head." Eco rolled his eyes up. "Then he stood on a chair, put the noose around his neck, and kicked the chair out of the way. His neck snapped. I like to think he died quickly." The slave regarded his master's face affectionately. "Such a waste! And all for the love of that worthless boy!"

"You're certain that's why he killed himself?"

"Why else? He was making a good living here in Neapolis, enough to send a bit back to his brother in Alexandria every now and again, and even to think of purchasing a second slave. I'm not sure how I'd have taken to that; I've been with him since he was a boy. I used to carry his wax tablets and scrolls for him when he was little and had his own tutor. No, his life was going well in every way, except for that horrible boy!"

"You know that Cleon died yesterday."

"Oh, yes. That's why the master killed himself."

"He hung himself *after* hearing of Cleon's death?"

"Of course! Only . . ." The old man looked puzzled, as if he had not previously considered any other possibility. "Now let me think. Yesterday was strange all around, you see. The master sent me out early in the morning, before daybreak, with specific instructions not to return until evening. That was very odd, because usually I spend all day here, admitting his pupils and seeing to his meals. But yesterday he sent me out and I stayed away until dusk. I heard about Cleon's death on my way home. When I came in, there was the master, hanging from that rope."

"Then you don't know for certain when he died—only that it must have been between daybreak and nightfall."

"I suppose you're right."

"Who might have seen him during the day?"

"Usually pupils come and go all day, but not so yesterday, on account of the games at the gymnasium. All his regular students took part, you see, or else went to watch. The master had planned to be a spectator himself. So he had canceled all his regular classes, you see, except for his very first of the day—and that he'd never cancel, of course, because it was with that wretched boy!"

"Cleon, you mean."

"Yes, Cleon and his sister, Cleio. They always came for the first hour of the day. This month they were reading Plato on the death of Socrates."

"Suicide was on Mulciber's mind, then. And yesterday, did Cleon and his sister arrive for their class?"

"I can't say. I suppose they did. I was out of the house by then."

"I shall have to ask Cleio, but for now we'll assume they did. Perhaps Mulciber was hoping to patch things up with Cleon." The slave gave me a curious look. "I know about the humiliating episode of the returned poems the day before," I explained.

The slave regarded me warily. "You seem to know a great deal for a man who's not from Neapolis. What are you doing here?"

"Only trying to discover the truth. Now, then: we'll assume that Cleon and Cleio came for their class, early in the morning. Perhaps Mulciber was braced for another humiliation, and even then planning suicide—or was he wildly hoping, with a lover's blind faith, for some impossible reconciliation? Perhaps that's why he dismissed you for the day, because he didn't care to have his old slave witness either outcome. But it must have gone badly, or at least not as Mulciber hoped, for he never showed up to watch the games at the gymnasium that day. Everyone seems to assume that it was news of Cleon's death that drove him to suicide, but it seems to me just as likely that Mulciber hung himself right after Cleon and Cleio left, unable to bear yet another rejection."

Eco, greatly agitated, mimed an athlete throwing a discus, then a man fitting a noose around his neck, then an archer notching an arrow in a bow.

I nodded. "Yes, bitter irony: even as Cleon was enjoying his greatest triumph at the gymnasium, poor Mulciber may have been snuffing out his own existence. And then, Cleon's death in the pool. No wonder everyone thinks that Eros himself brought Cleon down." I studied the face of the dead man. "Your master was a poet, wasn't he?"

"Yes," said the slave. "He wrote at least a few lines every day of his life."

"Did he leave a farewell poem?"

The slave shook his head. "You'd think he might have, if only to say good-bye to me after all these years."

"But there was nothing? Not even a note?"

"Not a line. And that's another strange thing, because the night before he was up long after midnight, writing and writing. I thought perhaps he'd put the boy behind him and thrown himself into composing some epic poem, seized by the muse! But I can't find any trace of it. Whatever he was writing so frantically, it seems to have vanished. Perhaps, when he made up his mind to hang himself, he thought better of what he'd written, and burned it. He seems to have gotten rid of some other papers, as well."

"What papers?"

"The love poems he'd written to Cleon, the ones Cleon returned to him—they've vanished. I suppose the master was embarrassed at the thought of anyone reading them after he was gone, and so he got rid of them. So perhaps it's not so strange after all that he left no farewell note."

I nodded vaguely, but it still seemed odd to me. From what I knew of poets, suicides, and unrequited lovers, Mulciber would almost certainly have left some words behind—to chastise Cleon, to elicit pity, to vindicate himself. But the silent corpse of the tutor offered no explanation.

As the day was waning, I at last returned to the house of Sosistrides, footsore and soul-weary. A slave admitted us. I paused to gaze for a long moment at the lifeless face of Cleon. Nothing had changed, and yet he did not look as beautiful to my eyes as he had before.

Sosistrides called us into his study. "How did it go, Finder?"

"I've had a productive day, if not a pleasant one. I talked to everyone I could find at the gymnasium. I also went to the house of your children's tutor. You do know that Mulciber hanged himself yesterday?"

"Yes. I found out only today, after I spoke to you. I knew he was a bit infatuated with Cleon, wrote poems to him and such, but I had no idea he was so passionately in love with him. Another tragedy, like ripples in a pond." Sosistrides, too, seemed to assume without question that the tutor's suicide followed upon news of Cleon's death. "And what did you find? Did you discover anything . . . significant?"

I nodded. "I think I know who killed your son."

His face assumed an expression of strangely mingled relief and dismay. "Tell me, then!"

"Would you send for your daughter first? Before I can be certain, there are a few questions I need to ask her. And when I think of the depth of her grief, it seems to me that she, too, should hear what I have to say."

He called for a slave to fetch the girl from her room. "You're right, of course; Cleio should be here, in spite of her . . . unseemly appearance. Her grieving shows her to be a woman, after all, but I've raised her almost as a son, you know. I made sure she learned to read and write. I sent her to the same tutors as Cleon. Of late she's been reading Plato with him, both of them studying with Mulciber . . ."

"Yes, I know."

Cleio entered the room, her mantle pushed defiantly back from her shorn head. Her cheeks were lined with fresh, livid scratches, signs that her mourning had continued unabated through the day.

"The Finder thinks he knows who killed Cleon," Sosistrides explained.

"Yes, but I need to ask you a few questions first," I said. "Are you well enough to talk?"

She nodded.

"Is it true that you and your brother went to your regular morning class with Mulciber yesterday?"

"Yes." She averted her tear-reddened eyes and spoke in a hoarse whisper.

"When you arrived at his house, was Mulciber there?"

She paused. "Yes."

"Was it he who let you in the door?"

Again a pause. "No."

"But his slave was out of the house, gone for the day. Who let you in?"

"The door was unlocked . . . ajar . . ."

"So you and Cleon simply stepped inside?"

"Yes."

"Were harsh words exchanged between your brother and Mulciber?"

Her breath became ragged. "No."

"Are you sure? Only the day before, your brother had publicly rejected and humiliated Mulciber. He returned his love poems and ridiculed them in front of others. That must have been a tremendous blow to Mulciber. Isn't it true that when the two of you showed up at his house yesterday morning, Mulciber lost his temper with Cleon?"

She shook her head.

"What if I suggest that Mulciber became hysterical? That he ranted against your brother? That he threatened to kill him?"

"No! That never happened. Mulciber was too—he would never have done such a thing!"

"But I suggest that he did. I suggest that yesterday, after suffering your brother's deceit and abuse, Mulciber reached the end of his tether. He snapped, like a rein that's worn clean through, and his passions ran away with him like maddened horses. By the time you and your brother left his house, Mulciber must have been raving like a madman—"

"No! He wasn't! He was—"

"And after you left, he brooded. He took out the love poems into which he had poured his heart and soul, the very poems that Cleon returned to him so scornfully the day before. They had once been beautiful to him, but now they were vile, so he burned them."

"Never!"

"He had planned to attend the games at the gymnasium, to cheer Cleon on, but instead he waited until the contests were over, then sneaked into the vestibule, skulking like a thief. He came upon Cleon alone in the pool. He saw the statue of Eros—a bitter re-minder of his own rejected love. No one else was about, and there was Cleon, swimming facedown, not even aware that anyone else was in the courtyard, unsuspecting and helpless. Mulciber couldn't resist—he waited until the very moment that Cleon passed beneath the statue, then pushed it from its pedestal. The statue struck Cleon's head. Cleon sank to the bottom and drowned."

Cleio wept and shook her head. "No, no! It wasn't Mulciber!"

"Oh, yes! And then, wracked with despair at having killed the boy he loved, Mulciber rushed home and hanged himself. He didn't even bother to write a note to justify himself or beg forgiveness for the murder. He'd fancied himself a poet, but what greater failure is there for a poet than to have his love poems rejected? And so he hung himself without writing another line, and he'll go to his fu-neral pyre in silence, a common murderer—"

"No, no, no!" Cleio clutched her cheeks, tore at her hair, and wailed. Eco, whom I had told to be prepared for such an outburst, started back nonetheless. Sosistrides looked at me aghast. I averted my eyes. How could I have simply told him the truth, and made him believe it? He had to be shown. Cleio had to show him.

"He *did* leave a farewell," Cleio cried. "It was the most beautiful poem he ever wrote!"

"But his slave found nothing. Mulciber's poems to Cleon had vanished, and there was nothing new—"

"Because I took them!"

"Where are they, then?"

She reached into the bosom of her black gown and pulled out two handfuls of crumpled papyrus. "These were his poems to Cleon! You never saw such beautiful poems, such pure, sweet love put down in words! Cleon made fun of them, but they broke my heart! And here is his farewell poem, the one he left lying on his threshold so that Cleon would be sure to see it, when we went to his house yesterday and found him hanging in the foyer, his neck broken, his body soiled . . . dead . . . gone from me forever!"

She pressed a scrap of papyrus into my hands. It was in Greek, the letters rendered in a florid, desperate hand. A phrase near the middle caught my eye:

> One day, even your beauty will fade;
> One day, even you may love unrequited!
> Take pity, then, and favor my corpse
> With a first, final, farewell kiss . . .

She snatched back the papyrus and clutched it to her bosom.

My voice was hollow in my ears. "When you went to Mulciber's house yesterday, you and Cleon found him already dead."

"Yes!"

"And you wept."

"Because I loved him!"

"Even though he didn't love you?"

"Mulciber loved Cleon. He couldn't help himself."

"Did Cleon weep?"

Her face became so contorted with hatred that I heard Sosistrides gasp in horror. "Oh, no," she said, "he didn't weep. Cleon laughed! He laughed! He shook his head and said, 'What a fool,' and walked out the door. I screamed at him to come back, to help me cut Mulciber down, and he only said, 'I'll be late for the games!'" Cleio collapsed to the floor, weeping, the poems scattering around her. "'Late for the games!'" she repeated, as if it were her brother's epitaph.

On the long ride back to Rome through the Campanian country-side, Eco's hands grew weary and I grew hoarse debating whether I had done the right thing. Eco argued that I should have kept my suspicions of Cleio to myself. I argued that Sosistrides deserved to know what his daughter had done, and how and why his son had died—and needed to be shown, as well, how deeply and callously his beautiful, beloved Cleon had inflicted misery on others.

"Besides," I said, "when we returned to Sosistrides's house, I wasn't certain myself that Cleio had murdered Cleon. Accusing the dead tutor was a way of flushing her out. Her possession of Mulciber's missing poems were the only tangible evidence that events had unfolded as I suspected. I tried in vain to think of some way, short of housebreaking, to search her room without either Cleio or her father knowing—but as it turned out, such a search would have found nothing. I should have known that she would keep the poems on her person, next to her heart! She was as madly, hopelessly in love with Mulciber as he was in love with Cleon. Eros can be terribly careless when he scatters his arrows!"

We also debated the degree and nature of Cleon's perfidy. When he saw Mulciber's dead body, was Cleon so stunned by the enormity of what he had done—driven a lovesick man to suicide—that he went about his business in a sort of stupor, attending the games and performing his athletic feats like an automaton? Or was he so cold that he felt nothing? Or, as Eco argued in an extremely convoluted series of gestures, did Mulciber's fatal demonstration of lovesick devotion actually stimulate Cleon in some perverse way, inflating his ego and inspiring him to excel as never before at the games?

Whatever his private thoughts, instead of grieving, Cleon blithely went off and won his laurel crown, leaving Mulciber to spin in midair and Cleio to plot her vengeance. In a fit of grief she cut off her hair. The sight of her reflection in Mulciber's atrium pool gave her the idea to pass as a boy; an ill-fitting tunic from the tutor's wardrobe completed her disguise. She carried a knife with her to the gymnasium, the same one she had used to cut her hair, and was prepared to stab her brother in front of his friends. But it turned out that she didn't need the knife. By chance—or guided by Eros—she found her way into the courtyard, where the statue presented itself as the perfect murder weapon.

As far as Cleio was concerned, the statue's role in the crime constituted proof that she acted not only with the god's approval but as an instrument of his will. This pious argument had so far, at least as of our leaving Neapolis, stayed Sosistrides from punishing her. I did not envy the poor merchant. With his wife and son dead, could he bear to snuff out the life of his only remaining offspring, even for so great a crime? And yet, how could he bear to let her live, knowing she had murdered his beloved son? Such a conundrum would test the wisdom of Athena!

Eco and I debated, too, the merits of Mulciber's poetry. I had begged of Sosistrides a copy of the tutor's farewell, so that I could ponder it at my leisure:

> Savage, sullen boy, whelp of a lioness,
> Stone-hearted and scornful of love,
> I give you a lover's ring—my noose!

No longer be sickened by the sight of me;
I go to the only place that offers solace
To the broken-hearted: oblivion!
But will you not stop and weep for me,
If only for one moment . . .

The poem continued for many more lines, veering between re-crimination, self-pity, and surrender to the annihilating power of love.

Hopelessly sentimental! More cloying than honey! The very worst sort of dreck, pronounced Eco, with a series of gestures so sweeping that he nearly fell from his horse. I merely nodded, and wondered if my son would feel the same in another year or so, after Eros had wounded him with a stray arrow or two and given him a clearer notion, from personal experience, of just how deeply the god of love can pierce the hearts of helpless mortals.

A GLADIATOR DIES
ONLY ONCE

"A beautiful day for it," I said begrudgingly. Cicero nodded and squinted up at the filtered red sunlight that penetrated the awning above our seats. Below, in the arena, the first pair of gladiators strode across the sand to meet each other in combat.

The month was Junius, at the beginning of what promised to be a long, hot summer. The blue sky and undulating green hills were especially beautiful here in the Etrurian countryside outside the town of Saturnia, where Cicero and I, traveling separately from Rome, had arrived the day before to attend the funeral of a local magistrate. Sextus Thorius had been struck down in the prime of life, thrown from his horse while riding down the Clodian Way to check on the progress of a slave gang doing repair work on the road. The next day, word of his demise reached Rome, where quite a few important persons had felt obligated to attend the funeral.

Earlier that morning, not a few of the senators and bankers who gathered to watch the funeral procession had raised an eyebrow at the sight of Gordianus the Finder among them; feeling the beady gaze of a prune-faced matron on me, I distinctly overheard her whisper to her husband, "What's *he* doing here? Does someone suspect foul play at work in the death of Sextus Thorius?" But Cicero, when he caught sight of me, smiled grimly and moved to join me, and asked no questions. He knew why I had come. A few years ago, facing the prospect of a ruinous business scandal, Thorius had consulted Cicero for legal advice, and Cicero had sent Thorius to me to get to the bottom of the affair. In the end, both scandal and litigation were averted. Thorius had rewarded me generously, and had subsequently sent quite a bit of business my way. The least I could do on the occasion of his death was to pack my best toga, spend the night at a seedy inn in Saturnia, and show up at his funeral.

We had followed the procession of musicians, hired mourners and family members to the little necropolis outside Saturnia, where, after a few speeches of remembrance, Thorius's remains had been set alight atop a funeral pyre. At the soonest opportunity to do so without seeming impolite, I had turned to leave, eager to start back to Rome, when Cicero caught my arm.

"Surely you're not leaving yet, Gordianus. We must stay for the funeral games."

"Games?" I meant to load the word with irony, but Cicero took the question in my voice literally.

"There's to be a gladiator show, of course. It's not as if Thorius was a nobody. His family wasn't rich, but they'll have spent whatever they can afford, I'm sure."

"I hate watching gladiators," I said bluntly.

"So do I. But they're a part of the funeral, no less than the procession and the eulogies. One has to stay."

"I'm not in the mood to see blood spilled."

"But if you leave now, people will notice," he said, lowering his voice. "You can't afford to have them think you're squeamish, Gor-dianus. Not in your line of work."

I glanced at the faces around us, lit by the funeral pyre. The prune-faced matron was among them, along with her husband and numerous others from the same social set back in Rome. Much as I might hate to admit it, I was dependent on the trust and good will of such people, the sort who had occasion to call on my services and means to pay for them. I ferreted out the truth, and in return they put bread on my table.

"But I have to get back to Rome," I protested. "I can't afford an-other night at that seedy inn."

"Then you'll stay with me," said Cicero. "I have accommodations with a local banker. Good food. Comfortable beds." He raised an eyebrow.

Why did Cicero want so badly for me to stay? It occurred to me that he was the squeamish one. To watch the gladiators, he wanted the company of someone who wouldn't needle him about his squea-mishness, as so many of his social equals were likely to do.

Begrudgingly, I acquiesced, and so found myself, that fine after-noon in Junius, seated in a wooden amphitheater constructed espe-cially for the funeral games to honor the passing of Sextus Thorius of Saturnia. Since I was with Cicero, I had been admitted into the more exclusive section of seats beneath the shade of the blood-red awning, along with the bereaved family, various local dignitaries, and important visitors from Rome. The local villagers and farmers sat in the sun-drenched seats across from ours. They wore brimmed hats for shade and waved brightly colored fans. For a brief moment, bemused by the fluttering fans, I had the illusion that the crowd had been covered by a swarm of huge butterflies flapping their wings.

There were to be three matches, all fought to the death. Any less than three would have seemed parsimonious on the part of the fam-ily. Any more would have begun to look ostentatious, and added to the cost. As Cicero had said, the family of Sextus Thorius, while eminently respectable, was not rich.

The three pairs of gladiators were paraded before us. Helmets hid their faces, but they were easy to tell apart by their different armor and their contrasting physiques. One stood out from all the rest because of his coloration, a Nubian whose muscular arms and legs shone beneath the hot sun like burnished ebony. As the fighters strode before us, each raised his weapon. The crowd responded with polite cheering, but I overheard two men behind us complaining:

"Pretty obscure outfit. Owned by some freedman from Ravenna, I'm told; fellow called Ahala. Never heard of him!"

"Me neither. How did the family settle on this crew? Probably came cheap. Still, I suppose the Nubian's something of a novelty . . ."

There followed the ritual inspection of weapons for sharpness and armor for soundness, performed by the local magistrate in charge of the games, then the gladiators departed from the arena. The magistrate invoked the gods and delivered yet another eulogy to Sextus Thorius. A few moments later, to a blare of trumpets, a pair of gladiators reemerged and the first bout commenced. The shorter, stockier fighter was outfitted in the Thracian manner with a small round shield and a short sword. His tall, lumbering opponent wore heavier Samnite armor and carried an oblong shield.

"Samnite versus Thracian—a typical match," noted Cicero, who often fell to lecturing when he was uneasy or nervous. "Did you know that the very first gladiatorial matches took place right here in Etruria? Oh, yes; we Romans inherited the custom from the Etruscans. They began by sacrificing captive warriors before the funeral pyres of their leaders—" Cicero gave a start as the sword of the Samnite struck one of the iron bosses on the shield of the Thracian with a resounding clang, then he cleared his throat and continued. "Eventually, instead of simply strangling the captives, the Etruscans decided to have them fight each other, allowing the victors to live.

We Romans took up the custom, and so developed the tradition of death matches at the funerals of great men. Of course, nowadays, anyone who was anyone must be honored with games at his funeral. I've even heard of gladiator matches at the funerals of prominent women! The result is a tremendous demand for fresh gladiators. You still see captive warriors among them, but more and more often they're simply slaves who've been trained to fight, or sometimes convicted criminals—murderers who'd otherwise be executed, or thieves who'd rather take a chance in the arena than have a hand chopped off."

Below us, the Thracian thrust past the Samnite's shield and scored a glancing cut across the man's sword-arm. Blood sprinkled the sand. Cicero shuddered.

"Ultimately, one should remember that it's a religious occasion," he noted primly, "and the people must have their religion. And quite candidly, I don't mind watching a death match if both the combatants are convicted criminals. Then at least there's something instructive about the bloodletting. Or even if the fighters are captured warriors; that can be instructive as well, to take a good look at our enemies and to see how they fight, and to celebrate the favor of the gods, who've put us in the stands and them down there in the arena. But more and more the trend is to have trained slaves do the fighting—"

The tall Samnite, after a staggering retreat under the Thracian's relentless assault, suddenly rallied and managed to score a solid thrust at the other's flank. Blood spattered the sand. From behind his helmet the Thracian let out a cry and staggered back.

Behind us, the two men who had earlier complained now both roared with excitement:

"That's how to turn the tables! You've got him now, Samnite!"

"Make the little fellow squeal again!"

Cicero fidgeted in his seat and cast a disapproving glance behind us, then looked sidelong at the young woman seated next to him. She was watching the bout with narrowed eyes, one hand touching her parted lips and the other patting her heaving bosom. Cicero looked at me and raised an eyebrow. "And then there's the unwholesome glamour which these gladiators exert on certain women—and on more than a few men, as well, I'm sad to say. The whole culture has gone gladiator-mad! Roman boys play at being gladiators instead of generals, Roman ladies swoon whenever they see one, and do you know, I've even heard of Roman citizens who've volunteered to fight as gladiators themselves. And not just for the money—although I understand even some slaves are paid handsomely if they can survive and make a name for themselves—but for some sort of perverse thrill. I can't begin to imagine—"

His objection was abruptly drowned out by the roar of the crowd. The stocky Thracian had rallied and was once again relentlessly pushing the taller Samnite back. Sword clanged against sword, until the Samnite, tripping, fell backwards. The Thracian stepped onto the shield the Samnite had drawn over his chest, pinning the man down. He pressed the tip of his sword against the Samnite's windpipe. The Samnite released his sword and instinctively grasped the blade, then drew back his hand, flinging blood from the cuts across his fingers.

The Samnite had been worsted. From behind the visor of his helmet, the triumphant Thracian scanned the stands, looking to the crowd for judgment. Following the ancient custom, those who thought the Samnite should be spared would produce handkerchiefs and wave them, while those who wanted to see him put to death would raise their fists in the air. Here and there I saw a few fluttering handkerchiefs, all but submerged in a sea of clenched fists.

"I don't agree," said one of the men behind us. "I rather liked the Samnite. He put up a good fight."

"Bah!" said his friend, shaking his fist in the air. "They're both amateurs! The whole match was barely acceptable; I wouldn't give a fig to watch either of them fight again. Send the loser straight to Hades, I say! Anything less would dishonor the memory of Sextus Thorius."

"I suppose you're right," said the other, and from the corner of my eye I saw him put away his handkerchief and raise his fist.

The Thracian looked to the magistrate in charge of the games for the final judgment. The man raised his fist and nodded curtly, and the Thracian drove the sword into the Samnite's throat. A great fountain of blood spurted from the wound, gushing across the Samnite's helmet and chest and onto the sand all around. The man thrashed and convulsed, very nearly throwing the Thracian off-balance. But the Thracian steadied himself, shifting more weight onto the shield that confined the Samnite and bearing down on his sword until it penetrated the back of the Samnite's neck and was driven firmly into the packed sand beneath.

With a roar of triumph, the Thracian stepped backed and thrust his fists in the air. The Samnite bucked his hips and thrashed his limbs, pinned to the earth by the sword through his neck. The Thracian performed a victory strut in a circle around him.

"Disgusting!" muttered Cicero, pressing a clenched fist to his lips and looking queasy.

"Delightful!" uttered one of the men behind us. "Now that's more like it! What a finish!"

Then, as a single body—myself included—the crowd drew a gasp. With one of his thrashing hands, the Samnite had managed to grab hold of the Thracian's ankle, and with his other hand he had somehow managed to regain his sword. He pounded the pommel against the sand, as if to still that arm from thrashing, so that the blade pointed rigidly upright. The Thracian lost his balance and, making circles in the air with his arms, began to tumble backward.

For a long, breathless moment, it looked as if no power in the heavens or on the earth could stop the Thracian from falling backward directly onto the upright blade of the Samnite's sword, impaling himself.

Even Cicero bolted forward, rigid with suspense. The woman next to him swooned. The men behind us bleated with excitement.

The Thracian swayed back—regained his balance—and swayed back again. The upright sword glinted in the sunlight.

Making a tremendous circle with his arms, the Thracian at last managed to propel himself forward. Wrenching his ankle from the Samnite's grasp, he took a few staggering steps forward, then wheeled about. The Samnite had stopped thrashing, but the sword in his fist still pointed skyward. Approaching cautiously, as one might a snake that seemed to have writhed its last but might yet strike, the Thracian squatted down and snatched the sword from the Samnite's grip—then jerked back in alarm as a bizarre noise emerged from the Samnite's throat, a gurgling death-rattle that froze my blood. Gripping the pommel in both hands, the Thracian pointed the sword downward. As one might strike a last blow to make sure that a snake was finished, he drove the blade deep into the Samnite's groin.

Again, the crowd gasped in unison. Like Cicero beside me, I put my hand to my groin and flinched. But the Samnite was now truly dead. Fresh blood stained the loincloth around the wound, but he did not move.

His chest heaving, the Thracian stood and recommenced his victory strut. After a moment of stunned silence, the exhilarated crowd rewarded him with thunderous cheering. The magistrate strode into the arena and rewarded him with a palm frond to mark his victory. Waving it over his head, the gladiator departed to raucous applause.

"Well!" declared Cicero, clearly impressed despite his avowed distaste for the games. "That will be hard to top."

The body of the Samnite was dragged away, the pools of blood were raked over with fresh sand, and the next match commenced. It was a novelty bout between two *dimacheri*, so-called because each wielded not one but two daggers. To compensate for their lack of shields, they wore more pieces of armor than other types of fighters— greaves to protect their forearms and shins, plated pectorals to guard their throats and chests, and various bands about their limbs and bits of metal over their naked flesh that suggested adornment as much as armor. Instead of the nerve-wracking banging of swords against shields, the sound of their match was a constant, grating slither of blade against blade as they engaged in a dizzying dance of parries and thrusts. One was swarthy and the other pale, but otherwise their physiques were much alike; not as muscular as either of the previous fighters, they had the lithesome bodies of dancers. Speed and agility counted for more than brute strength in such a match, and they were so evenly matched, and their maneuvers so elegant, that their contest seemed almost choreographed. Instead of grunts and cheers, they elicited "ahs" and "ohs" of appreciation from the crowd. Watching them whirl about, I felt the pleasure one feels from watching dancers rather than warriors, so that I almost forgot that for one of them, death waited at the end of the match.

Then, with a scraping noise that set my teeth on edge, a dagger slid over armor and successfully connected with unprotected flesh, and the first blood was spilled. The crowd exhaled an "Ah!" at a higher pitch than before, and I sensed the stirring of their collective bloodlust.

Both fighters seemed to be wearying, losing the unerring focus that had kept them from harming each other. More blood was spilled, though the wounds were minor, mere scratches that dabbed the blades with just enough blood to send red droplets flying through the air to mingle with the fine spray of sweat cast from the gladiators' glistening limbs.

Slowly but surely the pace of the parries and thrusts accelerated, even as their rhythm became more ragged and unpredictable. My heartbeat quickened. I glanced at Cicero and realized that he had not said a word throughout the match. He leaned forward, his eyes glittering with fascination.

The swarthy fighter suddenly seized the advantage. His arms became a blur of movement, like the wings of a bee. And like a bee he stung, managing to prick first the right hand of his opponent, then the left hand, so that the pale gladiator released both of his daggers and stood defenseless. Pressing his daggers to the other's wrists, the swarthy fighter forced the disarmed man to spread his arms wide open, like a crucified slave.

It was a brazen gesture on the part of the swarthy gladiator to humiliate his foe, but it contained a miscalculation. At such close quarters, almost chest-to-chest, the pale gladiator was able to thrust one knee into his opponent's groin, and simultaneously to butt his helmet against the other's. The swarthy gladiator was sent staggering back. The hushed crowd erupted in shrieks of laughter.

The pale gladiator's advantage was short-lived. He made a dash to recover one of his daggers, but the distance was too great. The swarthy gladiator was upon him like a pouncing lion, hemming him in with his daggers, jabbing and pricking him, forcing him to perform a spastic, backward dance, controlling him at every step. To pay him back, the swarthy gladiator kneed him not once but twice in the groin. The pale gladiator folded forward in agony, then abruptly performed the motion in reverse, straining upright onto his toes, for not one but two daggers were pressed against the soft, unarmored flesh beneath his chin. The movement was so neatly performed that it seemed like the climax to a dance which the two had been performing from the moment their bout commenced. They stood like statues, one with daggers poised, the other on tiptoes, quivering, empty hands at his sides, helpless. The crowd roared its approval.

The victor looked toward the magistrate, who raised an eyebrow and turned his head from side to side to assess the will of the crowd. Spontaneously, the crowd produced a multitude of fluttering hand-kerchiefs. Voices cried, "Spare him! Spare him!" Even the men be-hind me took up the chant: "Spare him! Spare him!"

In my experience, the judgment of the mob is like quicksilver, hard to pin down and impossible to predict. If I had turned at that moment and asked the men behind me, "Why spare the pale gladia-tor?", no doubt they would have given the rote answer: "Because he fought well, and deserves to fight another day." But the Samnite had fought just as bravely, if not as beautifully, and they had been eager to see him die. I think it was the fact that the two *dimacheri* had fought so well together that swayed the crowd to spare the loser; they were like a matched set that no one wished to see broken. The pale gladiator owed his life as much to his opponent as to himself; had they not been so precisely matched, those two daggers would have been thrust into his gullet in the blink of an eye. Instead, one by one, the daggers withdrew. The pale gladiator dropped to his knees, his head bowed to show deference both to the spectators who had spared him and to the man who had bested him, as the victor re-ceived his palm frond from the presiding magistrate.

"Well!" said Cicero, breaking his silence. "So far it's been a better show than any of us expected, I daresay. I wonder what the final match will bring?"

Sometimes, if the games are boring, spectators begin to vacate the stands after the first or second match, deciding they've ade-quately paid their respects to the dead and need stay no longer. On this day, for the final match, not a single spectator stirred from his seat. Instead, there was a new arrival. I was not the only one who no-ticed her; one of the men behind me released a wolf whistle.

"Feast your eyes on that beauty!" he murmured.

"Where?" said his friend.

"Right across from us, looking for a place to sit."

"Oh, yes, I see. A beauty, you say? Too dark for my taste."

"You need to broaden your palate then. Ha! I'll bet you've never had a Nubian."

"As if *you* had!"

"Of course I have. You forget that I spent a few years traveling around Libya and Egypt . . ."

I grew deaf to their prattling, fascinated by the newcomer. She was strikingly beautiful, with high cheekbones, full lips, and flashing eyes. Her dense black hair was piled on her head in the latest style and tied with ribbons, and she wore a tunica of pale blue that contrasted with the ebony sheen of her naked arms and throat. Her burnished-copper necklace and bracelets glinted in the bright sunlight. Her bosom heaved slightly, as if she were excited or slightly out of breath. One seldom saw in Italy a Nubian who was not a slave, but from her dress and the fact that she appeared to be out and about on her own, I took her to be a free woman. While I watched, a row of male spectators, clearly as struck by her beauty as I was, nudged one another and obligingly made room for her, giving her an aisle seat.

The two gladiators who strode into the arena for the final bout could not have been more different. The first was stoutly built, his chest and legs covered by curly red hair. He was outfitted in the manner of the Gauls, with a short sword and a tall, rectangular shield, a loose loincloth and bands of metal-plated leather wrapped around his midsection, leaving his legs and chest bare. His helmet covered not only his head but, tapering and flaring out again like an hourglass, extended down to cover his neck and breastbone as well.

Following him into the arena was a *retiarius*, to my mind the most fearsomely attired class of gladiators. *Retiarii* carry not a sword and shield, but a long trident and a net. This one was all the more striking because of his contrast to the red-haired Gaul, for he was the tall, smoothly muscled Nubian we had seen in the opening parade of gladiators, as ebon-hued as the woman who had just found a seat in the stands. I wondered briefly if there might be some connection between them—then drew in a breath as the Gaul made a rush at the *retiarius*, and the combat commenced.

Sword clanged against trident. Already heated to fever pitch by the previous matches, the crowd became raucously vocal at once, jumping from their seats and crying out for blood. The gladiators responded with a bout that exceeded anything we had previously seen that day. For two men so heavily muscled, they moved with surprising speed (although the *retiarius*, with his long legs, was considerably more graceful than his opponent). They seemed almost to read one another's thoughts, as blows were deflected or dodged at the last possible instant, and each attack was followed at once by a counterattack of equal cunning and ferocity. Beside me, Cicero repeatedly flinched and gasped, but did not look away. Neither did I, swept up by the primal fascination of watching two men in a struggle for life and death.

As the match continued, the attributes of each fighter became clear. The Gaul was stronger, the Nubian quicker; he would need to be, if he were to succeed in casting the net over his prey. Several times, when the Gaul closed the distance between them in order to slash and thrust, the net almost captured him, but the Gaul eluded it by dropping to the sand, rolling out of harm's way, and springing back to his feet.

"At this rate, the Gaul's going to exhaust himself," said one of the men behind me. "Then watch the Nubian catch him in that net like a fish out of water and start poking holes in him!"

Irritated, Cicero turned to shush the man, but I was thinking exactly the same thought. And indeed, almost more quickly than my eyes could apprehend it, the very thing happened. The Gaul rushed in, slashing his sword. Wielding the trident with one hand, the Nubian parried the Gaul's thrust, and with his other hand he spun the net in the air and brought it down directly over the Gaul. The lead weights sown at various points around the edge of the net caused it to collapse around the Gaul and swallow him, sword, shield, and all.

If the Gaul had tripped, which seemed almost inevitable, that would have been the end of him. But somehow he managed to stay upright, and when the Nubian, wielding his trident with both hands now, rushed toward him, he managed to spin about so that the three sharp prongs landed squarely against his shield. The prongs, failing to penetrate flesh, instead became enmeshed in the fabric of the net. The Nubian yanked at his trident to free it, but the net held it fast, and the Gaul, though pulled forward, managed to stand his ground.

Sensing more than seeing his advantage—for the net must have greatly blocked the view from his narrow visor—the Gaul rushed forward. Holding fast to the trident, the Nubian was unable to stand his ground and was pushed back. Tripping, he fell onto his rump and released the shaft of the trident with one hand, still gripping it with the other. The Gaul, using his bull-like strength, twisted to one side. The Nubian, his wrist unnaturally bent, gave a cry and released the trident altogether.

The Gaul, slashing at the net with his sword and thrusting upwards with his shield, managed to push the net up and over his head, taking the trident with it. Stepping free, he kicked the net behind him, and with it the now hopelessly entangled trident. The Nubian, meanwhile, managed to scramble to his feet, but he was now without a weapon.

The Gaul might have made short work of his opponent, but eschewing his sword, he used his shield as a weapon instead. Rushing headlong at the Nubian, he struck him with his shield, so hard that the Nubian was knocked backwards against the wooden wall of the arena. The spectators directly above him, unable to see, rushed forward from their seats and craned their necks, peering over the railing. Among them—not hard to pick out in that crowd—I saw the

Nubian woman. Even greater than the contrast of her dark flesh next to the paleness of those around her was the marked contrast of her expression. Submerged in a sea of faces that leered, gaped, and howled with bloodlust, she was silent and stricken, wearing a look of shock and dismay.

The Gaul played cat-and-mouse with his prey. He stepped back, allowing the Nubian to stagger forward, gasping for breath, then struck him full-force again with his shield, knocking him against the wall. Over and over, the Gaul struck the Nubian, knocking the breath out of him each time, until the man was barely able to stand. The Gaul delivered one last body-blow with his shield, and the Nubian, recoiling from the wall, fell forward onto his face.

Casting aside his shield, the Gaul grabbed hold of the Nubian's ankle and dragged him toward the center of the arena. The Nubian thrashed ineffectively, seemingly unable to catch a breath. To judge from the intermittent red trail he left in the sand, he was bleeding from some part of his body, perhaps from his mouth.

"Ha!" said one of the men behind me. "Who's the fish out of water now?"

The Gaul reached the center of the ring. Releasing the Nubian's ankle, he held up his fists and performed a victory strut in a circle around him. The crowd gasped at the man's audacity. The Thracian had behaved with the same careless bravado, and had very nearly paid for it with his life.

But the Nubian was in no condition to take advantage of any miscalculation by his opponent. At one point, he stirred and tried to raise himself on his arms, and the crowd let out a cry; but his arms failed him and he fell back again, flat on his chest. The Gaul stood over him and looked to the spectators for judgment.

The reaction from the stands was mixed. People rose to their feet. "Spare him!" cried some. "Send him to Hades!" cried others. The magistrate in charge turned his head this way and that, looking distinctly uncomfortable at the lack of consensus. Whichever course he chose, some in the crowd would be disappointed. At last he gave a sign to the waiting gladiator, and I was not surprised that he did the predictable thing. Mercy to a defeated fighter had already been granted once that day; mercy was the exception, not the rule. The crowd had come expecting to see bloodshed and death, and those who wanted to see the Nubian killed had more reason to see their expectation gratified than did those who preferred the novelty of allowing him to live. The magistrate raised his fist in the air.

There were cries of triumph in the stands, and groans of disappointment. Some cheered the magistrate, others booed. But to all this commotion I was largely deaf, for my eyes were on the Nubian woman directly across from me. Her body stiffened and her face froze in a grimace as the Gaul raised his sword for the death blow; I had the impression that she was struggling to contain herself, to exhibit dignity despite the despair that was overwhelming her. But as the sword descended, she lost all composure. She clutched her hair. She opened her mouth. The sound of her scream was drowned in the roar of the crowd as the Nubian convulsed on the sand, blood spurting like a fountain around the sword thrust between his shoulder blades.

For an instant, the Nubian woman's gaze met mine. I was drawn into the depths of her grief as surely as if I tumbled into a well. Cicero gripped my arm. "Steady, Gordianus," he said. I turned toward him. His face was pale but his tone was smug; at last, it seemed to say, he had found someone more squeamish at the sight of death than himself.

When I looked back, the woman had vanished.

With their palm fronds held aloft, the victors paraded once more around the arena. The magistrate invoked the memory of Sextus

Thorius and uttered a closing prayer to the gods. The spectators filed out of the amphitheater.

"Did you notice her?" I asked Cicero.

"Who, that hyperventilating young woman next to me?"

"No, the Nubian across from us."

"A Nubian female?"

"I don't think she showed up until the final bout. I think she was alone."

"That seems unlikely."

"Perhaps she's related somehow to the Nubian gladiator."

He shrugged. "I didn't notice her. How observant you are, Gordianus! You and your endless curiosity. But what did you think of the games?" I started to answer, but Cicero gave me no chance. "Do you know," he said, "I actually rather enjoyed myself, far more than I expected to. A most instructive afternoon, and the audience seemed quite uplifted by the whole experience. But it seems to me a mistake on the part of the organizers, simply as a matter of presentation, not to show us the faces of the gladiators at some point, either at the beginning or the end. Their individual helmets project a certain personality, to be sure, like masks in the theater. Or do you think that's the point, to keep them anonymous and abstract? If we could see into their eyes, we might make a more emotional connection—they'd become humans beings first, and gladiators second, and that would interfere with the pure symbolism of their role in the funeral games. It would thwart the religious intent . . ." Safe once more from the very real bloodshed of the arena, Cicero nattered on, falling into his role of aloof lecturer.

We arrived at Cicero's lodgings, where he continued to pontificate to his host, a rich Etrurian yokel who seemed quite overwhelmed to have such a famous advocate from Rome sleeping under his roof. After a parsimonious meal, I excused myself as quickly as I could and went to bed. I could not help thinking that the lice at the inn had been more congenial, and the cook more generous.

I fell asleep thinking of the Nubian woman, haunted by my final image of her—her fists tearing at her hair, her mouth opened to scream.

The next day I made my way back to Rome. I proceeded to forget about the funeral of Sextus Thorius, the games, and the Nubian woman. The month of Junius passed into Quinctilis.

Then, one day, as Rome sweltered through the hottest summer I could remember, Eco came to me in my garden to announce a visitor.

"A woman?" I said, watching his hands shape curves in the air.

Eco nodded. *Rather young*, he went on to say, in the elaborate system of gestures we had devised between us, *with skin the color of night*.

I raised an eyebrow. "A Nubian?"

Eco nodded.

"Show her in."

My memory did not do justice to her beauty. As before, her hair was done up with ribbons and she was attired in pale blue and burnished copper. Probably the outfit was the best she possessed. She had worn it to attend the funeral games; now she wore it for me. I was flattered.

She studied me for a long moment, a quizzical expression on her face. "I've seen you somewhere before," she finally said.

"Yes. In Saturnia, at the funeral games for Sextus Thorius."

She sucked in a breath. "I remember now. You sat across from me. You weren't like the rest—laughing, joking, screaming for blood. When Zanziba was killed, you saw the suffering on my face, and I could tell that you . . ." Her voice trailed off. She lowered her eyes. "How strange, the paths upon which the gods lead us! When I asked around the Subura for a man who might be able to help me, yours was the name people gave me, but I never imagined that I'd seen you before—and in that place of all places, on that day of all accursed days!"

"You know who I am, then?"

"Gordianus. They call you the Finder."

"Yes. And you?"

"My name is Zuleika."

"Not a Roman name."

"I had a Roman name once. A man who was my master gave it to me. But Zuleika is the name I was born with, and Zuleika is the name I'll die with."

"I take it you shed your slave name when you shed your former master. You're a freedwoman, then?"

"Yes."

"Let's sit here in the garden. My son will bring us wine to drink."

We sat in the shade, and Zuleika told me her story.

She had been born in a city with an unpronounceable name, in a country unimaginably far away—beyond Nubia, she said, even beyond the fabled source of the Nile. Her father had been a wealthy trader in ivory, who often traveled and took his family with him. In a desert land, at a tender age, she had seen her father and mother murdered by bandits. Zuleika and her younger brother, Zanziba, were abducted and sold into slavery.

"Our fortunes varied, as did our masters," she said, "but at least we were kept together as a pair; because we were exotic, you see." *And beautiful,* I thought, assuming that her brother's beauty matched her own. "Eventually we found ourselves in Egypt. Our new owner was the master of a mime troupe. He trained us to be performers."

"You have a particular talent?"

"I dance and sing."

"And your brother?"

"Zanziba excelled at acrobatics—cartwheels, balancing acts, somersaults in midair. The master said that Zanziba must have a pair

of wings hidden somewhere between those massive shoulders of his."
She smiled, but only briefly. "Our master had once been a slave himself. He was a kind and generous man; he allowed his slaves to earn
their own money, with the goal of eventually buying their freedom.
When we had earned enough, Zanziba and I, we used the money to
purchase Zanziba's freedom, with the intention of putting aside
more money until we could do the same for me.

"But then the master fell on hard times. He was forced to disband
the troupe and sell his performers piecemeal—a dancer here, a juggler there. I ended up with a new master, a Roman merchant living
in Alexandria. He didn't want me for my dancing or my singing. He
wanted me for my body." She lowered her eyes. "When Zanziba
came to him and said he wanted to buy my freedom, the man named
a very steep price. Zanziba vowed to earn it, but he could never hope
to do so as an acrobat, performing for coins in the street. He disappeared from Alexandria. Time passed, and more time. For such a
long time I heard no word from him that I began to despair, thinking
that my brother was dead, or had forgotten about me.

"Then, finally, money arrived—a considerable sum, enough to
buy my freedom and more. And with it came a letter—not in Zanziba's hand, because neither of us had ever learned to read or write,
but written for him by the banker who transmitted the money."

"What did the letter say?"

"Can you read?"

"Yes."

"Then read it for yourself." Zuleika handed me a worn and tattered scrap of parchment.

Beloved Sister, I am in Italy, among the Romans. I have become a
gladiator, a man who fights to the death to honor the Roman dead. It is
a strange thing to be. The Romans profess to despise our kind, yet all
the men want to buy us drinks in the taverns and all the women want

to sleep with us. I despise this life, but it is the only way a freedman can earn the sort of money we need. It is a hard, cruel life, not fit for an animal, and it comes to a terrible end. Do not follow or try to find me. Forget me. Find your way back to our homeland, if you can. Live free, sister. I, too, shall live free, and though I may die young, I shall die a free man. Your loving brother, Zanziba.

I handed the scrap of parchment back to her. "Your brother told you not to come to Italy."

"How could I not come? Zanziba hadn't forgotten me, after all. I was not going to forget him. As soon as I was able, I booked passage on a ship to Rome."

"Travel is expensive."

"I paid for the fare from the money Zanziba sent me."

"Surely he meant for you to live off that money."

"Here in Rome I make my own living." She raised her chin high. The haughty angle flattered her. She was beautiful; she was exotic; she was obviously clever. I could well imagine that Zuleika was able to demand a high fee for the pleasure of her company.

"You came to Rome. And then?"

"I looked for Zanziba, of course. I started with the banker who'd sent the money. He sent me to a gladiator camp near Neapolis. I talked to the man who owned the camp—the trainer, what you Romans call a *lanista*. He told me Zanziba had fought with his troupe of gladiators for a while, but had long since moved on. The *lanista* didn't know where. Most gladiators are captives or slaves, but Zanziba was a free agent; he went where the money was best. I followed his trail by rumor and hearsay. I came to one dead end after another, and each time I had to start all over again. If you're as good as people say, Gordianus the Finder, I could have used the skills of a man like you to track him down." She raised an eyebrow. "Do you have any idea how many gladiator camps there are in Italy?"

"Scores, I should imagine."

"Hundreds, scattered all over the countryside! Over the last few months I've traveled the length and breadth of Italy, looking for Zanziba without luck, until . . . until a man who knew Zanziba told me that he was fighting for a *lanista* named Ahala who runs a camp in Ravenna. But the man said I needn't bother going all the way to Ravenna, because Ahala's gladiators would be fighting at funeral games the very next day up in Saturnia."

"At the funeral of Sextus Thorius," I said.

"Yes. I wasn't able to leave Rome until the next morning. I traveled all day. I arrived just when Zanziba's match was beginning—excited, fearful, out of breath. Just in time to see—"

"Are you sure it was him?"

"Of course."

"But he wore a helmet."

She shook her head. "With or without the helmet, I'd have known him. By his limbs and legs. By the way he *moved*. 'Zanziba must have wings hidden between those massive shoulders,' the master in Alexandria used to say . . ." Her voice trembled and her eyes glittered with tears. "After all my travels, all my searching, I arrived just in time to see my brother die!"

I lowered my eyes, remembering the scene: the Nubian flat on his chest, the Gaul with his sword poised to strike, the uncertain magistrate, the raucous crowd, the death blow, the fountain of blood . . .

"I'm sorry you had to see such a thing, Zuleika. Did you attend to his body afterwards?"

"I wasn't even allowed to see him! I went to the quarters where the gladiators were kept, but the *lanista* wouldn't let me in."

"Did you tell him who you were?"

"If anything, that made him even more hostile. He told me it didn't matter whose sister I was, that I had no business being there. 'Clear off!' he shouted, and one of the gladiators shook a sword at me, and I ran away, crying. I should have stood up to him, I suppose, but I was so upset . . ."

Stood up to him? I thought. That would have been impossible. A freedwoman Zuleika might be, but that hardly gave her the privileges of a Roman citizen, or the prerogatives of being male. No one in Saturnia that day would have taken her side against the *lanista*.

I sighed, wondering, now that her story was told, why she had come to see me. "Your brother did an honorable thing when he sent you money to buy your freedom. But perhaps he was right. You shouldn't have followed him here. You shouldn't have tried to find him. A gladiator's life is brutish and short. He chose that life, and he saw it through to the only possible end."

"No!" she whispered, shaking her head, fixing me with a fiery gaze. "It wasn't the end."

"What do you mean?"

"It wasn't the end of Zanziba!"

"I don't understand."

"Zanziba didn't die that day. I know, because . . . because I've seen him!"

"Where? When?"

"Yesterday, here in Rome, in the marketplace down by the river. I saw Zanziba!"

Was the glint in her eyes excitement or madness? "Did you speak to him?"

"No. He was on the far side of the market. A cart blocked my way, and before I could reach him, he was gone."

"Perhaps you were mistaken," I said quietly. "It happens to me all the time. I see a face across a crowd, or from the corner of my eye, and I'm sure it's someone I know. But when I take a second look, I realize the familiarity was merely an illusion, a trick of the mind."

She shook her head. "How many men who look like Zanziba have you ever seen in the Roman market?"

"All the more reason why you might mistake such a fellow for your brother. Any tall, muscular man with ebony skin, glimpsed at a distance—"

"But it wasn't a glimpse! I saw him clearly—"

"You said a cart blocked the way."

"That was *after* I saw him, when I tried to move toward him. Before that, I saw him as clearly as I'm seeing you now. I saw his face! It was Zanziba I saw!"

I considered this for a long moment. "Perhaps, Zuleika, you saw his lemur. You wouldn't be the first person to see the restless spirit of a loved one wandering the streets of Rome in broad daylight."

She shook her head. "I saw a man, not a lemur."

"But how do you know?"

"He was buying a plum from a vendor. Tell me, Gordianus: do lemures eat plums?"

I tried to dissuade her from hiring me by naming the same fee I would have asked from Cicero, but she agreed to the figure at once, and paid me a first installment on the spot. Zuleika seemed quite proud of her financial resources.

It was her idea that we should begin our search in Rome, and I agreed, duly making the rounds of the usual eyes and ears. I quickly discovered that a large Nubian of Zanziba's description had indeed been seen around the marketplace, but no one could identify the man and no one knew where he'd come from, or where he'd gone. Zuleika wanted to visit every hostel and tavern in the city, but I counseled patience; put out a reward for information, I told her, and the information would come to us. Sure enough, a few days later, a street-sweeper in the Subura arrived at my door with word that the Nubian I was seeking had spent a single night at a seedy little hostel off the Street of the Coppersmiths, but had given no name and had moved on the next day.

Again I counseled patience. But days passed with no new information, and Zuleika grew impatient to commence with the next obvious step: to pay a call on Ahala, Zanziba's *lanista*, the man who had turned her away when she tried to see her brother's corpse. I remained dubious, but made preparations for the journey. Ravenna is a long way from Rome, especially when the traveler suspects in his heart of hearts that at journey's end lies bitter disappointment.

Zuleika traveled with me and paid all expenses—sometimes with coins, but more often, I suspected, by exchanging favors with tavern keepers along the way, or by plying her trade with other guests. How she made her living was her business. I minded my own.

During the day, we rode on horseback. Zuleika was no stranger to horses. One of her brother's acrobatic tricks had been to stand upright on the back of a cantering horse, and she had learned to do so as well. She offered to show me, but I dissuaded her; if she fell and broke her neck, who would pay my way home?

She was a good conversationalist, a skill that no doubt contributed to her ability to make a decent living; men pay for pleasure, but come back for good company. To pass the hours, we talked a great deal about Alexandria, where I had lived for a while when I was young. I was amused to hear her impressions of the teeming city and its risible inhabitants. In return, I told her the tale of the Alexandrian cat, whose killer I had discovered, and the terrible revenge exacted by the cat-worshipping mob of the city.

I was also intrigued by her newcomer's impressions of Rome and Italy. Her search for Zanziba had taken her to many places, and her livelihood had acquainted her with men from all levels of society. She knew both the city and the countryside, and due to the nature of her search she had inadvertently become something of an expert on the state of gladiators.

"Do you know the strongest impression I have of this land of yours?" she said one day, as we passed a gang of slaves working in a field along the Flaminian Way. "Too many slaves!"

I shrugged. "There are slaves in Alexandria, too. There are slaves in every city and every country."

"Perhaps, but it's different here. Maybe it's because the Romans have conquered so many other people, and become so wealthy, and brought in so many slaves from so many places. In Egypt, there are small farmers all along the Nile; they may own slaves, but they also till the earth themselves. Everyone pulls together; in years of a good inundation, everyone eats well, and in years when the Nile runs low, everyone eats less. Here, it seems to me the farmers are all rich men who live in the city, and slaves do every bit of the work, and the free men who should be farmers are all in Rome, crowded into tenements and living off the dole. It doesn't seem right."

"The farms are run well enough, I suppose."

"Are they? Then why does Rome import so much grain from Egypt? Look at how these field slaves are treated—how shabbily they're dressed, how skinny they are, how hard they're made to work, even under this blistering sun. An Egyptian farmer would be out in the fields alongside his slaves, pushing them to work harder, yes, but also seeing just how hard they do work, and making sure they're healthy and well fed so they're fit to work the next day, too. To an Egyptian, slaves are a valuable investment, and you don't squander them. Here, there's a different attitude: Work a slave as hard as you can, invest as little as possible in his upkeep, and when you've used him up, dispose of him and get another, because slaves are cheap and Rome's provinces provide an endless supply."

As if to illustrate her point, we passed a huddled figure in the gutter alongside the road, a creature so shriveled and filthy that I could tell neither its age nor its sex—an abandoned slave, kicked out by its master, no doubt. As we passed by, the creature croaked a few unintelligible words and extended a clawlike hand. Zuleika reached into her traveling bag and threw the unfortunate a crust of bread left over from her breakfast.

"Too many slaves," she repeated. "And far too many gladiators! I can scarcely believe how many camps full of gladiators I had occasion to visit since I arrived here. So many captured warriors, from so many conquered lands, all flowing into Italy. What to do with them all? Put on gladiator games and make them fight each other to the death! Put on a show with six gladiators, and three will likely be dead by the end of the day. But ten more will arrive the next day, bought cheap at auction! Not all of them are good fighters, of course; the ones who turn out to be clumsy or cowardly or nearsighted can be sent off to a farm or a ship's galley or the mines. The ones who remain have to be outfitted and trained, and fed reasonably well to keep them strong.

"That's how the *best* camps are run. But those *lanistas* charge a lot of money to hire out their gladiators. Not everyone can afford the best, but every Roman wants to host games at his father's funeral, even if it's only a single pair of fighters spilling each other's blood in a sheep pen while the family sit on the fence and cheer. So there's a market for gladiators who can be hired cheaply. You can imagine how those gladiators are kept—fed slop and housed in pens, like animals. But their lives are more miserable than any animal's, because animals don't fall asleep at night wondering if the next day they'll die a horrible death for a stranger's amusement. Such gladiators are poorly trained and armed with the cheapest weapons. Can you imagine a fight to the death where both men are armed with nothing better than wooden swords? There's no way to make a clean, quick kill; the result is a cruel, bloody farce. I've seen such a death match with my own eyes. I didn't know which man to pity more, the one who died, or the one who had to take the other's life using such a crude weapon."

She shook her head. "So many gladiators, scattered all over Italy, all trained to kill without mercy. So many weapons within easy reach. So much misery. I think, some day, there may be a reckoning."

When we reached the outskirts of Ravenna, I asked a man on the road for directions to the gladiator camp of the *lanista* Ahala.

The man eyed the two of us curiously for a moment, then saw the iron citizen's ring on my finger. "On the far side of town you'll come to a big oak tree where the road forks. Take the left branch for another mile. But unless you've come to hire some of his gladiators, I'd stay clear of the place. Unfriendly. Guard dogs. High fences."

"To keep the gladiators in?"

"To keep everybody else out! A while back, a neighbor's slave wandered onto the property. One of those dogs tore his leg off. Fellow bled to death. Ahala refused to make restitution. He doesn't like folks coming 'round."

Leaving Zuleika at a hostel near the town forum, I made my way alone to the oak tree on the far side of town and took the branch to the left. After a mile or so, just as the man had said, a rutted dirt road branched off the stone-paved highway. I followed the road around a bend and came to a gateway that appeared to mark the boundary of Ahala's property. The structure itself was probably enough to keep out most unwanted visitors. Nailed to the two upright posts were various bones bleached white by the sun, and adorning the beam above my head was a collection of human skulls.

I passed through the gate and rode on for another mile or so, through a landscape of thickets and wild brush. At last I arrived at a compound surrounded by a high palisade of sharpened stakes. From within I heard a man's voice shouting commands, and the clatter of wood striking wood—gladiators drilling with practice swords, I presumed. I heard other, more incongruous noises—the bleating of sheep and goats, a smith's hammer, and the sound of men laughing, not in a harsh or mean-spirited way, but quite boisterously. I approached a door in the palisade, but had no chance to knock; on the other side, so close and with such ferocity that I jerked back and my heart skipped a beat, dogs began to bark and jump against the gate, scraping their claws against the wood.

A shouting voice chastised the dogs, who stopped barking. A peephole opened in the gate, so high up that I assumed the man beyond was standing on a stool. Two bloodshot eyes peered down at me.

"Who are you and what do you want?"

"Is this the gladiator camp of Ahala?"

"Who wants to know?"

"Are you Ahala?"

"Who's asking?"

"My name is Gordianus. I've come all the way from Rome."

"Have you, indeed?"

"I saw some of your gladiators perform at Saturnia a while back."

"Did you, now?"

"I was most impressed."

"Were you?"

"More to the point," I said, improvising, "my good friend Marcus Tullius Cicero was impressed."

"Cicero, you say?"

"You've heard of him, I presume? Cicero's a man to be reckoned with, a rising politician and a very famous advocate who handles the legal affairs of some of the most powerful families in Rome."

The man lifted an eyebrow. "Don't think much of politicians and lawyers."

"No? Well, as a rule, Cicero doesn't think much of funeral games. But he thought your men put on quite a show." So far, everything I had said was true; when lying, I have found it best to begin with the truth and embellish only as necessary. "In his line of work, Cicero is frequently called upon to advise the bereaved. On legal matters such as wills, you understand. But they often ask his advice about all sorts of other things—such as who to call upon to produce a truly memorable afternoon of funeral games."

"I see. So this Cicero thought my boys put on a memorable show?"

"He did indeed. And as I happened to be coming to Ravenna on business of my own, and as you happen to have your camp here, I promised my good friend Cicero that I would call on you if I had a chance, to see what sort of operation you run—how many gladiators you've got, how long you've been in business, how much you charge, that sort of thing."

The man nodded. The peephole banged shut. The barking resumed, but receded into the distance, as if someone were dragging the dogs elsewhere. A bolt was thrown back. The gate swung open.

"Ahala—*lanista*—at your service." I had assumed the speaker was standing on something to reach the peephole, but I was wrong. Towering over me was a grizzled, hulking giant of a man. He looked like a gladiator himself, though few gladiators live long enough to attain such a magnificent mane of gray hair. Was Ahala the exception? It was not entirely unheard of for a fighter to survive long enough to buy his freedom and become a professional trainer; it was far less common for such a survivor to become the owner of a cadre of gladiators, as Ahala apparently was. Whatever his origins and history, he was obviously smarter than his lumbering physique and terse manner might suggest.

"Come in," he said. "Have a look around."

The compound within the palisade included several barnlike buildings set close together, separated by garden plots and pens for horses, goats, and sheep.

"You raise livestock," I said.

"Gladiators eat a lot of meat."

"And you grow your own garlic, I see."

"Gives the fellows extra strength."

"So I've heard." Whole treatises had been written about the proper care and feeding of gladiators.

At a shouted command, the clatter of wooden weapons resumed. The noise seemed to come from beyond another palisade of sharpened stakes. "This is the outer compound," Ahala explained. "Gladiators are kept in the inner compound. Safer that way, especially for visitors like you. Wouldn't want you to end up with your skull decorating that gate out by the highway."

I smiled uncertainly, not entirely sure the man was joking. "Still, I'd like to have a look at the gladiators."

"In a bit. Show you the armory first. Explain how I do business." He led me into a long, low shed festooned with chains, upon which were hung all manner of helmets, greaves, swords, shields, and tridents. There were also a number of devices I didn't recognize, including some tubes made of metal and wood that looked as if they might fit into a man's mouth. Ahala saw me looking at them, but offered no explanation. Some of the weapons also looked a bit odd to me. I reached out to touch a hanging sword, but Ahala seized my wrist.

"You'll cut yourself," he grumbled, then ushered me to the far end of the shed, where a trio of smiths in leather aprons were hammering a red-hot piece of metal.

"You make your own weapons?" I asked.

"Sometimes. A customized fit can make the difference between a good fighter and a great one. Mostly I keep these fellows busy with repairs and alterations. I like to keep the armory in tip-top shape."

He led me past the smiths, into another shed, where carpenters were whittling wood into pegs. "Amphitheater seeds, I call those," said Ahala with a laugh. "Some of the people who hire me want a temporary arena built especially for the games. Maybe they need to seat a hundred people, maybe a thousand. My carpenters can throw up a decent amphitheater practically overnight, provided there's a good source of local timber. Client pays for the materials, of course. But I've found it saves time and shaves considerable expense if I've got nails and pegs ready to go. All part of a complete package."

I nodded. "I'd never thought of that—the added expense of erecting a place to put on the games."

Ahala shrugged. "Funeral games don't come cheap."

We passed through a small slaughterhouse where the carcass of a sheep had been hung for butchering. Certain parts of slaughtered animals that might normally have been discarded had been saved and hung to dry. I stepped toward the back corner of the room to have a closer look, but Ahala gripped my elbow.

"You wanted to see the fighters. Step this way."

He led me to a gate in the inner palisade, lifted the bar, and opened the narrow door. "That way, to your right, are the barracks, where they eat and sleep. The training area is this way. Visitor coming!" he shouted. We walked through a covered passage and emerged on a sandy square open to the sky, where five pairs of men abruptly pulled apart and raised their wooden practice swords in a salute to their *lanista*.

"Carry on!" barked Ahala.

The men resumed their mock battles, banging swords against shields.

"I thought . . ."

"You thought we'd be above them, looking down, like in an amphitheater?" said Ahala.

"Yes."

He chuckled. "We don't stage exhibition bouts here. Only way to see the training area is to walk right in. Stand closer if you want. Smell the sweat. Look them in the eye."

I felt acutely vulnerable. I was used to seeing gladiators at a distance, in the arena. To stand among them, with nothing between them and me, was like entering a cage full of wild animals. Even the shortest man among them was a head taller than me. All ten wore helmets but were otherwise naked. Apparently they were training to receive blows to the head, because their rhythmic exercise consisted of exchanging repeated blows to each other's helmets. The blows were relatively gentle, but the racket was unnerving.

From his physique, I thought I recognized at least one of the gladiators from the games at Saturnia, the bull-necked Thracian who had triumphed in the opening bout. About the others I was less sure.

"I wonder, do you have any Nubians among your men?"

Ahala raised an eyebrow. "Why do you ask?"

"There was a Nubian that day in Saturnia, a *retiarius*. Cicero took particular note of him—'just the sort of exotic touch to ensure a memorable day,' he said."

Ahala nodded. "A *retiarius*? Ah, yes, I remember now. That fellow's dead, of course. But it just so happens that I *do* have another Nubian in the troupe. Tall, strapping fellow like the one you saw."

"Also a *retiarius*?"

"He can fight with net and trident, certainly. All my gladiators are trained to be versatile. They can fight in whatever style you wish."

"Yes, it's all about giving the spectators what they want, isn't it? Delivering a thrill and an eyeful." I watched the practicing pairs of gladiators advance and retreat, advance and retreat with the rhythmic precision of acrobats. "Can I see this Nubian?" I said.

"See him train, you mean?"

"Yes, why not?"

Ahala called to an assistant. "Bring the Nubian. This man wants to see him train with net and trident." He turned back to me. "While we wait, I'll explain how I calculate my prices, depending on the size of funeral games you need . . ."

For the next few moments, I had to struggle to keep my face a blank; I'd never imagined that funeral games could be so costly. To be sure, a *lanista* faced considerable expenses, but I suspected that Ahala was making a considerable profit as well. Was that why Zanziba had come to him, because Ahala had the wherewithal to pay him handsomely?

"Are they all slaves?" I asked, interrupting Ahala as he was reciting a complicated formula for payment on installment plans.

"What's that?"

"Your gladiators—are they all slaves? One hears occasionally of free men who hire themselves out as gladiators. They make good money, I'm told. Have their choice of women, too."

"Are you thinking of taking it up?" He looked me up and down and laughed, rather unkindly, I thought.

"No. I'm merely curious. That Nubian who fought in Saturnia, for example—"

"Who cares about him?" snapped Ahala. "Gone to Hades!" He scowled, then brightened. "Ah, here's his replacement."

Seen at such close quarters, the *retiarius* who entered the training area was a magnificent specimen of a man, tall and broad and elegantly proportioned. He immediately engaged in a mock combat with the gladiator who had accompanied him, putting on a lively demonstration for my benefit. Was it the same Nubian I had seen in Saturnia? I thought so—or was I doing what I had accused Zuleika of doing, seeing what I wanted or expected to see?

"Enough fighting!" I said. "I want to see his face."

"His face?" Ahala stared at me, perplexed.

"I've seen a Nubian fight—I've seen one die, at Saturnia—but

I've never seen one this close, face-to-face. Indulge my curiosity, *lanista*. Show me the fellow's face."

"Very well." At Ahala's signal, the gladiators drew apart. Ahala beckoned the Nubian to come to us. "Take off your helmet," he said.

The Nubian put aside his weapons, removed his helmet, and stood naked before me. I had never seen the face of the Nubian who fought in Saturnia. I had never seen Zanziba's face. But those two brown eyes which stared back at me—had I seen them before? Were they Zuleika's soulful eyes, set in a man's face? Was this the face of her brother, Zanziba? The high cheekbones were much the same, as were the broad nose and forehead. But I could not be sure.

"What is your name, gladiator?"

He hesitated, as slaves not used to being addressed by strangers often do. He glanced at Ahala, then looked straight ahead. "Chiron," he said.

"Like the centaur? A good name for a gladiator, I suppose. Were you born with that name?"

Again he hesitated and glanced at Ahala. "I don't know."

"Where do you come from?"

"I . . . don't know."

"How odd. And how long have you been at this camp, with Ahala as your *lanista*?"

"I . . ."

"Enough of this!" snapped Ahala. "Can't you see the fellow's simple-minded? But he's a damned good fighter, I guarantee. If you want the personal history of each and every gladiator, put some sesterces on my table first and hire them! Now the tour is over. I've other things to do. If your friend Cicero or some of his rich clients have need of funeral games, they'll know where to find me. You men, get back to your training. Gordianus, allow me to show you the way out."

As the gate to the compound slammed shut behind me, the dogs, silent throughout my visit, recommenced their barking.

"It's him!" insisted Zuleika. "It must be. Describe him again, Gordianus."

"Zuleika, I've described the man to you a dozen times. Neither of us can say if it was Zanziba I saw, or not."

"It *was* him. I know it was. But if he died in Saturnia, how can he be alive now?"

"That's a very good question. But I have a suspicion . . ."

"You know something you're not telling me. You saw something, there in the compound!"

"Perhaps. I'll have to go back and have another look, to be sure."

"When?"

I sighed, looking around the little room we had been given to share at the hostel in Ravenna. It was a plain room, with two hard beds, a small lamp, and a single chamber pot, but to my weary eyes, as the long summer day faded to twilight, it looked very inviting. "Tonight, I suppose. Might as well get it over with."

"What if the *lanista* won't let you in?"

"I don't intend to ask him."

"You're going to sneak in? But how?"

"I do have *some* experience at this sort of thing, Zuleika. I noticed a particular spot in the palisade where the posts are a bit shorter than elsewhere. If I climb over at that point, and manage not to impale myself, I think I can drop right onto the roof of the slaughterhouse. From there I can easily climb down—"

"But the dogs! You heard dogs barking. The man on the road said a dog tore a slave's leg off."

I cleared my throat. "Yes, well, the dogs do pose a challenge. But I think I know, from the sound of their barking, where their kennel is located. That's why I bought those pieces of meat at the butcher shop this afternoon; and why I travel with that small pouch full of various powders and potions. In my line of work, you never know when you might have need of a powerful soporific. A few pieces of steak, generously dusted with pulverized harpy root and tossed over the palisade . . ."

"But even if you put the dogs to sleep, there are all those gladiators, men who've been trained to kill—"

"I shall carry a dagger for self-defense."

"A dagger! From the way you describe Ahala, the *lanista* himself could kill you with his bare hands." She shook her head. "You'll be taking a terrible risk, Gordianus."

"That's what you're paying me for, Zuleika."

"I should go with you."

"Absolutely not!"

Some distance from the compound, I tethered my horse to a stunted tree and proceeded on foot. Hours past midnight, the half-moon was low in the sky. It shed just enough light for me to cautiously pick my way, while casting ample shadows to offer concealment.

The compound was quiet and dark; gladiators need their sleep. As I drew near the palisade, one of the dogs began to bark. I tossed bits of steak over the wall. The barking immediately ceased, followed by slavering sounds, followed by silence.

The climb over the palisade was easier than I expected. A running start, a quick scamper up the rough bark of the poles, a leap of faith over the sharp spikes, and I landed solidly atop the roof of the slaughterhouse, making only a faint, plunking noise. I paused for breath, listening intently. From outside the compound I heard a quiet, scurrying noise—some nocturnal animal, I presumed—but within the compound there was only a deep silence.

I climbed off the roof and proceeded quickly to the gate that opened into the inner compound, where the gladiators were quartered. As I suspected, it was unbarred. At night, the men inside were free to come and go at will.

I returned to the slaughterhouse and stepped inside. As I had thought, the organs I had seen hanging to dry in the back corner were bladders harvested from slaughtered beasts. I took one down and examined it in the moonlight. Ahala was a frugal man; this bladder already had been used at least once, and was ready to be used again. The opening had been stitched shut but then carefully un-stitched; a gash in the side had been repaired with some particularly fine stitch work. The inside of the bladder had been thoroughly cleaned, but by the moonlight I thought I could nonetheless discern bits of dried blood within.

I left the slaughterhouse and made my way to the armory shed, by night a hanging forest of weird shapes. Navigating through the dark-ness amid dangling helmets and swords, I located one of the peculiar wood-and-metal tubes I had noticed earlier. I hefted the object in my hand, then put it in my mouth. I blew through it, cautiously, qui-etly—and even so, gave myself a fright, so uncanny was the gurgling death-rattle that emerged from the tube.

It frightened the other person in the shed, as well; for I was not alone. A silhouette behind me gave a start, whirled about, and col-lided with a hanging helmet. The helmet knocked against a shield with a loud, clanging noise. The silhouette staggered back and col-lided with more pieces of hanging armor, knocking some from their hooks and sending them clattering across the floor.

The cacophony roused at least one of the drugged canines. From the kennel, I heard a blood-curdling howl. A moment later, a man began to shout an alarm.

"Gordianus! Where are you?" The stumbling, confused silhou-ette had a voice.

"Zuleika! I told you not to follow me!"

"All these hanging swords, like an infernal maze—Hades! I've cut myself . . ."

Perhaps it was her blood that attracted the beast. I saw its silhouette enter from the direction of the kennels and career toward us, like a missile shot from a sling. The snarling creature took a flying leap and knocked Zuleika to the ground. She screamed.

Suddenly there were others in the armory—not dogs, but men. "Was that a woman?" one of them muttered.

The dog snarled. Zuleika screamed again.

"Zuleika!" I cried.

"Did he say . . . *Zuleika?*" One of the men—tall, broad, majestic in silhouette—broke away from the others and ran toward her. Seizing a hanging trident, he drove it into the snarling dog—then gave a cry of exasperation and cast the trident aside. "Numa's balls, I grabbed one of the fakes! Somebody hand me a *real* weapon!"

I was closest. I reached into my tunic, pulled out my dagger, and thrust it into his hand. He swooped down. The dog gave a single plaintive yelp, then went limp. The man scooped up the lifeless dog and thrust it aside.

"Zuleika!" he cried.

"Zanziba?" she answered, her voice weak.

In blood, fear, and darkness, the siblings were reunited.

The danger was not over, but just beginning; for having discovered the secret of Ahala's gladiator camp, how could I be allowed to live? Their success—indeed, their survival—depended on absolute secrecy.

If Zuleika had not followed me, I would have climbed over the palisade and ridden back to Ravenna, satisfied that I knew the truth and reasonably certain that the Nubian I had seen earlier that day was indeed Zanziba, still very much alive. For my suspicion had been confirmed: Ahala and his gladiators had learned to cheat death. The bouts they staged at funeral games looked real, but in fact were shams, not spontaneous but very carefully choreographed. When they appeared to bleed, the blood was animal blood that spurted from animal bladders concealed under their scanty armor or loincloths, or from the hollow, blood-filled tips of weapons with retractable points, cleverly devised by Ahala's smiths; when they appeared to expire, the death rattles that issued from their throats actually came from sound-makers like the one I had blown through. No doubt there were many other tricks of their trade which I had not discovered with my cursory inspection, or even conceived of; they were seasoned professionals, after all, an experienced troupe of acrobats, actors, and mimes making a very handsome living by pretending to be a troupe of gladiators.

Any doubt was dispelled when I was dragged from the armory into the open and surrounded by a ring of naked, rudely awakened men. The torches in their hands turned night to day and lit up the face of Zuleika, who lay bleeding but alive on the sand, attended by an unflappable, gray-bearded physician; it made sense that Ahala's troupe would have a skilled doctor among them, to attend to accidents and injuries.

Among the assembled gladiators, I was quite sure I saw the tall, lumbering Samnite who had "died" in Saturnia, along with the shorter, stockier Thracian who had "killed" him—and who had put on such a convincing show of tottering off-balance and almost impaling himself on the Samnite's upright sword. I also saw the two *dimacheri* who had put on such a show with their flashing daggers that the spectators had spared them both. There was the redheaded Gaul who had delivered the "death blow" to Zanziba—and there was Zanziba himself, hovering fretfully over his sister and the physician attending to her.

"I can't understand it," the physician finally announced. "The dog should have torn her limb from limb, but he seems hardly to have broken the skin. The beast must have been dazed—or drugged." He shot a suspicious glance at me. "At any rate, she's lost very little blood. The wounds are shallow, and I've cleaned them thoroughly. Unless an infection sets in, that should be the end of it. Your sister is a lucky woman."

The physician stepped back and Zanziba knelt over her. "Zuleika! How did you find me?"

"The gods led me to you," she whispered.

I cleared my throat.

"With some help from the Finder," she added. "It *was* you I saw at the funeral games in Saturnia that day?"

"Yes."

"And then again in Rome?"

He nodded. "I was there very briefly, some days ago, then came straight back to Ravenna."

"But Zanziba, why didn't you send for me?"

He sighed. "When I sent you the money, I was in great despair. I expected every day to be my last. I moved from place to place, plying my trade as a gladiator, expecting death but handing it out to others instead. Then I fell in with these fellows, and everything changed." He smiled and gestured to the men around him. "A company of free men, all experienced gladiators, who've realized that it simply isn't necessary to kill or be killed to put on a good show for the spectators. Ahala is our leader, but he's only first among equals. We all pull together. After I joined these fellows, I *did* send for you—I sent a letter to your old master in Alexandria, but he had no idea where you'd gone. I had no way to find you. I thought we'd lost each other forever."

Regaining her strength, Zuleika rose onto her elbows. "Your fighting is all illusion, then?"

Her brother grinned. "The Romans have a saying: A gladiator dies only once. But I've died in the arena many, many times! And been paid quite handsomely for it."

I shook my head. "The game you're playing is incredibly dangerous."

"Not as dangerous as being a real gladiator," said Zanziba.

"You've pulled it off so far," I said. "But the more famous this troupe becomes, the more widely you travel and the more people see you—some of them on more than one occasion—the harder it will become to maintain the deception. The risk of discovery will grow greater each time you perform. If you're found out, you'll be charged with sacrilege, at the very least. Romans save their cruelest punishments for that sort of crime."

"You're talking to men who've stared death in the face many times," growled Ahala. "We have nothing to lose. But you, Gordianus, on the other hand . . ."

"He'll have to die," said one of the men. "Like the others who've discovered our secret."

"The skulls decorating the gateway?" I said.

Ahala nodded grimly.

"But we can't kill him!" protested Zanziba.

"He lied about his purpose in coming here," said Ahala.

"But his purpose was to bring Zuleika to me . . ."

So began the debate over what to do with me, which lasted through the night. In the end, as was their custom, they decided by voting. I was locked away while the deliberations took place. What was said, I never knew; but at daybreak I was released, and after making me pledge never to betray them, Ahala showed me to the gate.

"Zuleika is staying?" I said.

He nodded.

"How did the voting go?"

"The motion to release you was decided by a bare majority of one."

"That close? How did you vote, Ahala?"

"Do you really want to know?"

The look on his face told me I didn't.

I untethered my horse and rode quickly away, never looking back.

On my first day back in Rome, I saw Cicero in the Forum. I tried to avoid him, but he made a beeline for me, smiling broadly.

"Well met, Gordianus! Except for this beastly weather. Not yet noon, and already a scorcher. Reminds me of the last time I saw you, at those funeral games in Saturnia. Do you remember?"

"Of course," I said.

"What fine games those were!"

"Yes," I agreed, a bit reluctantly.

"But do you know, since then I've seen some even more spectacular funeral games. It was down in Capua. Amazing fighters! The star of the show was a fellow with some barbaric Thracian name. What was it, now? Ah, yes: Spartacus, they called him. Like the city of warriors, Sparta. A good name for a gladiator, eh?"

I nodded and quickly changed the subject. But for some reason, the name Cicero had spoken stuck in my mind. As Zuleika had said, how strange are the coincidences dropped in our paths by the gods; for in a matter of days, that name would be on the lips of everyone in Rome and all over Italy.

For that was the month that the great slave revolt began, led by Spartacus and his rebel gladiators. It would last for many months, spreading conflagration and chaos all over Italy. It would take me to the Bay of Neapolis for my first fateful meeting with Rome's richest man, Marcus Licinius Crassus, and a household of ninety-nine slaves all marked for death; but that is another story.

What became of Zanziba and Zuleika? In the ensuing months of warfare and panic, I lost track of them, but thought of them often. I especially remembered Zuleika's comments on Roman slavery. Were her sympathies inflamed by the revolt? Did she manage to persuade her brother and his comrades, if indeed they needed persuading, to join the revolt and take up arms against Rome? If they did, then almost certainly things went badly for them; for eventually Spartacus and his followers were trapped and defeated, hunted and slaughtered like animals, and crucified by the thousands.

After the revolt was over and the countryside gradually returned to normal, I eventually had occasion to travel to Ravenna again. I rode out to the site of Ahala's compound. The gate of bones was still there, but worn and weathered and tilted to one side, on the verge of collapsing. The palisade was intact, but the gate stood open. No weapons hung in the armory. The animals pens were empty. Spider webs filled the slaughterhouse. The gladiator quarters were abandoned.

And then, many months later, from across the sea I received a letter on papyrus, written by a hired Egyptian scribe:

To Gordianus, Finder and Friend: By the will of the gods, we find ourselves back in Alexandria. What a civilized place this seems, after Rome! The tale of our adventures in Italy would fill a book; suffice to say that we escaped by the skin of our teeth. Many of our comrades, including Ahala, were not so lucky.

We have saved enough money to buy passage back to our native land. In the country of our ancestors, we hope to find family and make new friends. What appalling tales we shall have to tell of the strange lands we visited; and of those lands, surely none was stranger or more barbaric than Rome! But to you it is home, Gordianus, and we wish you all happiness there. Farewell from your friends, Zuleika and her brother Zanziba.

For many years, I have saved that scrap of papyrus. I shall never throw it away.

POPPY AND THE
POISONED CAKE

"Young Cicero tells me that you can be discreet. Is that true, Gordianus? Can you keep a confidence?"

Considering that the question was being put to me by the magistrate in charge of maintaining Roman morals, I weighed my answer carefully. "If Rome's finest orator says a thing, who am I to contradict him?"

The censor snorted. "Your friend Cicero said you were clever, too. Answer a question with a question, will you? I suppose you picked that up from listening to him defend thieves and murderers in the law courts."

Cicero was my occasional employer, but I had never counted him as a friend, exactly. Would it be indiscreet to say as much to the censor? I kept my mouth shut and nodded vaguely.

Lucius Gellius Poplicola—Poppy to his friends, as I would later find out—looked to be a robust seventy or so. In a time wracked by civil war, political assassinations, and slave rebellions, to reach such a rare and venerable age was proof of Fortune's favor. But Fortune must have stopped smiling on Poplicola—else why summon Gordianus the Finder?

The room in which we sat, in Poplicola's house on the Palatine Hill, was sparsely appointed, but the few furnishings were of the highest quality. The rug was Greek, with a simple geometric design in blue and yellow. The antique chairs and the matching tripod table were of ebony, with silver hinges. The heavy drapery drawn over the doorway for privacy was of plush green fabric shot through with golden threads. The walls were stained a somber red. The iron lamp in the middle of the room stood on three griffin feet and breathed steady flames from three gaping griffin mouths. By its light, while waiting for Poplicola, I had perused the little yellow tags that dangled from the scrolls which filled the pigeon-hole bookcase in the corner. The censor's library consisted entirely of serious works by philosophers and historians, without a lurid poet or frivolous playwright among them. Everything about the room bespoke a man of impeccable taste and high standards—just the sort of fellow whom public opinion would deem worthy of wearing the purple toga, a man qualified to keep the sacred rolls of citizenship and pass judgment on the moral conduct of senators.

"It was Cicero who recommended me, then?" In the ten years since I had met him, Cicero had sent quite a bit of business my way.

Poplicola nodded. "I told him I needed an agent to investigate . . . a private matter. A man from outside my own household, and yet someone I could rely upon to be thorough, truthful, and absolutely discreet. He seemed to think that you would do."

"I'm honored that Cicero would recommend me to a man of your exalted position and—"

"Discretion!" he insisted, cutting me off. "That matters most of all. Everything you discover while in my employ—*everything*—must be held in the strictest confidence. You will reveal your discoveries to me and to no one else."

From beneath his wrinkled brow he peered at me with an intensity that was unsettling. I nodded and said slowly, "So long as such discretion does not conflict with more sacred obligations to the gods, then yes, Censor, I promise you my absolute discretion."

"Upon your honor as a Roman? Upon the shades of your ancestors?"

I sighed. Why must these nobles always take themselves and their problems so seriously? Why must every transaction require the invocation of dead relatives? Poplicola's earth-shattering dilemma was probably nothing more than an errant wife or a bit of blackmail over a pretty slaveboy. I chafed at his demand for an oath and considered refusing, but the fact was that my daughter, Diana, had just been born, the household coffers were perilously depleted, and I needed work. I gave him my word, upon my honor and my ancestors.

He produced something from the folds of his purple toga and placed it on the little table between us. I saw it was a small silver bowl, and in the bowl there appeared to be a delicacy of some sort. I caught a whiff of almonds.

"What do you make of that?" he said.

"It appears to be a sweet cake," I ventured. I picked up the little bowl and sniffed. Almonds, yes; and something else . . .

"By Hercules, don't eat any of it!" He snatched the bowl from me. "I have reason to believe it's been poisoned." Poplicola shuddered. He suddenly looked much older.

"Poisoned?"

"The slave who brought me the cake this afternoon, here in my study—one of my oldest slaves, more than a servant, a companion really—well, the fellow always had a sweet tooth . . . like his master, that way. If he shaved off a bit of my delicacies every now and then, thinking I wouldn't notice, where was the harm in that? It was a bit of a game between us. I used to tease him; I'd say, 'the only thing that keeps me from growing fat is the fact that you serve my food!' Poor Chrestus . . ." His face became ashen.

"I see. This Chrestus brought you the cake. And then?"

"I dismissed Chrestus and set the bowl aside while I finished reading a document. I came to the end, rolled up the scroll, and filed it away. I was just about to take a bite of the cake when another slave, my doorkeeper, ran into the room, terribly alarmed. He said that Chrestus was having a seizure. I went to him as quickly as I could. He was lying on the floor, convulsing. 'The cake!' he said. 'The cake!' And then he was dead. As quickly as that! The look on his face—horrible!" Poplicola gazed at the little cake and curled his lip, as if an adder were coiled in the silver bowl. "My favorite," he said in a hollow voice. "Cinnamon and almonds, sweetened with honey and wine, with just a hint of aniseed. An old man's pleasure, one of the few I have left. Now I shall never be able to eat it again!"

And neither shall Chrestus, I thought. "Where did the cake come from?"

"There's a little alley just north of the Forum, with bakery shops on either side."

"I know the street."

"The place on the corner makes these cakes every other day. I have a standing order—a little treat I give myself. Chrestus goes down to fetch one for me, and I have it in the early afternoon."

"And was it Chrestus who fetched the cake for you today?"

For a long moment, he stared silently at the cake. "No."

"Who, then?"

He hunched his thin shoulders up and pursed his lips. "My son, Lucius. He came by this afternoon. So the doorkeeper tells me; I didn't see him myself. Lucius told the doorkeeper not to disturb me, that he couldn't stay; he'd only stopped by to drop off a sweet cake for me. Lucius knows of my habit of indulging in this particular sweet, you see, and some business in the Forum took him by the street of the bakers, and as my house was on his way to another errand, he brought me a cake. The doorkeeper fetched Chrestus, Lucius gave Chrestus the sweet cake wrapped up in a bit of parchment, and then Lucius left. A little later, Chrestus brought the cake to me . . ."

Now I understood why Poplicola had demanded an oath upon my ancestors. The matter was delicate indeed. "Do you suspect your son of tampering with the cake?"

Poplicola shook his head. "I don't know what to think."

"Is there any reason to suspect that he might wish to do you harm?"

"Of course not!" The denial was a little too vehement, a little too quick.

"What is it you want from me, Censor?"

"To find the truth of the matter! They call you Finder, don't they? Find out if the cake is poisoned. Find out who poisoned it. Find out how it came about that my son . . ."

"I understand, Censor. Tell me, who in your household knows of what happened today?"

"Only the doorkeeper."

"No one else?"

"No one. The rest of the household has been told that Chrestus collapsed from a heart attack. I've told no one else of Lucius's visit, or about the cake."

I nodded. "To begin, I shall need to see the dead man, and to question your doorkeeper."

"Of course. And the cake? Shall I feed a bit to some stray dog, to make sure . . ."

"I don't think that will be necessary, Censor." I picked up the little bowl and sniffed at the cake again. Most definitely, blended with the wholesome scent of baked almonds, was the sharper odor of the substance called bitter-almond, one of the strongest of all poisons. Only a few drops would suffice to kill a man in minutes. How fiendishly clever, to sprinkle it onto a sweet almond–flavored confection, from which a hungry man with a sweet tooth might take a bite without noticing the bitter taste until too late.

Poplicola took me to see the body. Chrestus looked to have been fit for his age. His hands were soft; his master had not overworked him. His waxy flesh had a pinkish flush, further evidence that the poison had been bitter-almond.

Poplicola summoned the doorkeeper, whom I questioned in his master's presence. He proved to be a tightlipped fellow (as doorkeepers should be), and added nothing to what Poplicola had already told me.

Visibly shaken, Poplicola withdrew, with instructions to the doorkeeper to see me out. I was in the foyer, about to leave, when a woman crossed the atrium. She wore an elegant blue stola, and her hair was fashionably arranged with combs and pins atop her head into a towering configuration that defied logic. Her hair was jet black, except for a narrow streak of white above her left temple that spiraled upward like a ribbon into the convoluted vortex. She glanced at me as she passed, but registered no reaction. No doubt the censor received many visitors.

"Is that the censor's daughter?" I asked the doorkeeper.

"No."

I raised an eyebrow, but the tightlipped slave did not elaborate. "His wife, then?"

"Yes. My mistress Palla."

"A striking woman." In the wake of her passing, a kind of aura seemed to linger in the empty atrium. Hers was a haughty beauty that gave little indication of her age. I suspected she must be older than she looked, but she could hardly have been past forty.

"Is Palla the mother of the censor's son, Lucius?"

"No."

"His stepmother, then?"

"Yes."

"I see." I nodded and took my leave.

I wanted to know more about Poplicola and his household, so that night I paid a visit to my patrician friend Lucius Claudius, who knows everything worth knowing about anyone who counts in the higher circles of Roman society. I intended to be discreet, honoring my oath to the censor, and so, after dinner, relaxing on our couches and sharing more wine, in a roundabout way I got onto the topic of elections and voting, and thence to the subject of census rolls. "I understand the recent census shows something like eight hundred thousand Roman citizens," I noted.

"Indeed!" Lucius Claudius popped his pudgy fingers into his mouth one by one, savoring the grease from the roasted quail. With his other hand, he brushed a ringlet of frizzled red hair from his forehead. "If this keeps up, one of these days citizens shall outnumber slaves! The censors really should do something about restricting citizenship."

My friend's politics tend to be conservative; the Claudii are patricians, after all. I nodded thoughtfully. "Who are the censors nowadays, anyway?"

"Lentulus Clodianus . . ." he said, popping a final finger into his mouth, ". . . and old Lucius Gellius Poplicola."

"Poplicola," I murmured innocently. "Now why does that name sound familiar?"

"Really, Gordianus, where is your head? Poplicola was consul two years ago. Surely you recall that bit of unpleasantness with Spartacus? It was Poplicola's job as consul to take the field against the rebel slaves, who gave him a sound whipping—not once, but twice! The disgrace of it, farm slaves led by a rogue gladiator, thrashing trained legionnaires led by a Roman consul! People said it was because Poppy was just too old to lead an army. He's lucky it wasn't the end of his career! But here it is two years later, and Poppy's a censor. It's a big job. But safe—no military commands! Just right for a fellow like Poppy—been around forever, honest as a stick."

"Just what do the censors do?"

"Census and censure, their two main duties. Keep the roll of voters, assign the voters to tribes, make sure the patrician tribes carry the most weight in the elections—that's the way of it. Well, we can hardly allow those seven hundred and ninety nine thousand common citizens out there to have as much say in electing magistrates as the thousand of us whose families have been running this place since the days of Romulus and Remus; wouldn't make sense. That's the census part."

I nodded. "And censure?"

"The censors don't just say who's a citizen and who's not; they also say what a citizen should be. The privilege of citizenship implies certain moral standards, even in these dissolute days. If the censors put a black mark for immoral conduct by a man's name in the rolls, it's serious business. They can expel a fellow from the Senate. In fact . . ." He leaned forward and lowered his voice to emphasize the gravity of what he was about to say. "In fact, word has it that the censors are about to publish a list of *over sixty men* they're throwing out of the Senate for breach of moral character—taking bribes, falsifying documents, embezzling. Sixty! A veritable purge! You can imagine the mood in the Senate House. Everyone suspicious of everyone else, all of us wondering who's on the list."

"So Poplicola is not exactly the most popular man in the Forum these days?"

"To put it mildly. Don't misunderstand, there's plenty of support for the purge. I support it myself, wholeheartedly. The Senate needs a thorough housecleaning! But Poppy's about to make some serious enemies. Which is ironic, because he's always been such a peacemaker." Lucius laughed. "Back when he was governor of Greece in his younger days, they say Poppy called together all the bickering philosophers in Athens and practically pleaded with them to come to some sort of consensus about the nature of the universe. 'If we cannot have harmony in the heavens, how can we hope for anything but discord here on earth?' " His mimicry of the censor's reedy voice was uncanny.

"Census and censure," I murmured, sipping my wine. "I don't suppose ordinary citizens have all that much to fear from the censors."

"Oh, a black mark from the censor is trouble for any man. Ties up voting rights, cancels state contracts, revokes licenses to keep a shop in the city. That could ruin a man, drive him into poverty. And if a censor really wants to make trouble for a fellow, he can call him before a special Senate committee to investigate charges of immorality. Once that sort of investigation starts, it never ends—just the idea is enough to give even an honest man a heart attack! Oh, yes, the censorship is a powerful office. That's why it has to be filled with men of absolutely irreproachable character, completely untainted by scandal—like Poppy." Lucius Claudius suddenly frowned and wrinkled his fleshy brow. "Of course, there's that terrible rumor I heard only this afternoon—so outrageous I dismissed it out of hand. Put it out of my mind so completely that I actually forgot about it until just now . . ."

"Rumor?"

"Probably nothing—a vicious bit of slander put about by one of Poppy's enemies . . ."

"Slander?"

"Oh, some nonsense about Poppy's son, Lucius, trying to poison the old man—using a sweet cake, if you can believe it!" I raised my eyebrows and tried to look surprised. "But these kinds of stories always get started, don't they, when a fellow as old as Poppy marries a woman young enough to be his daughter, and beautiful as well. Palla is her name. She and her stepson, Lucius, get along well—what of it? People see them out together now and again without Poppy, at a chariot race or a play, laughing and having a good time, and the next thing you know, these nasty rumors get started. Lucius, trying to poison his father so he can marry his stepmother—now that would be a scandal! And I'm sure there are those who'd like to think it's true, who'd love nothing better than to see Poppy pulled down into the muck right along with them."

The attempted poisoning had taken place that afternoon—and yet Lucius Claudius had already heard about it. How could the rumor have spread so swiftly? Who could have started it? Not Poplicola's son, surely, if he were the poisoner. But what if Poplicola's son were innocent of any wrongdoing? What if he had been somehow duped into passing the deadly cake by his father's enemies, who had then gone spreading the tale prematurely . . .

Or might the speed of the rumor have a simpler explanation? It could be that Poplicola's doorkeeper was not nearly as tightlipped as his terse answers had led me to think. If the doorkeeper told another slave in the household about the poison cake, who then told a slave in a neighbor's house, who then told his master . . .

I tried to keep my face a blank, but Lucius Claudius saw the wheels spinning in my head. He narrowed his eyes. "Gordianus— what are you up to? How did we get onto the subject of Poplicola, anyway? Do you know something about this rumor?"

I was trying to think of some way to honor my oath to the censor without lying to my friend, when I was saved by the arrival of Lucius

Claudius's beloved Momo. The tiny Melitaean terrier scampered into the room, as white as a snowball and almost as round; lately she had grown as plump as her master. She scampered and yapped at Lucius's feet, too earthbound to leap onto the couch. Lucius summoned a slave, who lifted the dog up and placed it on his lap. "My darling, my sweet, my adorable little Momo!" he cooed, and seemed to forget all about Poplicola, to my relief.

Bitter-almond is a difficult poison to obtain. I am told that it is extracted from the pits of common fruits, but the stuff is so lethal—a man can die simply from having it touch his skin, or inhaling its fumes—that most of the shady dealers in such goods refuse to handle it. The rare customer looking for bitter-almond is usually steered into purchasing something else for his purpose, "just as good," the dealer will say, though few poisons are as quick and certain as bitter-almond.

My peculiar line of work has acquainted me with all sorts of people, from the highest of the high, like Poplicola, to the lowest of the low—like a certain unsavory dealer in poisons and potions named Quintus Fugax. Fugax claimed to be immune to every poison known to man, and even boasted that on occasion he tested new ones on himself, just to see if they would make him sick. To be sure, no poison had yet killed him, but his fingers were stained permanently black, there was a constant twitch at the corner of his mouth, his skin was disfigured with strange splotches, his head was covered with scabs and bald spots, and one of his eyes was clouded with a rheumy yellow film. If anyone in Rome was unafraid to deal in bitter-almond, it was Quintus Fugax.

I found him the next day at his usual haunt, a squalid little tavern on the riverfront. I told him I wanted to ask some general questions about certain poisons and how they acted, for my own edification. So long as I kept his wine cup full, he agreed to talk with me.

Several cups later, when I judged that his tongue was sufficiently loosened by the wine, I asked him if he knew anything about bitter-almond. He laughed. "It's the best! I always tell people so, and not just because I'm about the only dealer who handles it. But hardly anybody wants it. Bitter-almond carries a curse, some say. People are afraid it'll turn on them, and they'll end up the dead one. Could happen; stuff can practically kill you just by you looking at it."

"Not much call for bitter-almond, then?"

"Not much." He smiled. "But I did sell a bit of it, just yesterday."

I swirled my wine and pretended to study the dregs. "Really? Some fishmonger wanting to do in his wife, I suppose."

He grinned, showing more gaps than teeth. "You know I never talk about my customers."

I frowned. "Still, it can't have been anyone very important. I'd have heard if some senator or wealthy merchant died from sudden convulsions after eating a hearty meal."

Fugax barked out a laugh. "Ha! Try a piece of cake!"

I caught my breath and kept my eyes on the swirling dregs. "I beg your pardon?"

"Customer wanted to know if you could use bitter-almond in an almond sweet cake. I said, 'just the thing!'"

"What was he, a cook? Or a cook's slave, I suppose. Your customers usually send a go-between, don't they? They never deal with you face-to-face."

"This one did."

"Really?"

"Said she couldn't trust any of her slaves to make such a sensitive purchase."

"*She?*"

He raised his eyebrows and covered his mouth, like a little boy caught tattling, then threw back his head and cackled. "Gave that much away, didn't I? But I can't say who she was, because I don't know. Not poor, though. Came and went in a covered litter, all blue like her stola. Made her bearers stop a couple of streets away so they couldn't see where she went and I wouldn't see where she came from, but I sneaked after her when she left. Watched her climb into that fancy litter—hair so tall she had to stoop to get in!"

I summoned up a laugh and nodded. "These crazy new hairstyles!"

His ravaged face suddenly took on a wistful look. "Hers was pretty, though. All shiny and black—with a white streak running through it, like a stripe on a cat! Pretty woman. But pity the poor man who's crossed her!"

I nodded. "Pity him indeed . . ."

The enviable corner spot on the street of the bakers was occupied by a family named Baebius; so declared a handsomely painted sign above the serving counter that fronted the street. A short young blonde, a bit on the far side of pleasingly plump but with a sunshiny smile, stepped up to serve me. "What'll you have today, citizen? Sweet or savory?"

"Sweet, I think. A friend tells me you make the most delicious little almond cakes."

"Oh, you're thinking of Papa's special. We're famous for it. Been selling it from this shop for three generations. But I'm afraid we don't have any today. We only make those every other day. However, I can sell you a wonderful cheese-and-honey torte—very rich."

I pretended to hem and haw and finally nodded. "Yes, give me one of those. No, make it three—hungry mouths at home! But it's too bad you don't have the almond cakes. My friend raves about them. He was by here just yesterday, I think. A fellow named Lucius Gellius."

"Oh, yes, we know him. But it's not him who craves the almond cakes, it's his father, the censor. Old Poplicola buys one from every batch Papa bakes!"

"But his son Lucius *was* here yesterday?"

She nodded. "So he was. I sold him the sweet cake myself and wrapped it up in parchment for him to take to his father. For himself and the lady he bought a couple of little savory custards. Would you care to try—"

"The lady?"

"The lady who was waiting for him in the blue litter."

"Is she a regular customer, too?"

The girl shrugged. "I didn't actually see her; only got a glimpse as Lucius was handing her the custard, and then they were off toward the Forum. There, taste that and tell me it's not fit for the gods."

I bit into the cheese-and-honey torte and feigned an enthusiastic nod. At that moment, it could have been ambrosia and I would have taken no pleasure in it.

I made my report to Poplicola that afternoon. He was surprised that I could have concluded my investigation so swiftly, and insisted on knowing each step in my progress and every person I had talked to. He stood, turned his back to me, and stared at the somber red wall as I explained how I came to suspect the use of bitter-almond; how I questioned one of the few men who dealt in that particular poison, plied him with wine, and obtained a description that was almost certainly of Palla; how the girl at the bakery shop not only confirmed that Lucius had purchased the cake the previous day, but saw him leave in a blue litter with a female companion.

"None of this amounts to absolute proof, I admit. But it seems reasonably evident that Palla purchased the bitter-almond in the morning, that Lucius was either with her at that time, and stayed in the litter, or else joined her later, and then the two of them went to the bakery shop, where Lucius purchased the cake. Then one or both of them together sprinkled the poison onto the cake—"

Poplicola hunched his gaunt shoulders and produced a stifled cry, a sound of such despair that I was stunned into silence. When he turned to face me, he appeared to have aged ten years in an instant.

"All this is circumstantial evidence," he said, "not legal proof."

I spoke slowly and carefully. "Legal proof is narrowly defined. To satisfy a court of law, all the slaves involved would be called upon to testify—the litter-bearers, your doorkeeper, perhaps the personal attendants of Palla and Lucius. Slaves see everything, and they usually know more than their masters think. They would be tortured, of course; the testimony of slaves is inadmissible unless obtained by torture. Acquiring that degree of proof is beyond my means, Censor."

He shook his head. "Never mind. We both know the truth. I knew it all along, of course. Lucius and Palla, behind my back—but I never thought it would come to this!"

"What will you do, Censor?" It was within Poplicola's legal rights, as *paterfamilias*, to put his son to death without a trial or any other formality. He could strangle Lucius with his own hands or have a slave do it for him, and no one would question his right to do so, especially under the circumstances. He could do the same thing to his wife.

Poplicola made no answer. He had turned to face the wall again, and stood so stiff and motionless that I feared for him. "Censor . . . ?"

"What will I do?" he snapped. "Don't be impertinent, Finder! I hired you to find out a thing. You did so, and that's the end of your concern. You'll leave here with some gold in your purse, never fear."

"Censor, I meant no—"

"You vowed an oath, on your ancestors, to speak of this affair to no one but me. I shall hold you to it. If you're any sort of Roman—"

"There's no need to remind me, Censor," I said sharply. "I don't make oaths lightly."

He reached into a pouch within his purple toga, counted out some coins, laid them on the little table before me, and left the room without saying another word.

I was left to show myself out. On my way to the foyer, addled by anger, I took a wrong turn and didn't realize it until I found myself in a large garden surrounded by a peristyle. I cursed and turned to re-trace my steps, then glimpsed the couple who stood beneath the colonnade at the far corner of the garden, their heads together as if engaged in some grave conversation. The woman was Palla. Her arms were crossed and her head was held high. The man, from his manner toward her, I would have taken to be her husband had I not known better. Lucius Gellius looked very much like a younger replica of his father, even to the chilly stare he gave me as I hastily withdrew.

In the days that followed, I kept my ears perked for any news of de-velopments at the house of Poplicola, but there was only silence. Was the old man plotting some horrible revenge on his son and wife? Were they still plotting against him? Or had the three of them some-how come together, with confessions of guilt and forgiveness all around? I hardly saw how such a reconciliation could be possible, af-ter such a total breach of trust.

Then, one morning, I received a note from my friend Lucius Claudius:

Dear Friend, Dinner Companion, and Fellow Connoisseur of Gossip,
    We never quite finished our discussion about Poplicola the other day, did we? The latest gossip (horrible stuff): On the very eve of the great purge in the Senate, one hears that certain members are planning to mount a prosecution against the censor's son, Lucius Gellius, ac-cusing him of sleeping with his stepmother and plotting to kill

Poppy. *Such a trial will stir up a huge scandal—what will people think of a magistrate in charge of morals who can't stop his own son and wife from fornicating and scheming to do him in? Opponents (and likely targets) of the purge will say, "Clean up your own house, Poplicola, before you presume to clean ours!"*

Who knows how such a trial might turn out? The whole family will be dragged through the mud—if there's any dirt on any of them, the prosecutors will dig it up. And if Lucius is found guilty (I still can't believe it), they won't allow him exile—he'll be put to death along with Palla, and to save face, Poplicola will have to play stern paterfamilias and watch while it's done! That would be the death of Poppy, I fear. Certainly, it would be the end of his political career. He'd be utterly humiliated, his moral authority a joke. He couldn't possibly continue as Censor. No purge of the Senate, then, and politics can go on as usual! What an age we live in.

Ah well, come dine with me tonight. I shall be having fresh pheasant, and Cook promises to do something divine with the sauce . . .

The pheasant that night was succulent. The sauce had an intriguing insinuation of mint that lingered teasingly on the tongue. But the food was not what I had come for.

Eventually we got around to the subject of the censor and his woes.

"There's to be a trial, then," I said.

"Actually . . . no," said Lucius Claudius.

"But your note this morning—"

"Invalidated by fresh gossip this afternoon."

"And?"

Lucius leaned back on his couch, stroked Momo, and looked at me shrewdly. "I don't suppose, Gordianus, that you know more about this affair than you're letting on?"

I looked him in the eye. "Nothing that I could discuss, even with you, my friend, without violating an oath."

He nodded. "I thought it must be something like that. Even so, I don't suppose you could let me know, simply yes or no, whether Lucius Gellius and Palla really—Gordianus, you look as if the pheasant suddenly turned on you! Well, let no one say that I ever gave a dinner guest indigestion by pressing an improper question. I shall simply have to live not knowing. Though in that case, why I should tell *you* the latest news from the Forum, I'm sure I don't know."

He pouted and fussed over Momo. I sipped my wine. Lucius began to fidget. Eventually his urge to share the latest gossip got the better of him. I tried not to smile.

"Very well, since you must know: Poppy, acting in his capacity as censor, has convoked a special Senate committee to investigate his own son on a charge of gross immorality—namely this rumor about adultery and attempted parricide. The committee will take up the investigation at once, and Poppy himself will preside over it."

"But how will this affect the upcoming trial?"

"There won't be a trial. The investigation supersedes it. It's rather clever of Poppy, I suppose, and rather brave. This way he heads off his enemies who would have made a public trial into a spectacle. Instead, he'll see to the question of his son's guilt or innocence himself, behind closed doors. The Senate committee will make the final vote, but Poppy will oversee the proceedings. Of course, the whole thing could spin out of his control. If the investigating committee finds Lucius Gellius guilty, the scandal will still be the ruin of Poppy." He shook his head. "Surely that won't happen. For Poppy to take charge of the matter himself, that must mean that his son is innocent, and Poppy knows it—doesn't it?" Lucius raised an eyebrow and peered at me expectantly.

"I'm not sure what it means," I said, and meant it.

The investigation into the moral conduct of Lucius Gellius lasted two days, and took place behind the closed doors of the Senate House, where none but scribes and witnesses and the senators themselves were allowed. Fortunately for me, Lucius Claudius was among the senators on the investigating committee, and when the investigation was done he invited me once again to dine with him.

He greeted me at the door himself, and even before he spoke, I could tell from his round, beaming face that he was pleased with the outcome.

"The committee reached a conclusion?" I said.

"Yes, and what a relief!"

"Lucius Gellius was cleared of the charges?" I tried not to sound skeptical.

"Completely! The whole business was an absurd fabrication! Nothing to it but vicious rumors and unfounded suspicions."

I thought of the dead slave, Chrestus. "There was no evidence at all of Lucius Gellius's guilt?"

"No such evidence was presented. Oh, so-and-so once saw Palla and Lucius Gellius sitting with their legs pressed together at the Circus Maximus, and another so-and-so saw them holding hands in a marketplace one day, and someone else claims to have seen them kiss beneath some trees on the Palatine Hill. Nothing but hearsay and rubbish. Palla and Lucius Gellius were called upon to defend themselves, and they both swore they had done nothing improper. Poplicola himself vouched for them."

"No slaves were called to testify?"

"This was an investigation, Gordianus, not a trial. We had no authority to extract testimony under torture."

"And were there no other witnesses? No depositions? Nothing regarding the poisoned cake that was rumored?"

"No. If there *had* been anyone capable of producing truly damning evidence, they'd have been found, surely; there were plenty of senators on the committee hostile to Poppy, and believe me, since the rumors first began, they've been scouring the city looking for evidence. It simply wasn't there."

I thought of the poison dealer, and of the blond girl who had waited on me at the bakery shop. I had tracked them down with little enough trouble; Poplicola's enemies would have started out with less to go on, but surely they had dispatched their own finders to search out the truth. Why had the girl not been called to testify, at least? Had no one made even the simple connection between the rumor of the poisoned cake and the bakery shop which produced Poplicola's favorite treat? Could the forces against the censor have been so inept?

Lucius laughed. "And to think of the meals I left untouched, fretting over Poppy! Well, now that he and his household have been vindicated, he can get on with his work as censor. Tomorrow Poppy will post his list of senators who've earned a black mark for immoral conduct. Good riddance, I say. More elbow room for the rest of us in the Senate chambers!" He sighed and shook his head. "Really, all that grief, and the whole thing was a farce."

Yes, I thought warily, so it had ended up—a farce. But what role had I played in it?

The next day I went to the street of the bakers, thinking to finally taste for myself one of the famous almond sweet cakes baked by the Baebius family—and also to find out if, indeed, no one from the Senate committee had called upon the blond girl.

I strolled up the narrow, winding little street and arrived at the corner with a shock. Instead of the blond girl's smiling face behind the serving counter, I saw a boarded-up storefront. The sign bearing the family name, there for three generations, had been obliterated with crude daubs of paint.

A shopkeeper down the street saw me gaping and called to me from behind his counter.

"Looking for the Baebii?"

"Yes."

"Gone."

"Where?"

"No idea."

"When?"

He shrugged. "A while back. Just up and left overnight, the whole lot of them. Baebius, his wife and daughter, the slaves—here one day, all gone the next. Poof! Like actors falling through a trap-door on a stage."

"But why?"

He gestured that I should step closer, and lowered his voice. "I suspect that Baebius must have gotten himself into serious trouble with the authorities."

"What authorities?"

"The Senate itself!"

"Why do you say that?"

"Just a day or two after he vanished, some pretty rough-looking strangers came snooping up and down the block, asking for Baebius and wanting to know where he'd gone. They even offered money, but nobody could tell them. And then, a few days after that, here come more strangers asking questions, only these were better dressed and carried fancy-looking scrolls; claimed they were conducting some sort of official investigation, and had 'senatorial authority.' Not that it mattered; people around here still didn't know what had become of Baebius. It's a mystery, isn't it?"

"Yes . . ."

"I figure Baebius must have done something pretty bad, to get out of town that sudden and not leave a trace behind." He shook his head. "Sad, though; his family had been in that shop a long time. And you'd think he might have given me his recipe for those almond cakes before he disappeared! People come by here day and night, asking for those cakes. Say, could I interest you in something sweet? These honey-glazed buns are fresh out of the oven. Just smell that aroma . . ."

Is it better to visit a poison dealer on a full stomach or an empty one? Empty, I decided, and so I declined the baker's bun and made my way across the Forum and the cattle market to the riverfront, and thence to the seedy little tavern frequented by Quintus Fugax.

The interior seemed pitch-dark after the bright sunshine. I had to squint as I stumbled from bench to bench, searching among the derelicts. Only the most hardened drinkers were in such a place at that time of day. The place stank of spilled wine and river rot.

"Looking for someone?" asked the tavern keeper.

"A fellow called Fugax."

"The scarecrow with the rheumy eye and the bad breath?"

"That's him."

"You're out of luck, then, but not as out of luck as your friend."

"What do you mean?"

"They dragged him out of the river a couple of days ago."

"What?"

"Drowned. Poor sod must have fallen in; not my fault if a man leaves here too drunk to walk straight. Or maybe . . ." He gave me a significant look. "Maybe somebody pushed him in."

"Why do you say that?"

"Fugax had been strutting around here lately, claiming he was about to come into a big sum of money. Crazy fool! Saying a thing like that in this neighborhood is asking for trouble."

"Where was he going to get this money?"

"That's what I wondered. I asked him, 'What, are you planning to sell your garden villa on the Tiber?' He laughed and said he had something to sell, all right—information, important information that powerful people would pay a lot for; pay to get it, or pay to keep others from getting it. Not likely, I thought! 'What could a river rat like you know that anybody would give a fig to find out?' He just laughed. The fellow was half-crazy, you know. But I figure maybe somebody heard him bragging, tried to rob him, got angry when they didn't find much, and threw him in the river. The dock workers that found him say it looked like he might have hit his head on something—hard to tell with all those scabs and rashes. Did you know him well?"

I sighed. "Well enough not to mourn too much over his death."

The tavern keeper looked at me oddly. "You need something to drink, citizen."

I had declined the baker's bun, but I accepted the tavern keeper's wine.

The doorkeeper at Poplicola's house tersely informed me that his master was not receiving visitors. I pushed past him and told him I would wait in the red study.

I waited for quite a while, long enough to peruse a few of the scrolls in Poplicola's little library: Aristotle on ethics, Plato on the examined life. There was a movement at the green curtain drawn over the doorway. It was not Poplicola who entered, but Palla.

She was shorter than I had thought; her elaborate turret of hair gave an illusion of height. But she was actually more beautiful than I had realized. By the reflected light of the red walls, her skin took on a smooth, creamy luster. The bland youthfulness of her face was at odds with the worldliness in her eyes. At such close range, it was harder than ever to calculate her age.

"You must be Gordianus," she said.

"Yes."

"My husband is physically and emotionally exhausted by the events of the last few days. He can't possibly see you."

"I think he should."

"Has he not paid you yet?"

I gritted my teeth. "I'm not an instrument to be used and then disposed of. I helped him discover the truth. I brought him certain information. Now I find that an innocent family has been driven into hiding, and another man is dead, very likely murdered to keep him quiet."

"If you're talking about that wretch Fugax, surely the whole city is better off being rid of such a creature."

"What do you know about his death?"

She made no answer.

"I insist that your husband see me," I said.

She looked at me steadily. "Anything you might wish to say to Poppy, you may say to me. We have no secrets from each other—not anymore. Everything has come into the open between us."

"And your son-in-law?"

"Father and son are reconciled."

"The three of you have worked it all out?"

"Yes. But that's really none of your business, Finder. As you say, you were hired to find out a thing, and you did. There's an end of it."

"An end of Chrestus, and of Fugax, you mean. And who knows what's become of the baker and his family?"

She drew a deep breath and gave me a sour look. "The slave Chrestus belonged to my husband. His death was an injury to my husband's property. Chrestus was old and slow, he pilfered from his master's food and might not have survived another winter; his market value was nil. It's for Poppy and Poppy alone to seek

recompense for the loss, and if he chooses to overlook it, then neither you nor anybody else has any business poking further into the
matter."

She crossed her arms and paced slowly across the room. "As for
Fugax, as I say, his death is no loss to anyone. A public service, I
should think! When the trial began to loom, and then the investigation, he tried to blackmail us. He was a stupid, vile, treacherous little man, and now he's dead. That, too, is none of your business."

She reached the far corner and turned around. "As for the baker
and his family, they were paid a more than adequate compensation
for their trouble."

"The man's family had been in that shop for generations! I can't
believe he left of his own free will."

She stiffened her jaw. "True, Baebius was not completely cooperative, at first. A certain amount of pressure was required to make
him see reason."

"Pressure?"

"A black mark from a censor could have made a great deal of
trouble for Baebius. Once that was explained to him, Baebius saw
that it would be best if he and his family left Rome altogether and
set up shop elsewhere. I'm sure his almond cakes will be just as popular in Spain as they were here in Rome. Poppy shall miss them,
alas." She spoke without a shred of irony.

"And what about me?"

"You, Gordianus?"

"I knew more than anyone."

"Yes, that's true. To be candid, I thought we should do something
about you; so did my stepson. But Poppy said that you had sworn an
oath of secrecy upon your ancestors, that you gave him your word,
Roman to Roman. That sort of thing counts for a great deal with
Poppy. He insisted that we leave you alone. And he was right; you

kept silent. He expects you to remain silent. I'm sure you won't let him down."

She flashed a serene smile, without the least hint of remorse. It struck me that Palla resembled a bit of poisoned cake herself.

"So you see," she said, "it's all worked out for the best, for everyone concerned."

Legally and politically, the affair of Poplicola and the poisoned cake was at an end. The court of public opinion, however, would continue to try and retry the case for years to come.

There were those who insisted that the Senate investigation had been rigged by Poplicola himself; that vital witnesses had been intimidated, driven off, even killed; that the censor was morally bankrupt, unfit for his office, and that his happy household was a sham.

Others defended Poplicola, saying that all the talk against him originated with a few morally depraved, bitter ex-senators. There were even those who argued that the episode was proof of Poplicola's wisdom and profound sense of judgment. Upon hearing such shocking charges against his son and wife, many a man would have rushed to avenge himself on them, taking their punishment into his own hands; but Poplicola had exercised almost superhuman restraint, called for an official inquiry, and ultimately saw his loved ones vindicated. For his patience and cool-headed perseverance, Poplicola was held up as a model of Roman sagacity, and his loyal wife, Palla, was admired as a woman who held her head high even when enduring the cruelest slanders.

As for his son, Lucius Gellius's political career advanced more or less unimpeded by the scandal. He became more active than ever in the courts and in the Senate House, and openly expressed his ambition to someday be censor, following in his father's footsteps. Only rarely did his unproved crimes come back to haunt him, as on the occasion when he sparred with Cicero in a rancorous debate and threatened to give the great orator a piece of his mind—to which Cicero replied, "Better that, Lucius Gellius, than a piece of your cake!"

THE CHERRIES OF LUCULLUS

"Once a thing is done, it's done. The accomplished fact takes on an air of inevitability, no matter how uncertain it might have seemed beforehand. Do you not agree, Gordianus?" Cicero flashed a quizzical smile.

"I'm not sure what you mean," I said.

We were strolling across the Forum on a fine spring morning. Ahead of us, fluffy white clouds were heaped on the horizon beyond the Capitoline Hill, like a vast nimbus crowning the Temple of Jupiter, but in every other direction the sky was an immaculate blue. The mild, warm air carried strains of birdsong from yew trees that grew along the slope of the Palatine Hill that rose steeply to our left. We continued to stroll at a slow pace, but paused when a group of Vestals emerged from the round temple of their goddess and crossed our path, holding their chins high and wearing haughty expressions. One of them deigned to cast a glance at Cicero, and I saw him give her a faint nod. I recognized his sister-in-law Fabia; once, years ago, I had rescued her from the terrible fate that awaits any Vestal who dares to break her vow of chastity. Fabia did not appear to notice me, or else deliberately avoided meeting my gaze. So it sometimes goes with those who call on Gordianus the Finder in their time of trouble; when the trouble is over, and they no longer need me, I vanish to their eyes, as the smoke from a censer can be dispersed by a puff of air, leaving no trace to the senses.

Cicero, tired of walking, indicated that he wished to sit for a while on the stone bench beside the steps of the Temple of Castor and Pollux. He gestured to the space beside him, but I told him I preferred to remain standing for a while.

"What's this you were saying, about inevitability?" I asked.

Cicero hummed thoughtfully. "How did the playwright Ennius put it? 'It is done now. The workings of the Fates I surmise; how could the outcome have been otherwise?'"

"Ennius was talking about the murder of Remus by Romulus, as I recall. But what in Hades are *you* talking about, Cicero?"

He shrugged and narrowed his eyes, as if searching his mind for an example, but I suspected the point he wished to make was already fully formed in his mind and he was simply taking his time to get around to it, wanting his words to seem spontaneous rather than rehearsed. Cicero was a lawyer, and this is how lawyers speak; they never go straight to the point when they can practice circumlocution. There was no sense in pressing him. I sighed and decided to sit down after all.

"Well, Gordianus, consider: a mere ten years ago—say, during the consulship of my good friend Lucullus—who could have foreseen with any certainty the future course of the Roman Republic? To the west, the rebel general Sertorius was luring malcontents in the Senate to Spain, with the aim of setting up a rival republic; Sertorius and his followers claimed that they represented the true Rome, and showed every intention of returning someday to claim the city as their own. Meanwhile, to the east, the war against King Mithridates had taken a turn for the worse; it was beginning to look as if Rome had bitten off more than she could chew when she invaded Mithridates's holdings in Asia Minor, and we were likely to choke on our mistake.

"And *then*, to compound the situation, our enemies decided to join forces against us! Sertorius sent his right-hand man, Marcus Varius, to lead Mithridates's army, and so Rome found herself embattled against Roman generals on both sides. The development was all the more unnerving because Sertorius had only one eye—as did Varius! One had lost his right eye in battle, the other his left; I can never remember which had lost which. Notwithstanding Aristotle and his disdain for coincidence, any historian will tell you that Fortune loves odd synchronisms and curious parallels—and what a curious turn of events, if Rome had been bested by two of her own generals, a pair of men who between them possessed a pair of eyes such as most men take for granted. I must confess, Gordianus, in my darker moods it seemed to me that Sertorius and Mithridates together would triumph and split the world between them; history would have taken a very different course, and Rome would be a different place today."

"But that's not what happened," I said.

"No. Sertorius, with his overbearing personality, at last became so insufferable to his own followers that they murdered him. Sertorius's one-eyed henchman Varius proved to be not such a capable general after all; in a sea battle off the island of Lemnos, Lucullus took him captive and destroyed his army. King Mithridates was bested on every front, and stripped of his most prized territories, which now pay their tribute to Rome. What's done is done, and the outcome seems to have been inevitable all along; Rome's triumph was assured from the beginning, by the grace of the gods, and it could never have been otherwise."

"You believe in destiny, then?"

"*Rome* believes in destiny, Gordianus, for at every stage of her history, her destiny has been manifest."

"Perhaps," I said, but doubtfully. It was in the nature of my work to poke and prod and peer beneath the surface of things, to turn back rugs, so to speak, and examine the detritus swept underneath; and from my experience, no man (and by extension, no nation) possessed such a thing as a manifest destiny. Every man and nation proceeded through life in fits and starts, frequently heading off in the wrong direction and then doubling back, usually making a host of catastrophic mistakes and desperately trying to cover them over before moving on to make the next mistake. If the gods took any part in the process, it was generally to have a bit of sport at the expense of hapless mortals, not to light the way to some predetermined path of greatness. Only historians and politicians, blessed by keen self-interest and blurry hindsight, could look at the course of events and see the workings of divine intention.

If Cicero entertained another view, I was hardly surprised. At that moment, he was swiftly and surely approaching the apogee of his political career. His work as an advocate in the courts had gained him the friendship of Rome's most powerful families. His advancement through the magistracies had been marked by one successful election campaign after another. In the coming run for the consulship he was considered a clear front-runner. When I first met him, many years before, he had been young, untested, and much more cynical about the ways of the world; since then, success had tamed him and given him the rosy, self-satisfied aura of those who begin to think their success was inevitable, along with the success of the city and the empire they served.

"And yet," I observed, "if things had gone only a little differently, Sertorius might have become king of the West, with his capital in Spain, and Mithridates might still be undisputed king of the East, and Rome might have been reduced to a mere backwater over which the two of them would be squabbling."

Cicero shuddered at the thought. "A good thing, then, that Sertorius was killed, and Mithridates soundly defeated by Lucullus."

I cleared my throat. It was one thing for Cicero to engage in philosophical speculation about destiny, but another to contradict the facts of recent history. "I believe it's been left for Pompey to finally end the war with Mithridates, once and for all."

"Pompey is charged with *ending* the war, yes; but Lucullus fought Mithridates for years, all over Asia Minor, before he was recalled to Rome and forced to cede his command to Pompey. If Pompey appears to be making quick work of Mithridates, it's only because Lucullus softened the ground for him." Cicero snorted. "Ever since Lucullus came back to Rome, he's been owed a triumph for his many victories in the East, but his political enemies have successfully conspired to deprive him of it. Well, their obstructionism is about to be ended, and within a year, Lucullus will finally celebrate his triumph; perhaps—and I should be only too honored—during the year of my consulship, should the gods favor my election. So please, Gordianus, don't subject me to this line of argument about Pompey being the sole conqueror of the East. Lucullus broke the enemy's back, and Pompey merely moved in for the kill."

I shrugged. It was a controversy about which I had no firm opinion.

Cicero cleared his throat. "Anyway . . . how would you like to join him for a leisurely meal this afternoon?"

"Join *whom?*"

"Why, Lucullus, of course."

"Ah . . ." I nodded. So that was the true purpose of Cicero's desire to see me that morning, and the point of his digressions. The subject all along had been Lucullus.

"Has Lucullus invited me?"

"He has. And, let me assure you, Gordianus, no man in his right mind would refuse an invitation to sup with Lucullus. His conquests in the East made him very, very wealthy, and I've never known anyone who more greatly enjoys spending his wealth. His dinners are legendary—even those he consumes by himself!"

I nodded. Lucullus was a well-known Epicurean, devoted to enjoying the good life and indulging every sensory pleasure. Even during military campaigns he had been noted for the extravagance of his table. The multitudes in Rome were eagerly looking forward to his triumph, which, along with a fabulous procession, would also feature public entertainments, banquets, and a distribution of gifts to all who attended.

"If Lucullus desires my company, why does he not contact me directly? And to what do I owe the honor of this invitation?" *In other words: What sort of trouble had Lucullus gotten himself into, and what would he expect me to do about it?* I could leave the question of payment to another time; Lucullus was not miserly and could afford to be generous.

Cicero looked at me askance. "Gordianus, Gordianus! Always so suspicious! First of all, Lucius Licinius Lucullus is not the sort of fellow to dispatch a slave to deliver an invitation to a fellow citizen he hasn't yet met. Not his style at all! He obtains new friends through those who are already his friends. He's very strict about that sort of thing; decorum matters greatly to him. Which is not to say he's stuffy; quite the opposite. Do you follow me?"

I raised a dubious eyebrow.

Cicero snorted. "Very well, then, it was *I* who mentioned your name to him and suggested he might wish to make your acquaintance. And not for any nefarious purpose; the context was entirely innocent. What do you know about Lucullus's circle of friends?"

"Nothing, really."

"Yet if I were to mention their names, you'd no doubt recognize them. Famous men, well regarded in their fields, the best of the best. Men like Antiochus of Ascalon, the Greek philosopher; Arcesislaus, the sculptor; and of course Aulus Archias, the poet. Those three are Lucullus's constant companions."

"I've heard of them, of course. Is it Lucullus's habit to collect friends whose names all begin with the same letter?"

Cicero smiled. "You're not the first to notice that; 'the three A's,' Lucullus sometimes calls them. A mere coincidence, signifying nothing—as I'm sure Aristotle would agree, notwithstanding his own initial. Anyway, as you can imagine, the conversation at Lucullus's table can be rather elevated, with discussions of philosophy and art and poetry and so on; even I sometimes find it a bit challenging to carry my weight—if you can imagine that!" He laughed aloud at this self-deprecation; to be polite, I managed a chuckle.

"Of late," he continued, "Lucullus has been most interested in discourse on the subjects of truth and perception—how we know what we know, and how we distinguish truth from falsehood."

"Epistemology, I think the philosophers call it."

"Exactly! You see, Gordianus, you are not entirely without refinement."

"I don't recall claiming that I was."

Cicero laughed, but I did not join him. "Anyway, Lucullus was saying that he's grown weary of hearing the same points of view expounded over and over. He already knows what Antiochus and Arcesislaus and Archias will say, given their points of view—the philosopher, the artist, the poet. And he knows what I will say—the politician! Apparently some particular problem is bothering him, though he won't come out and say what it is, and our tired ideas are of no use to him. So, when I dined with him a few days ago, I told him I knew a fellow who might very well have something new to offer: Gordianus the Finder."

"Me?"

"Are you not as obsessed with truth as any philosopher? Do you not see the true shape of things as keenly as any sculptor and cut through falsehood as cleverly as any playwright? And are you not as sharp a judge of character as any politician? More importantly, would you not enjoy an unforgettably lavish meal as much as any other man? All your host shall ask in return is your company and your conversation."

Put that way, I could see no reason to refuse. Still, it seemed to me there must be more to the matter than Cicero was willing to admit.

To reach the villa of Lucullus, one passed outside the city walls at the Fontinalis Gate, traveled a short distance up the Flaminian Way, and then ascended the Pincian Hill. A stone wall surrounded the property; entry could be obtained only through a guarded iron gate. Even after one passed through the gate, the villa could not be seen, for it was surrounded by extensive gardens.

The gardens had excited much comment, for Lucullus had collected hundreds of trees, flowers, vines, and shrubberies from all over Asia Minor and had transported them, at great expense, back to Rome, along with a veritable army of gardeners. Some of the plants had taken root in the soil of Italy, while others had not, and so the garden was still a work in progress, with here and there a bare spot or a plant that appeared less than content. Nonetheless, the consummate artistry of Lucullus's landscapers was evident at every turn. To follow the stone-paved path that wound up the hillside toward the villa, decorated here and there with a rustic bench, or a statue, or a splashing fountain, was to encounter one delightfully framed vista after another. Unfamiliar flowers bloomed in profusion. The leaves of exotic trees shivered in the warm breeze. Trellises were overgrown with vines that bore strange fruit. Occasionally, through the lush greenery, I caught a glimpse of the temples atop the Capitoline Hill in the distance, or the glimmer of the sinuous, faraway Tiber, and the sight compelled me to pause and take it in.

Cicero accompanied me. He had been up this winding path many times before, but seemed happy to take his time and indulge my wide-eyed wonderment.

At last we reached the villa. A slave greeted us, told us that his master awaited us in the Apollo Room, and asked us to follow him.

I heard Cicero release a gasp and then a groan. "The Apollo Room!" he muttered under his breath.

"You know the place?" I asked, my wonderment increasing as we traversed terraces, porticoes, and galleries. Everywhere I looked, I saw bits and pieces of Asia Minor that Lucullus had brought back to adorn his Roman home. Greek statues, ornamental plaques, sculptural reliefs, carved balustrades, dazzling tiles, magnificent rugs, shimmering draperies, colorful paintings in encaustic wax, superbly crafted tables and chairs, even entire marble columns had been shipped over the sea and up the Tiber to confront Lucullus's engineers, architects, and decorators with the formidable task of creating from their disparate elements a harmonious whole. By some miracle, they had succeeded. Opulence and abundance greeted the eye at every turn; gaudiness and ostentation were nowhere to be seen.

"Lucullus entertains guests in various rooms, depending on his mood," Cicero explained. "To each room is accorded a specific budget for the meal. The simplest meals—and they could be called simple only by the standards of Lucullus—are served in the Hercules Room; the plates are of simple silver, the food is traditional Roman fare, and the wines are of a vintage only slightly beyond the means of most of us mere senators. Lucullus finds the Hercules Room suitable for a simple afternoon repast when entertaining a few intimate friends—and that's where I presumed we would be eating. But the Apollo Room! The couches are sumptuous, the silver plate is stunning, and the food is fit for the gods! The wine will be Falernian, you may be sure. No delicacy which Lucullus's cook can imagine will be denied to us. If only Lucullus had warned me, I should have avoided eating altogether for the last few days, in preparation. My poor stomach is already grumbling in dread!"

For as long as I had known him, Cicero had suffered from irritable bowels. He suffered least when he maintained a simple diet, but like most successful politicians his life had become a whirlwind of meals and parties, and to refuse a host's offerings would seem churlish. "My stomach is no longer my own," he had complained to me once, groaning and clutching his belly after a particularly rich banquet.

At last we passed through a doorway into a magnificent hall. Along one wall, doors opened onto a terrace overlooking the gardens, with a view of the Capitoline Hill in the distance. The opposite wall was covered with a glorious painting celebrating the god Apollo and his gifts to mankind—sunlight, art, and music—with the Graces and the Muses in his retinue. At one end of the room, set in a niche, was a towering statue of the god, scantily clad and resplendent in his beauty, carved from marble but painted in such lifelike colors that for the barest instant I was fooled into thinking I saw a being of flesh and blood.

The room might have accommodated scores of guests, but the gathering that day was much smaller. A group of dining couches had been pulled into a semicircle near the terrace, where the guests could enjoy the warm, jasmine-scented breeze.

We were apparently the last to arrive, for only two of the couches remained empty, those situated at either side of our host. Lucullus, reclining at the center of the semicircle, looked up at our arrival, but did not stand. He was dressed in a saffron tunic with elaborate red embroidery and a belt of silver chain; his hair, gray at the temples but still plentiful for a man of forty-six, was combed back to show his prominent forehead. Despite his reputation for high living, his complexion was clear and his waist no larger than that of most men his age.

"Cicero!" he exclaimed. "How good to see you—and just in time for the mullet course. I had them delivered from Cumae this morning, from Orata's fish farm. Cook's trying a new recipe, something about grilling them on a stick with an olive stuffing; he tells me I shall wish to die after one taste, resolved that life's pleasures can achieve no higher pinnacle."

"No matter what the pleasure, there's always another to top it," responded one of the guests. The man's features were so like those of our host that I realized he had to be Lucullus's younger brother, Marcus Licinius. They were said to be very close; indeed, Lucullus had held off running for his first office until his brother Marcus was also old enough to run, so that they could both be elected to the curule aedileship as partners; the games they had put on for the populace that year, the first to ever feature elephants in combat with bears, had become legendary. To judge by his comment, and by his clothes— a Greek chiton with an elegantly stitched border of golden thread— Marcus was as much an Epicurean as his older brother.

"Wanting to die after eating a mullet! Have you ever heard anything so absurd?" This comment, followed by a laugh to soften its harshness, came from the guest seated opposite Marcus, whom I recognized at once: Cato, one of the most powerful senators in Rome. Cato was anything but an Epicurean; he was a Stoic, known for expounding old-fashioned virtues of frugality, restraint, and service to the state. His hair was closely cropped and he wore a simple white tunic. Despite their philosophical differences, he and Lucullus had become staunch political allies, firm friends, and—with Lucullus's marriage the previous year to Cato's half- sister, Servilia—brothers-in-law.

Reclining next to Cato was Servilia herself. To judge by the os- tentation of her red gown, silver jewelry, and elaborately coiffed hair, she shared her husband's Epicurean tastes rather than her brother's Stoic values. Her tinted cheeks and painted lips were not to my taste, but she projected a kind of ripe sensuality that many men would have found attractive. Her generous figure made it hard to be certain, but it looked to me that she was just beginning to show signs of carrying a child. Servilia was Lucullus's second wife; he had divorced the first, one of the Clodia sisters, for flagrant infidelity.

The three other guests were the Greek companions of Lucullus whom Cicero had previously mentioned to me. The poet Archias was perhaps ten years older than his patron, a small man with a neatly trimmed white beard. Antiochus the philosopher was the most corpulent person in the room, with several chins obscuring his neck. The sculptor Arcesislaus was the youngest of us, a strikingly handsome and exceedingly muscular fellow; he looked quite capable of wielding a hammer and chisel and moving heavy blocks of marble. I realized that it must be his Apollo in the niche at the end of the room, for the face of the god was uncannily like a self-portrait; it was likely that he had painted the wall as well, which gave the same face to Apollo. Clearly, Arcesislaus was an artist of immense talent.

I felt an unaccustomed quiver of discomfort. After years of dealing with Rome's elite, often seeing them at their weakest or worst, I seldom felt self-conscious in any company, no matter how exalted. But here, in the company of Lucullus's brilliant inner circle, in a setting so overwhelmingly opulent yet so impeccably refined, I felt decidedly out of my depth.

Cicero introduced me. Most of the guests had some knowledge of me; their not-unfriendly nods at the mention of my name reassured me, if only a little. Lucullus indicated that Cicero should take the couch to his right and that I should recline to his left.

The meal was spectacular—grilled eel, succulent venison, roasted fowl, and a wide variety of spring vegetables with delicate sauces, all washed down with the finest Falernian. As more wine flowed, the conversation grew more relaxed, punctuated by peals of laughter. The members of Lucullus's circle were completely at ease with one another, so much so that they seemed to speak a sort of secret language, full of veiled references and coded innuendoes. I felt very much an outsider, with little to contribute; mostly I listened and observed.

Servilia showed off a new piece of jewelry, a necklace of pearls linked by a finely wrought gold chain, and boasted of the bargain she had negotiated; the cost was roughly the value of my house on the Esquiline Hill. This prompted a discussion about money and investments, which led to a general consensus, myself abstaining, that land around Rome had become more expensive than it was worth, but a country house in Etruria or Umbria, complete with slaves to run it, could still be obtained at a bargain.

Marcus Licinius asked Cicero if the rumor he had heard was true, that Cicero's chief rival in the coming race for consul was likely to be the radical patrician, Catilina. Cicero replied by quoting a Greek epigram; the point was obscure to me, but the others were moved to laughter. There was more talk of politics. Cato complained about a fellow senator who had employed an obscure but ancient point of procedure to outmaneuver his opponents; declining to name the man, Cato instead referred to him using a vaguely indecent nickname—presumably a pun, but it meant nothing to me. I think he was talking about Julius Caesar.

It seemed that Archias was in the midst of composing an epic poem about Lucullus's campaigns in the East, hoping to complete it in time for his patron's eventual triumph. At the urging of Cicero, Archias quoted a new passage. The scene was one the poet had witnessed himself: the sinking of the fleet of the one-eyed Roman rebel Marcus Varius off the island of Lemnos. His words were spellbinding, conjuring images full of terror, gore, and glory. At one point, he quoted Lucullus's order to his men regarding the fate of the Roman rebel:

Take Varius alive, not dead;
Put no one-eyed man to the sword.
Disobey, and I'll pluck the eyes from your head
And throw you overboard!

It seemed to me that a shadow crossed Lucullus's face as he listened to these words, but afterwards he applauded as heartily as the rest of us, and promised Archias a place of honor at his triumph.

Over pheasant with pine-nut sauce, the conversation took a philosophical turn. Antiochus was a proponent of the so-called New Academy, a school of thought which argues that mankind possesses an innate faculty for distinguishing truth from falsehood and reality from fantasy. "The existence of such a faculty may be inferred if we consider the opposite case, that no such faculty exists," said the corpulent philosopher, dabbing a bit of sauce from his chin. "Perception comes from sensation, not from reason. I see the cup before me; I reach for it and I pick it up. I know the cup exists because my eyes and my hand tell me so. Ah, but how do I know I can trust my eyes and my hand in this instance? Sometimes, after all, we see a thing that turns out not to be there after all, or at least not what we thought it was; or we touch a thing in the dark and think we know what it is, then discover it to be otherwise when we see it in the light. Thus, sensation alone is not entirely reliable; indeed, it can be quite the opposite. So how do I know, in this instance, that this is a cup I hold before me, and not some other thing, or an illusion of a cup?"

"Because the rest of us can see it, too!" said Marcus, laughing. "Reality is a matter of consensus."

"Nonsense! Reality is reality," said Cato. "The cup would exist whether Antiochus or the rest of us saw it or not."

"I agree with you there, Cato," said the philosopher. "But the point remains: how do I *know* the cup exists? Or rather, let me change the emphasis of that question: How do *I* know the cup exists? Not by my eyes and hand alone, for those two are not always trustworthy, and not because we all agree it exists, despite what Marcus may say."

"By logic and reason," offered Cicero, "and the accumulated lessons of experience. True, our senses sometimes deceive us; but when they do, we take note of it, and learn to recognize that particular experience, and to differentiate it from instances where we *can* trust our senses, based also on past experience."

Antiochus shook his head. "No, Cicero. Quite apart from logic and reason and the lessons of experience, there exists in every man an innate faculty, for which we as yet have no name and governed by we know not which organ; yet that faculty determines, for each man, what is real and what is not. If we could but explore and cultivate that faculty, who knows to what greater degree of awareness we could elevate mankind?"

"What do you mean by a 'greater degree of awareness'?" said Marcus.

"A realm of perception beyond that which we presently possess."

Marcus scoffed. "Why do you assume such a state exists, if no mortal has yet attained it? It's a presumption with no basis in experience *or* logic; it's an idea plucked out of thin air."

"I agree," said Cato. "Antiochus is espousing mysticism, not philosophy, or at least not any brand of philosophy suitable for a hardheaded Roman. It's all very well for Greeks to spend their time pondering imponderables, but we Romans have a world to run."

Antiochus smiled, to show that he took no offense at Cato's words. He opened his mouth to reply, but was cut off by our host, who abruptly turned his gaze to me.

"What do *you* think, Gordianus?" said Lucullus.

I felt the eyes of the others converge on me. "I think . . ."

I looked to Cicero, who smiled, amused at my hesitation. I felt slightly flushed, and cleared my throat. "I think that most men are like myself, and don't give much thought to such questions. If I see a cup, and if I want what's in the cup, I pick it up and drink it, and that's the end of that. Now, if I were to reach for the cup and pick up a hedgehog instead, *that* would give me pause. But as long as a cup is a cup—and up is up, and down is down, and the sun comes up in the morning—I don't think most people ever think about epistemology."

Antiochus raised a condescending eyebrow. It was one thing for the others to challenge his ideas with other ideas, but quite another to dismiss the importance of the topic he had raised. In his eyes, I had shown myself to be hardly better than a barbarian.

My host was more indulgent. "Your point is well taken, Gordianus, but I think you're being just a bit disingenuous, aren't you?" said Lucullus.

"I don't know what you mean."

"Well, in your line of work—insofar as Cicero has explained it to me—I should think you rely a great deal on reason or instinct, or some faculty such as that which Antiochus speaks of, in order to determine the truth. A murder is committed; a relative comes to you, asking you to discover the killer. If a man's stopped breathing, it doesn't take an Aristotle to determine that he's dead; but how do you go about the rest of it—finding out who did it, and how, and when, and why? I suppose some evidence is concrete and indisputable, of the sort you can hold in the palm of your hand—a bloody dagger, say, or an earring separated from its match. But there must be a vast gray area where the indicators are not so certain. Witnesses to a crime sometimes tell different versions of events—"

"They inevitably do!" asserted Cicero with a laugh.

"Or a clue may point in the wrong direction," continued Lucullus, "or an innocent man may deliberately incriminate himself, so as to protect another. Lies must be sorted from truth, important facts must be placed above trivialities. The warp and woof of reality must be minutely examined for meaningful patterns and inconsistencies that might elude the scrutiny of a less conscientious . . . 'finder,' as I believe Cicero calls you. Indeed, Gordianus, I should think that you must have frequent occasion to apply the tenets of epistemology more rigorously than anyone else in this room. I suspect it's become second nature to you; you swim in a sea of practical philosophy and never think about it, as the dolphin never thinks of being wet."

"Perhaps," I acknowledged, dubious of his point but thankful that he had rescued me from looking like a cretin.

"So how *do* you go about it?" said Lucullus. "Ascertaining the truth, I mean? Do you apply a particular system? Or do you rely on intuition? Can you tell if a man is lying, simply by looking in his eyes? And if so, would that not be an indication that some innate faculty such as that suggested by Antiochus must indeed exist, perhaps more developed in some men—men like yourself—than in others?"

The guests looked at me intently now, seriously interested to see what I would say. I took a deep breath. "In fact, Lucullus, I *have* given some thought to such questions over the years. If we accept that a thing must be either true or false—either one thing or the other— then even the most complex questions can be approached by breaking them into smaller and smaller questions, and determining in each case which proposition is true and which is false. Smaller units of truth combine into greater units, until eventually a greater truth emerges. Sometimes, investigating the circumstances of a crime, I imagine I'm building a wall of bricks. Each brick must be solid, or else the whole wall will come down. So it's simply a matter of testing each brick before it's put into place. Is this brick true or false? True, and it goes into the wall; false, and it's discarded. Of course, sometimes one makes a mistake, and realizes it only after several courses of bricks have been laid, and it can be a messy business going back and making the repair."

"Ah, but how does such a mistake occur in the first place?" asked Antiochus, in a tone that showed he had warmed to me somewhat.

"Carelessness, confusion, a lapse of concentration."

"And how do you recognize the mistake?"

I shrugged. "Sooner or later, you step back and look at the wall, and you can see there's something wrong. Something's off-kilter; one of the bricks doesn't quite match the others."

"Ah, but there you have yet another indication of the existence of the faculty I speak of!" said Antiochus. "'One knows it when one sees it,' goes the commonplace. But how? Because of an innate ability to distinguish truth from falsehood."

"An innate sense that doesn't always work, apparently," said Marcus, with a laugh.

"That this faculty isn't infallible is hardly evidence against it," asserted Antiochus. "On the contrary, it's yet another sign of its existence. No other human faculty is infallible, so why should this one be? Perfection exists only in that ideal world which Plato postulated . . ."

Here the talk drifted to other matters philosophical, about which Lucullus did not question me; gratefully, I withdrew from the conversation. But it seemed to me that my brief foray into the debate had been deliberately engineered by Lucullus, so that he might observe and form a judgment of me. For what purpose? I did not know. Had I satisfied his expectations? That, too, I did not know.

I spent the rest of the meal observing the others. The corpulent Antiochus was the most vocal and self-assertive, and in such a company, that was saying a great deal. Cato tended to enter the debate only in reaction to the others, usually to chide or taunt them. His sister Servilia spoke only when the conversation involved gossip or money, and was silent about politics and philosophy. The poet Archias every so often contributed an epigram, some more appropriate to the conversation than others. Marcus Licinius seemed a contented sort who enjoyed every course of the meal and every turn of the conversation. Cicero was talkative and high-spirited, but occasionally I saw him touch his belly and wince. As he had feared, the meal was too rich for his dyspeptic constitution.

The one who spoke least—hardly at all, in fact—was the sculptor Arcesislaus. Like me, he seemed content merely to enjoy the food and wine and to observe the others. But he wore a vaguely scornful expression; even when Archias came out with an epigram that made the rest of us hoot with laughter, he hardly smiled. Was he shy and retiring, as are many artists, or was he haughty, as might be the case with a handsome young man of great talent? Or was he brooding about something? I could not make him out.

The generally buoyant mood dimmed only once, when the conversation turned to the father of Lucullus, and his sad end. Cicero had been talking—boasting, in fact—of his first important appearance as an advocate before the Rostra, defending a citizen accused of parricide. Cicero had retained my services to investigate the matter, and that was how we first met. The outcome of the trial had made Cicero a famous man in Rome and set him on the path to his present pinnacle of success. He never tired of telling the tale, even to those who already knew it, and would have gone on telling it had not Cato interrupted.

"It was the same with you, was it not, Lucullus?" said Cato. "Your first appearance in the courts made your reputation—even though you lost the case."

"I suppose," said Lucullus, suddenly reticent.

"Indeed, I remember it well, though it seems a lifetime ago," said Cato. "Your father was sent to put down the great slave revolt in Sicily. Things went well for him at first, then badly, and he was recalled. No sooner did he arrive back in Rome than one of his enemies accused him of official misconduct and prosecuted him in the courts. He was found guilty and sent into exile, poor fellow. But his sons didn't forget him! As soon as he was old enough to argue before the Rostra, our Lucullus dug up some dirt on his father's accuser and brought the man to trial. Everyone in Rome took sides; there was rioting and bloodshed in the Forum. When it was all over, Lucullus lost the case and the fellow got off—but the real winner was our Lucullus, whose name was on everyone's lips. Friends and foes alike acknowledged him as the very model of a loyal Roman son."

"And a fellow not to be tangled with," added Marcus, looking at his brother with admiration.

I was only vaguely aware of this tale regarding Lucullus's father and Lucullus's own younger days, and would have liked to have heard more, but our host was clearly not in a mood to discuss it. He lowered his eyes and raised a hand dismissively. An abrupt silence filled the room, and stretched awkwardly until Archias, clearing his throat, delivered one of his epigrams:

> Right are the Thracians, when they mourn
> The infant on the very morning of its birth.
> Right, also, when they rejoice that death has snatched
> Some aged mortal from the earth.
> Why not? This cup of life is full of sadness;
> Death is the healing draught for all its madness.

He raised his cup. The rest of us, including Lucullus, did likewise, and the wine we shared dispelled the chill that had fallen on the room.

The meal lasted at least three hours, but had begun so early that the sun was still well above the horizon when Lucullus announced that it was time for the final course.

"Something sweet, I hope," said Antiochus.

"Sweet, indeed," said Lucullus. "In fact, the final course is the principal reason for asking you all here today, so that you can share in my bounty." He rose from his couch and gestured that we should do likewise. "Up, everyone! Up, on your feet, and follow me! The first of the cherries are ripe, and today we shall devour them!"

From the others, as they stirred, I heard a murmur of pleasant anticipation. I stepped beside Cicero and spoke in his ear. "What are these 'cherries' that Lucullus speaks of?"

"A most exquisite fruit, which he brought back from the realm of Pontus on the Euxine Sea. They grow on small trees and come in many varieties, all with shiny skins in various shades of red. All sweet, all splendidly delicious! I was privileged to taste some of Lucullus's cherries last year at this time. What a delight that he should invite me back again to taste this year's crop!" Cicero smiled. "His brother Marcus says that if Lucullus's wars against Mithridates had yielded nothing else, they would still have been worth the effort for bringing cherries back to Rome!"

Lucullus led the way onto the terrace and then down a flagstone path that meandered through a small orchard of low, leafy trees. The branches were heavy with a fruit the likes of which I had never seen before. The cherries, as they were called, hung in great clusters. The type varied from tree to tree; some were blood-red, some were pink, and others were almost black. Lucullus demonstrated the ease with which they could be picked by reaching out and plucking off a whole handful at once.

"Be warned: the juice might stain your garments. And be careful of the pit." To demonstrate, he popped a cherry into his mouth, then spat the seed into his hand. His features assumed a sublime expression. He swallowed and smiled. "All this talk of philosophy and politics—how irrelevant it all seems when one can know the simple, unadulterated joy of devouring a cherry. And then another, and another!"

With much laughter, the rest of us joined him in plucking cherries from the branches and popping them into our mouths. Some of the most sophisticated individuals in Rome were reduced to a childlike euphoria by the unbridled joy of eating cherries.

"Sensational!" said Archias, with cherry juice running down his chin. "I must compose a poem to celebrate this crop of cherries."

Cicero sighed. "More wonderful than I remembered."

Even the dour Arcesislaus smiled as he shared the joy of eating cherries.

I felt a hand on my shoulder, and turned to see that it belonged to my host. "Come, Gordianus," he said in a low voice. "There's something I want you to see."

Leaving the others behind, Lucullus led me to a tree at the farthest corner of the cherry orchard. Its branches were more gnarled and its leaves more lustrous than those of the other trees, and its cherries were the largest and plumpest I had yet seen, of a hue that was almost purple.

"Of all the cherry trees I brought back from Pontus, this variety is the most extraordinary. The Greek-speakers of Pontus have preserved the ancient name which the aboriginal barbarians gave to this cherry. I find the word impossible to pronounce, but they tell me it translates as 'Most-Precious-of-All'—which these cherries are. Their flavor is sweet and very complex—at first subtle, then almost overwhelming. And their skins are very, very delicate. Most other cherries travel well; you could pack them in a basket and carry them across Italy to share with a friend. But these are so tender that they can scarcely survive a fall from the tree. To appreciate them, you literally must eat them from the tree—and even then, they may burst if you pluck them too carelessly."

Lucullus reached for one of the dark, plump cherries. He seemed not to tug at all; rather, the heavy fruit appeared to tumble into his palm of its own volition.

"Here is something evanescent," he murmured, "a sensation too unique to be described, capable only of being experienced: the cherry that can be eaten only beneath the tree, so fragile is it. As such, it has another, practical advantage: it can't have been poisoned."

I raised an eyebrow. "Is that a concern?"

Lucullus smiled without mirth. "A man like myself is never without enemies."

"Yet I saw no tasters at the meal."

"That is because you were meant to see no tasters."

He extended his arm and offered the cherry to me. "For you, Gordianus, the season's very first Most-Precious-of-All."

"You do me a great honor, Lucullus." *For which you will doubtless ask something in return*, I thought. Nevertheless, I accepted the cherry and slipped it between my lips.

The skin was sleek and warm, and so thin that it seemed to dissolve at the merest contact with my teeth. The meat of the cherry pressed sensuously against my tongue. The sweet juice flooded my mouth. At first I was disappointed, for the flavor seemed less intense than the cherries I had just tasted. Then, as I located the pit with my tongue and worked it toward my lips, the full flavor of the cherry suffused my senses with an intensity that was intoxicating. Lucullus saw my reaction and smiled.

I swallowed. Gradually, the precedence claimed by my sense of taste receded and my other senses returned to the fore. I became aware of a change in the light as the lowering sun shot rays of dark gold through the leafy orchard. I heard the distant laughter of the others, who had not yet followed us.

"Why did you ask me here today, Lucullus?" I said quietly. "What is it you want from me?"

He sighed. He picked another of the cherries, but did not eat it;

instead he held it in the cup of his palm, gazing at it. "How fleeting and elusive are the pleasures of life; how lasting the pain and bitterness, the disappointments and the losses. When I became a general, I was determined to be the best general possible, and never to repeat my father's failure; but I was determined also never to wreak destruction when destruction was not called for. So many generations of men have labored so hard to build up the few great storehouses of beauty and knowledge in this world, yet by fire and sword their accomplishments can be destroyed in minutes, their memory reduced to ashes. The power of the Roman legions is a great responsibility; I swore that Sulla would be my model, as he had been my mentor in other matters. When he had the chance to sack Athens and level it to the ground, instead Sulla saved it, and so passed on a great gift to future generations. What I least wanted was to ever gain a reputation such as that of Mummius of our grandfathers' time—the Mummius who ruthlessly destroyed the city of Corinth and never passed a Greek temple without plundering it. And yet . . ."

Lucullus pondered the cherry in his hand, as if it contained some mystery. "This tree came from an orchard near a town called Amisus, in Pontus. Did you ever hear of Amisus?"

I shook my head.

"It was not a particularly beautiful or wealthy city, but it did have the distinction of having been founded long ago as a colony of Athens; Amisus was an outpost of civilization at the farthest reaches of the world. Of all the horrors and atrocities that occurred during my war with Mithridates, the siege of Amisus caused me the greatest despair. The enemy commander who held the city saw that my forces must ultimately overwhelm him, so he engineered an escape by setting part of the city on fire. The fire distracted my men, held them back for a while, and concealed the movement of the enemy troops toward the sea, where they boarded ships and sailed away, leaving the city defenseless. When I realized the situation, I was determined to maintain the discipline of my troops. I gave orders that the fires should be extinguished and the city occupied in orderly fashion. But that was not what happened.

"The men were restless after the long siege; they were full of pent-up fury, frustrated that the city had been taken without bloodshed and eager for plunder. My officers were unable to restrain them. They surged into the defenseless city, raping boys and women, killing old men to slake their bloodlust, toppling statues, smashing furniture, breaking anything that was breakable for the sheer joy of destruction. They were heedless of the fire; they even helped to spread it, for night had fallen and they wanted light to continue their rampage, so they lit torches and carelessly threw them aside, or even deliberately set houses and even people aflame. The destruction of Amisus was a long, bloody night of fire and chaos. I stood by and watched, unable to stop them."

He gazed at the cherry a moment longer, then dropped it. It struck a paving stone and burst open with a spray of blood-red pulp. "Do you see, Gordianus? I meant to be Sulla; instead, I was Mummius."

"Even with the best intentions, each of us is helpless before the Fates," I said.

He nodded. "And something good did come of the siege of Amisus. I brought back to Rome this tree that bears the cherry they call Most-Precious-of-All."

I heard a burst of laughter from the others. Eating their way from tree to tree, they had drawn nearer. "Your other guests will join us soon," I said. "If there was something else you wished to say to me . . ."

He nodded, drawn back to the moment. "Yes—yes, there is a matter I wish to discuss. Look there, Gordianus. Do you see that gardener at work across the way, tending to a rose bush?"

I peered past leaves and branches. The man was bent over, pruning the cane of a rose bush. The last rays of daylight glittered on his sharp blade.

"I see him," I said, though because of the broad-brimmed hat he wore, I could see little of the man's face except his grizzled jaw.

"Do you remember earlier, Gordianus, when Archias quoted from the poem he's composing for my triumph—that bit about the rebel general Varius?"

"Of course: 'Put no one-eyed man to the sword . . . .'"

"Exactly. When Archias spoke those lines, a shadow crossed my face; you saw it."

"Perhaps."

"Don't be coy, Gordianus! I felt your eyes on me. You notice things that others do not."

"Yes, Lucullus, I saw your reaction, and I wondered at it."

"The poem is accurate, up to a point. I wanted Marcus Varius to be captured alive, and he was. My men brought him before me in chains."

"You showed mercy to him."

He flashed a joyless smile. "Not exactly. My intention was to keep him alive so that eventually he could be marched through the streets of Rome during my triumph. You know what happens to a captured enemy in such a procession; the people spit at him, curse him, pelt him with offal. And afterwards, like the traitor he was, Marcus Varius would be thrown from the Tarpeian Rock to his death."

"You speak as if none of this will happen."

"No; because Varius escaped. On my voyage home, just in sight of Sicily, somehow he slipped from his shackles, fought his way to the deck, and jumped overboard. We turned about and sailed after him, but the sun was in our eyes and we lost sight of him. The current was strong. The coast was a long way off, not impossible, perhaps, for a strong swimmer to reach, but Varius would have been weak from confinement, and one of my men was sure that he had wounded him; it seemed almost certain that Varius was swallowed by the sea and drowned."

"Have you received information to the contrary?"

"Not even the slightest rumor. I know what you're thinking: Varius was a man of considerable importance, with a bounty on his head and a distinguishing characteristic—his lack of one eye. If he did survive, he's either fled beyond Rome's reach, or buried himself in such obscurity that he might as well be dead."

"It would seem that either way—alive or dead—Varius is of no use to you now. You'll have to do without him as an ornament for your triumph."

Lucullus raised an eyebrow. "Cicero warned me of your penchant for sarcasm. But you strike to the heart of the matter. I spared the life of Varius for the specific purpose of bringing him back to Rome alive. He eluded me and thwarted my plans. I might as well have had the soldiers bring me his head on a pike, after all. And yet . . ." He turned his attention again to the slave who was pruning the rose bushes. "You, there! Gardener!"

The man stopped what he was doing and looked up. When he saw who spoke, he quickly lowered his head, so that his eyes were hidden by the brim of his hat; I never quite saw his face. "Yes, Master?" he called.

"Come here."

The gardener shuffled toward us, keeping his head bowed.

"There, that's close enough," said Lucullus. The man was still several paces distant. "How long have you been here, working in my gardens?"

"Only since the start of spring, Master. I was purchased in Athens by one of your agents and brought here to tend to your roses. It's what I've done all my life, Master—tend to roses." The man spoke passable Latin with a Greek accent. He continued to avert his gaze, as if awed by his master.

"What is your name?" said Lucullus. "Yes, yes, I know I've asked you before, but tell me again."

"Motho, Master." The man fiddled nervously with the pruning knife in his hand.

"Let me see your face."

Motho lifted his chin. He blinked and squinted as the last ray of the sun struck his single eye; the other eye was missing. The injury had long ago healed over. Scarred flesh covered the place where the eye should have been.

"How did you lose that eye, Motho?" said Lucullus. His voice was oddly flat.

The man sighed. He had told this story before. "It happened a long time ago, Master. Pricked it on a rose thorn. Seemed a small wound at first, but then it went bad. Had a fever for days; nearly died. In the end I got better—except for the eye."

Lucullus nodded. "Go back to your work now . . . Motho."

Looking relieved to be dismissed, the man shuffled back to the rose bush.

Lucullus seized my elbow in a grip far stronger than necessary and pulled me into the deep shadows beneath the cherry tree. "Did you see, Gordianus?"

"See what?"

"He has but one eye!"

"So I noticed. What of it?"

Lucullus lowered his voice to a whisper. "His face—it's no longer the same. Different somehow—leaner, more lined . . . but a man can change his face if he has a will to. And his voice is different, I must admit—but anyone can pretend to speak with an accent . . ."

"What are you saying, Lucullus?"

"That slave, the gardener who calls himself Motho—I'm almost certain the man is actually . . . Marcus Varius."

"What? Surely not! Can't you tell for certain, simply by looking at him?"

"Eyes are unreliable; eyes deceive a man. There is that other faculty, which Antiochus postulates, a sense of *knowing*—"

"It hardly seems likely that Varius would escape from your clutches only to turn up as a rose-tender in your garden, Lucullus." I almost laughed, but the look on his face stopped me. He was dead serious. "Surely there must be men who knew Varius here in Rome, before he turned traitor and joined Sertorius, men who could identify him without any doubt. Round up a few such fellows and ask them to have a look at this Motho—"

"I've already done that, Gordianus."

"And the result?"

"To a man, they deny that this fellow is Marcus Varius."

"Well, then . . ."

"They're lying! Or else by some trickery Varius has deceived them."

I shook my head. "I don't understand. What makes you think he's Varius?"

"I don't *think* it. I *know* it. The knowledge came to me in a flash, the moment I laid eyes on the man. It must be as Antiochus says: we have a faculty for discerning truth from falsehood, which comes from a source not limited to the five senses, or to what we call reason. That man *is* Marcus Varius. I simply know it!"

I looked at the gardener across the way. He was stooped over, still pruning the rose bush despite the failing light. I felt a prickle of dread, imagining the end to which Lucullus's wild notion might lead, if he was determined to pursue it. "Lucullus, is this why you invited me here today—to ask me about this man, and any . . . uncertainty . . . regarding his identity?"

"I know the circumstances are strange, Gordianus, very strange. But I haven't yet told you the strangest thing, which even I can't account for."

My sense of dread increased. Above the pounding of my heart I heard the laughter of the other guests, who were now quickly moving to join us; I saw them as shadows converging upon us in the twilight. "What is it, Lucullus?" I whispered.

"This fellow who calls himself Motho—do you remember which of his eyes is missing? Think carefully!"

"I don't need to think," I said. "I just saw him. It's his right eye that's missing."

"Are you certain of that, Gordianus?"

I narrowed my eyes. I conjured the man's face in memory. "Absolutely certain. He has no right eye."

The expression on Lucullus's face was ghastly. "And yet, always before, Varius was missing his *left* eye. Now here he is, pretending to be this slave Motho, and as you yourself can testify, he's missing his *right* eye. How can that be, Gordianus? *How can such a thing be?*"

"How I should love to have been there, Gordianus! Tell me again about those cherries." My good friend Lucius Claudius smiled wanly and gestured to the slave behind him to recommence wafting a long pole surmounted by a fan of peacock feathers, so as to stir the sluggish air. We reclined on couches beneath the shade of a fig tree in Lucius Claudius's garden at his house on the Palatine Hill. The weather was much warmer than the previous day.

My dear friend, always portly, was heavier than I had ever seen him; his complexion, always ruddy, had become alarmingly florid. His orange curls hung limply over his forehead, and his breathing, even at rest, was slightly labored. It was now some fourteen years since I first met him; time had begun to take a toll on him. It struck me that a rich meal such as the one Lucullus had served the previous day was the last thing Lucius Claudius needed.

"You've not tasted Lucullus's cherries?" I said.

"Never! I've heard about them, of course, and about how fabulous the house and the gardens are; but I've not yet been invited. Imagine that! Gordianus the Finder has trumped me on the social front! I'm really quite envious. But then, I've never felt at home in the rarefied intellectual circle of the Lucullus brothers; all that arty-farty philosophical blather rather puts me off my wine. And I seldom stray far from my own house anyway, these days. The litter-bearers complain that I've become too heavy for them to carry up and down the Seven Hills."

"They do not!"

"Not out loud, perhaps; but I hear them wheezing and grumbling. And now that the warm weather has begun, it's too hot to go out. I shall settle here under the shade of this fig tree and stay put until autumn."

"What about your Etruscan estate? You love it in the summer."

He sighed. "I should give it to you, Gordianus. Would you like a farm to retreat to?"

"Don't be ridiculous! What do I know about farming?"

"Yet you constantly complain of the indignities of city life. Perhaps I should leave the farm to you in my will."

"I'm touched, Lucius, but you'll probably outlive me by a good ten years." I said this lightly, but felt a prick of anxiety that Lucius should speak of wills; did he feel unwell? "Besides, you're changing the subject. I was hoping you could tell me a bit more about Lucullus." Lucius Claudius was always a fountain of gossip, especially about the movers and shakers of the ruling class.

A mischievous glint lit his eyes. "Ah, let me think. Well, for one thing, it sounds as if Cato rather glossed over the matter of Lucullus's father and his scandalous end."

"Yes, I was wondering about that." Twice at the banquet I had seen a shadow cross Lucullus's face: first, when Archias recited his lines about the capture of one-eyed Varius, and then again, when

Cato told the anecdote about Lucullus's father. "It seems rather extreme that the elder Lucullus should have been exiled simply because his campaign against the slave revolt in Sicily stalled."

"Oh, his offense was much more serious than merely losing a battle or two! When the Senate recalled the elder Lucullus from his command, it was his subsequent behavior that was so unforgivable—and quite inexplicable as well, at least to those who knew him, because the elder Lucullus had always been a model of probity and even temper. You see, instead of doing the honorable thing, the normal thing, when he was recalled—leaving his provisions and maps and dossiers of information for the use of his successor—the elder Lucullus instead destroyed the whole lot. Smashed weapons, dumped stores of food in the sea, even burned maps and records of troop movements. It was most strange, because he'd never been known as a spiteful man; his personality was more like that of his sons, and you've seen how pleasant and easygoing they both are. That's one reason his punishment was so controversial; many of his friends and allies here in Rome simply refused to believe that the elder Lucullus had done such a contemptible thing. But the proof was irrefutable, and the court unanimously condemned him of malversation and sent him into exile."

"How old were his sons at the time?"

"Mere boys. Our Lucullus was probably no more than ten years old."

"His father's trial must have been a terrible ordeal for him."

"I'm sure it was; yet eventually he turned it to his advantage. Instead of retreating from the world out of shame or bitterness, as soon as he was old enough, Lucullus dug up some dirt on the man who'd prosecuted his father and brought the fellow to trial. Everyone knew it was a prosecution motivated by revenge, but many people still felt warmly toward the exiled Lucullus and they were proud to see his son so full of spirit. The prosecution failed—but Lucullus's reputation was made."

"So I gathered."

Lucius Claudius hummed and nodded. "Let's see, what else can I tell you about Lucullus?" He was lost in thought for a moment, then the mischievous glint returned to his eyes. "Well—since you don't care to discuss *my* will—there's the matter of Lucullus's. I don't suppose *that* subject came up during the conversation?"

"Lucullus's will? No."

"Naturally; the one thing on everyone's mind would be the one thing no one mentioned!"

"Tell me more."

"Apparently, for the longest time, Lucullus had no will; he's one of those fellows who thinks he'll live forever. But just last month he drew up a will and left a copy in the keeping of the Vestal virgins. When a man as rich as Lucullus makes a will, that's news. Of course, the copy was sealed, and no one is supposed to know the details, but . . ."

"But *you* happen to have a tidbit or two, nonetheless?" I shook my head in wonder. How was it that Lucius Claudius, without ever leaving his garden, could know so much about the secret life of the city?

"Well, this is only secondhand, you understand, and there are no earth-shaking surprises. It's rather what you might expect: his beloved younger brother Marcus is his principal heir, and is also named as the guardian of Lucullus's son, if indeed the child Servilia is expecting turns out to be a male; if it's a daughter, the child is left to the care of her mother and her mother's family, which means her uncle Cato, I suppose."

I nodded; my supposition that Servilia was pregnant was correct. "And Servilia? What sort of provision is made for her?"

"Ah! As you may remember, Lucullus's last marriage ended in an acrimonious divorce; they say he picked the wrong Clodia—as if there might be a right one!" Lucius Claudius laughed at this little jest; each of the three Clodia sisters had become notorious for carrying on behind her husband's back. "Right now, Lucullus is still very keen on Servilia, especially since she's to give him a child. But Lucullus is wary; once burned, and all that. They say there are all sorts of provisions in the will to keep Servilia from getting so much as a sesterce if there should be the least hint of infidelity on her part."

"Has there been?"

Lucius Claudius raised an eyebrow. "She was known to have a wild streak when she was younger."

"Motherhood takes that out of some women."

"Perhaps. But you've seen the lady with your own two eyes. If she did wish to go fishing, she possesses all the right bait."

"She's not to my taste, but I'll take your word for it. It's curious that Servilia seems so different from her brother. Cato is so prim, so proper."

Lucius Claudius laughed. "For one thing, they're only half-siblings; perhaps Servilia inherited her wild streak from her father. And you know what they say: one Stoic in the family is more than enough!"

I nodded. "Speaking of Cato, is he mentioned in the will—beyond his role as guardian to his prospective niece?"

"Oh, yes, there's quite a generous provision for him. Cato has been instrumental in pushing through the proposal for Lucullus's triumph, and for that, Lucullus is grateful. The two have become staunch allies in the Senate; the new Gemini, some call them."

"Despite their differing philosophies?"

"Opposites attract. Look at you and me, Gordianus; could two Romans be more different? Yet this very day I've decided to make you heir to my Etruscan farm."

"Stop jesting, Lucius! Your farm would be useless to me—except, perhaps, for the fine wine that comes from your vineyards, another cup of which I would gladly accept right now." Lucius clapped his hands; a slave came at once and refilled my cup. "What about Cicero?"

He nodded. "Also named in the will, and generously provided for. And Jupiter knows *he* could use the money, what with bankrolling his campaign for the consulship this year! Really, it's a scandal how expensive it's become to run for office. Cicero's already been forced to borrow; he's in debt not just to Lucullus but to several other of his wealthy friends."

I nodded. "And the three A's, Lucullus's little coterie of Greek companions?"

"All named in the will, in gratitude for their many years of loyalty and inspiration."

I thought for a moment. "Let me understand what you've just told me, Lucius: Lucullus only recently made a will, and everyone who supped with him yesterday—except me—stands to profit enormously from his demise?"

Lucius frowned. "Is Lucullus in danger? Has he been threatened? I thought he called you there to investigate one of his gardeners, that one-eyed slave who, Lucullus imagines, is actually the fugitive traitor Varius."

"Yes, that was his ostensible reason for consulting me. Lucullus is utterly convinced of the man's identity."

"Is such a thing possible?"

"No. Motho can't be Varius. For one thing, his missing eye is on the wrong side!"

"You're sure of that?"

"I am. Only yesterday, Cicero reminded me that Sertorius had lost an eye on one side, his compatriot Varius an eye on the other; as Cicero put it, between them they possessed a full complement of eyes such as the rest of us take for granted. I know that Sertorius was missing his *right* eye—I once met the man myself—and so it follows that Varius was missing his *left*, as Lucullus himself asserts. Yet the gardener Motho is missing his right eye, and so cannot possibly be Varius. The most bizarre thing is that Lucullus knows this—yet remains convinced that Motho is Varius, nonetheless!"

"Do you think that Lucullus could be the victim of some elaborate hoax?"

"Toward what end?"

"Perhaps someone is deliberately trying to confuse him, make him doubt his sanity, drive him to suicide. It may sound farfetched, but have we not seen even subtler and more outrageous plots, Gordianus, especially when an estate as large as that of Lucullus is involved?"

I shook my head. "No, this delusion arose from Lucullus's own mind; no one suggested it to him."

"I suppose you looked into Motho's background?"

"Of course. Away from Lucullus and the other guests, I questioned the slave at length; if he's not a native Greek speaker for whom Latin is a second language, then he's a better actor than the celebrated Roscius! I also questioned Lucullus's agent, the man who purchased Motho in Athens for the express purpose of bringing him to Rome to tend to Lucullus's roses. Motho was born a slave and has been a slave all his life. He started as a field hand for some wealthy Athenian, but with aptitude and hard work he eventually became a highly skilled gardener. There's no reason to think he's anyone other than he appears to be. Poor fellow!"

"Why do you call him that?"

"Because, unless someone can convince him of his error, Lucullus almost certainly intends to proceed as if Motho *is* Varius. The wretched slave will be dressed up like a captured general, marched through the streets of Rome, jeered at and humiliated, mercilessly beaten by guards, and finally thrown to his death from the Tarpeian Rock."

"Surely not! Wasn't it the whole point of your visit, to verify the man's identity and put Lucullus's mind at rest?"

"Quite the opposite; Lucullus expects me to find proof that Motho *is* Varius, despite all evidence to the contrary. To Hades with logic or common sense; he wants me to validate what he already 'knows'—whether it's true or not!"

"Oh, dear. But if Lucullus tries to pass this gardener off as Varius, word will surely get out about the mistake that's been made, if not before the triumph, then afterwards. Lucullus will become a laughingstock—"

"And Motho will suffer a horrible death."

"The situation is mad!" exclaimed Lucius.

"And yet," I said, "Lucullus is hardly a madman. Madmen don't conquer half of Asia, and build the most impressive gardens in Rome, and oversee vast financial empires—do they? Madmen don't speak of saving cities for the greater good of posterity; they don't love philosophy and art and culture."

"It's all very strange. Unless . . ."

"What are you thinking, Lucius?"

He looked at me shrewdly. "Exactly what you're thinking, old friend. After all these years, can we not read one another's thoughts? Sometimes sane men *become* mad—because of some horrible event, or because the gods chose to make them so, or simply as a side effect . . ."

I nodded. "Yes, exactly what I was thinking: a side effect. As we have observed over the years, there are many poisons, given in doses that stop short of killing the victim outright, that can cause a derangement of the mind. If someone named in Lucullus's will has grown impatient, and has been making an effort to hurry him along . . ."

"But all of Lucullus's food is tasted in advance; he himself told you of his need for caution in that regard."

"And yet," I said, "if a man—or woman—were clever enough, and determined enough, that person might find a way to administer a poison even to a man as cautious and well-guarded as Lucullus."

"Clever and determined—that would certainly describe any member of Lucullus's inner circle." Lucius gazed at me darkly, then grimaced and shook his head. "No, no, Gordianus, surely we're mistaken! These aren't cutthroats and vipers we're talking about. Men like Cicero and Cato do not resort to murder for personal advancement! Marcus most certainly loves his older brother; and so far as we know, Servilia loves her husband. As for the three A's, each one is a genius in his own right. It's absurd that we should sit here and ponder which of them might be a cold-blooded poisoner, especially when we can't even say how a poison might be administered to Lucullus."

His vehemence sobered me. "Perhaps you're right, Lucius. I don't wish to be reckless. Yet I can't stand by and see an innocent man subjected to such a horrible fate."

Lucius shrugged. "We don't know for a fact that Lucullus is actually in danger, do we?"

"I didn't mean Lucullus! I meant the slave, Motho."

"Ah!" he nodded dubiously. All in all, I loved Lucius Claudius dearly; but he was a creature of his patrician upbringing, trained from birth never to feel empathy for a slave, and he simply could not equate the fate of a man like Motho with that of a man like Lucullus. He looked at me shrewdly. "Perhaps there's a poison involved, but without anyone intending there to be."

"What do you mean?" I said.

"Well, I'm wondering—how much do we actually know about these so-called cherries? Are they truly safe to eat?"

"Surely they must be."

"Must they? We both know of plants which can affect a man

strangely. Some of them, when ingested, or burned and inhaled, can cause light-headedness, or flights of fancy, or even hallucinations. Did you not discover that for yourself once, Gordianus, when my friend Cornelia retained your services because she was haunted by lemures?"

Even after so many years, I shivered, remembering that episode. "But all of us ate the cherries, not just Lucullus. And while the fruit may be new to Rome, it's been known for generations in its native region. If eating cherries could cause hallucinations or delusions, I think Lucullus would know."

"Yes, I suppose you're right." Lucius smiled wanly, and I could see that he was growing tired. "This is good, Gordianus—to sit and ponder with you like this. It reminds me of the affair which first brought us together; that, too, involved a will, and what appeared to be a resurrection from the dead. And here we are again, come full circle, and alpha meets omega."

I frowned. "Alpha is the beginning, and omega is the end. What are you implying, Lucius Claudius?"

He sighed. "We are all getting older, Gordianus. I know I am." He looked at me plaintively.

"Nonsense! You'll live to be a hundred!" I invested the words with as much enthusiasm as I could muster, but even to my ears they rang false.

A hoax? A poison? Or something else?

As I mused on the problem of Lucullus and his strange belief, my suspicions increasingly centered on the three A's.

It was the poet Archias who had first mentioned Varius at the supper, causing a shadow to cross Lucullus's face. Did Archias refer to Varius merely by chance, or did he know of his patron's belief regarding the gardener, and wished deliberately to disconcert him?

Was it possible that Archias had suggested the idea to Lucullus in the first place? Poets could induce an idea in a listener by using words that carried meanings beyond the obvious.

It was Antiochus the philosopher who had convinced Lucullus of the existence of some organ of perception which could discern truth from falsehood without resorting to accepted methods of logic and deduction. Such a belief reinforced Lucullus's tenacious insistence that Motho was Varius, despite the evidence of his own eyes and his own memory. Did the philosopher have some other, more direct connection to Lucullus's delusion?

And what of the artist Arcesislaus? While the rest of the company had engaged in spirited conversation, he had kept quiet and watched, wearing an enigmatic expression. His smug silence and lack of sociability aroused my suspicion.

Lucullus had given me permission to wander his estate and to talk to any of his guests or slaves. The next day, I took a stroll through his gardens, delighting in the scent of roses. I came upon Motho, who was on his hands and knees mulching one of the bushes. He lifted his head at the sound of my footsteps; because his empty, scarred eye socket was toward me, he had to turn his face to an awkward angle to get a glimpse of me. The posture was grotesque; he looked like a hunchback or some other malformed unfortunate. I felt a stab of pity, and yet, at the same time, I seemed to detect something almost sinister about the man. Had Lucullus experienced the same reaction—a natural shiver of distaste for another's misfortune—and allowed it to become an obsession, crowding out all reason? Or had Lucullus genuinely detected some menace in the presence of Motho? We seldom sense danger by means of reason; the realization comes to us more swiftly than that, and with indisputable conviction. What if Lucullus was right? What if Motho was, by whatever dark magic could make such a thing possible, the same man as Marcus Varius? To embrace such an idea was to relinquish the bonds of reason. That way lay madness, surely . . .

I gazed down into the one good eye of Motho, and came to my senses. He was nothing more than he appeared: a clever, hardworking man who had suffered the misfortune of being born into slavery, and then the further misfortune of losing an eye, and who now faced the ultimate misfortune of dying a horrible death to satisfy another man's deluded whim. It was to Motho that I owed the truth, even more than I owed it to Lucullus in exchange for the fee he had agreed to pay me. Silently, I vowed that I would not fail him.

I turned away and strode toward the house. On another of the garden paths, glimpsed through leafy foliage, I saw Lucullus's brother, Marcus, strolling beside Archias. They passed a little statue of the rampant god Priapus. "Out of scale, isn't he?" said Marcus. "Too small to fit that space?"

"Godhead is known from deeds, not size or shape," the poet uttered in his usual declamatory singsong. Did he always speak in epigrams?

I drew near to the house. Through an open window I was able to see into the main room of Lucullus's library, which was almost as talked about in Rome as the gardens or the Apollo Room. Lucullus had assembled the largest collection of scrolls this side of Alexandria; scholars and bibliophiles came from distant lands for the privilege of reading his books. Through the window I saw row upon row of upright bookcases, their pigeon holes stuffed with scrolls. Pacing back and forth before the window was Cicero, who moved his lips slightly as he pored over a tattered scroll; occasionally he lowered the scroll, gazed into the middle distance, and uttered disconnected phrases—"Sons of Romulus, I beseech you!" and "I come not to challenge a rival, but to save Rome from a scoundrel!" and so on. I gathered he was studying some treatise on oratory and cribbing rhetorical flourishes to use in his campaign against Catilina.

At the far end of the room, Cato and Antiochus stood in a

doorway, talking in whispers. Cato uttered an exclamation and tapped a rolled scroll against Antiochus's chest for emphasis. Antiochus threw back his head and laughed. Cicero stopped his pacing and shushed them loudly.

I followed the pathway that circled the house. A short flight of steps brought me to the terrace outside the Apollo Room. The doors were open. I stepped inside. The sunlight on the terrace had dazzled me, so that the room appeared dark; for a long moment I thought I was alone, until I realized otherwise.

"Do you mind? You're blocking my light."

It was Arcesislaus the artist who spoke, looking at me over his shoulder with a petulant expression. He stood before the long wall that boasted the painting of Apollo and his gifts to mankind. I smelled the singular odor of encaustic wax and saw that Arcesislaus was working with a thin blade and a palette of pigments, applying a new layer of colored wax over the existing one.

"And you're blocking *my* view," said a feminine voice. I turned about and saw Servilia, who reclined on a couch near the door to the terrace. Apparently, I had wandered into her line of sight and was blocking her view of the artist's handiwork—or was it her view of the artist himself?

I stepped to one side. "You're reworking part of the painting?"

Arcesislaus made a face that indicated that he did not care to explain himself, but finally sighed and gave me a curt nod. "Yes; Lucullus wants cherries. He's decided that cherries must have been created by Apollo—'Greatest of all the god's gifts!' he says—and so cherries must appear in this painting."

"Where is Lucullus, by the way?" I said.

Servilia answered. "My husband is out in the orchard now, eating more cherries. He's mad for them; cherry-mad!" She laughed—rather unpleasantly, I thought.

Arcesislaus stared at the painting, arms crossed, brooding. " 'Here, in this corner,' he told me. 'A cherry tree, if you please.' Never mind that it completely unbalances the composition. I'll have to add some new element to that other corner, as well. More work for me!"

"But isn't that what you artists live for—to work?"

He snorted. "That's a misconception commonly held by those who possess no talent. Like any sane man, I prefer leisure—and plea-sure—to working." Did he steal a look at Servilia, or simply look be-yond me? "I sculpt and I paint because Lucullus pays me to do so, and very handsomely."

"Money matters a great deal to you?"

He gave me a withering glance. "I'm no different from any other man! Except for my ability to do *this*." He scraped the blade against a daub of red wax on the palette, touched the blade to the painting, and as if by magic a cherry appeared, so glossy and plump that it made my mouth water.

"Remarkable!" I said.

He smiled begrudgingly, pleased by the compliment. "There's a trick to it—painting cherries. I could paint cherries all day long." He laughed, as if at some private joke. Servilia laughed as well.

A chill ran up my spine. I looked from the face of Arcesislaus to the face of Apollo—his self-portrait, there could be no doubt, for man and god shared the same sardonic smile. I thought of how mer-ciless, selfish, and cruel the god could be, in spite of his beauty.

I looked at the palette of pigmented wax. Not all paints were so thick. Other techniques called for paints that were quite thin, hardly more than colored water. With a thin liquid and a tiny horsehair brush, one could *paint* cherries—or paint *cherries* . . .

I backed out of the Apollo Room, onto the terrace, then turned and ran to the cherry orchard.

Lucullus was where I expected to find him, seated on a folding chair beneath the tree that bore the cherries called Most-Precious-of-All.

As I approached, I saw him reach up, pluck a cherry, gaze at it admiringly, and then lower it toward his open mouth.

"No!" I shouted. "Don't eat it!"

He turned his head, but continued to lower the cherry toward his lips—until I knocked it from his hand.

"Gordianus! What in Hades do you think you're doing?"

"Saving your life, quite possibly. Or perhaps just your sanity."

"What are you talking about? This is outrageous!"

"What was it you said to me about these cherries? So fragile they can be eaten only beneath the tree—which gives them a more practical advantage, that they can't have been poisoned."

"Yes; they're the only things I ever eat without having a taster test them first."

"And yet, they could be poisoned, here on the tree."

"But how? No one could soak them, or cut them open, or . . ." He shook his head. "I didn't call on your services for the purpose of finding a poisoner, Gordianus. I require of you one single task, and that regards—"

"They could be *painted*," I said. "What if someone diluted a poison, and with a brush applied the solution to the cherries while they yet hang on the branch? You might consume only a little at a time, but eventually, considering how many of these cherries you've eaten—"

"But Gordianus, I have suffered no ill effects. My digestion is fine; my lungs are clear; my eyes are bright."

But your mind is deranged, I wanted to say—but how could one say such a thing to a man like Lucullus? I would have to find another way; I would have to go roundabout, perhaps approach Marcus and win him over, make him see that his older brother needed looking after. Yes, I thought, that was the answer, considering how famously close was the bond between the two brothers. A very public family tragedy had struck them early in life; sometimes such an event drives a wedge between siblings, but quite the opposite had occurred with the brothers Lucullus. Their father's self-destructive behavior had very nearly ruined them, but together they had regained the city's respect and made a name for themselves that exceeded anything their ancestors had achieved. One might even say that Lucullus owed his success to the failure of his father—that he owed everything to his father . . .

Then I saw, in a flash, that cherries had nothing to do with Lucullus's dilemma. The will, yes—but not the cherries . . .

A slave, hearing his master's voice raised, appeared and stood at a respectful distance, a quizzical look on his face.

"Go find your master's brother. Ask him to come here," I said.

The slave looked to Lucullus, who peered at me for a long moment, then nodded. "Do as this man requests. Bring Marcus only— no one else."

While we waited, neither of us spoke. Lucullus moved his eyes here and there, never meeting my gaze.

Marcus appeared. "What's this? The slave told me he heard raised voices, an argument, and then Gordianus asked for me."

"He seems to think that my beloved cherries have been poisoned somehow," muttered Lucullus.

"Yes, but that was a false notion," I said. "And realizing that it was false, I gave it up. If only you could do the same, Lucullus."

"This is about Motho, isn't it?" said Marcus, regarding his brother with a pained look.

"Call him by his true name—Varius!" cried Lucullus.

"Why did you recently decide to write a will?" I said. The two brothers both looked at me sharply, taken aback at the change of subject.

"What a peculiar question to ask!" said Lucullus.

"For many years you had no will. You were far from Rome, fighting battles, accumulating a vast fortune and repeatedly putting your life at risk. Yet you saw no cause to write a will then."

"Because I thought I'd live forever! Men cling to the illusion of immortality for as long as they can," said Lucullus. "I think Archias once wrote a poem on the subject. Shall I summon him to deliver an epigram?"

"'The closer I cut to the bone, the more he laughs, denying all danger,'" I said, quoting Ennius. "How's that for a suitable epigram?"

"What are you talking about?" snapped Marcus. But the tremor in his voice gave him away; he was beginning to see the train of my thoughts.

"*You* encouraged him to write a will. Didn't you?"

Marcus stared at me for a long moment, then lowered his eyes. "Yes. The time had come."

"Because of a change in Lucullus's health? Because of some other threat to his life?"

"Not exactly." Marcus sighed. "Dear brother, he knows. There's no use hiding the truth from him."

"He knows nothing. There is nothing to know!" said Lucullus. "I have employed Gordianus for a single purpose: to prove to the world, and to *you*, Marcus, that I am not mistaken in what I know about Varius, or Motho, or whatever we should call him. I know what I know, and the world must be made to know it, too!"

"Did your father say things like that, after he was recalled from Sicily and made to stand trial?" I said, as gently as I could.

Marcus drew a deep breath. "Similar things, yes. He had strange notions; he fixated upon impossible ideas that no one could talk him out of. His emotions became inappropriate, his logic inexplicable, his behavior unpredictable. It began in a small way, but grew, until toward the end there was almost nothing left of the man we had known. There was only the slightest hint of the change before he

left to take up the command in Sicily—so slight, no one really noticed it at the time, but only in retrospect. By the time he returned
to Rome and stood trial, the change was obvious to those closest to
him—our mother, our uncles. My brother and I were mere children,
of course; we had no way of understanding. It was a very difficult
time for everyone. We spoke of it only within the family. It became
a source of shame to us, greater than the shame of my father's conviction and exile."

"A family secret," I said. "Had such a thing happened before, in
earlier generations?"

"Don't answer, Marcus!" said Lucullus. "He has no right to ask
such a question."

Unheeding, Marcus nodded. "Something similar befell our father's father. An early dotage, a softening of the wits; we think it
must be a kind of a malady that passes from father to son, a coiled
serpent in the mind that waits to strike until a man is at the peak of
his powers."

"All supposition!" snapped Lucullus. "Just as likely, it was the ha-
rassment of his enemies that drove our father to distraction, not
some affliction from within."

"As you see, Gordianus, my brother has always preferred to deny
the truth of this matter," said Marcus. "He denied it concerning our
father. He denies it now, when it begins to concern himself."

"And yet," I said, "he acceded to writing a will when you urged
him to—now, rather than later, when his faculties may have eroded
to a greater degree. That indicates to me that at some level, Lucullus
knows the truth of what's happening to him, even if he continues
outwardly to deny it. Is that not so, Lucullus?"

He gazed at me angrily, then his features gradually softened. His
eyes glistened. A tear ran down one cheek. "I have led an honorable
life. I have served Rome to the very best of my ability. I have been
generous to my friends, forgiving to my enemies. I love life dearly. At

last, I am about to have a child! Why must this shameful fate befall me? If the child is a son, will it befall him as well? My body is still strong; I may live many years yet. What's to become of me in the time I have left, if I lose my senses? Have the gods no mercy?"

I looked upon Lucullus and shivered. I saw a man surrounded by opulence beyond measure, at the summit of his career, adored by the multitude, beloved by his friends—yet utterly alone. Lucullus possessed everything and nothing, because he had no future.

"The gods have much to answer for," I said quietly. "But while you still can, you must struggle against your delusions, especially those which pose a danger to others. Renounce this idea you have about Motho, Lucullus. Say it aloud, so that Marcus can hear."

His face became a tragedy mask. The struggle within him was so great that he trembled. Marcus, weeping more openly than his brother, gripped his arm to steady him.

"Motho . . . is *not* Varius. There, I've said it! Though every fiber of my being tells me it's a lie, I'll say it again: Motho is not Varius."

"Say that you won't harm him," I whispered.

Lucullus shut his eyes tightly and clenched his fists. "I shall not harm him!"

I turned and left the brothers alone, to find what comfort they could beneath the branches of the cherry tree called Most-Precious-of-All.

So I came to taste my first cherry; so I made the acquaintance of Lucullus, to whom I never spoke again.

The months that followed marked the pinnacle of a life which, to any outsider, must have appeared especially blessed by the gods. Lucullus celebrated a magnificent triumph (at which the rebel general Varius did not appear). Also, a son was born to him, healthy and whole. Lucullus named the boy Marcus, and was said to dote upon him shamelessly. His marriage to Servilia was less happy; he eventually accused her of adultery and divorced her. Whether the charge was true, or the result of a delusion, I never knew.

Those months brought other changes, some very sad. Our conversation about Lucullus was one of my last encounters with my dear friend, Lucius Claudius, who fell dead one autumn afternoon in the Forum, clutching his chest. To my astonishment, Lucius did make me heir to his Etruscan farm—he had not been jesting that day in his garden. At about the same time, Cicero defeated Catilina and won his campaign for the consulship, making him a New Man among the nobility—the first of his family to attain Rome's highest office. Of my move to the Etruscan countryside, and of the great and tragic events of Cicero's consulship, I have written elsewhere.

An era of enormous tumult was beginning. Steadfast Republicans like Cicero and Cato desperately looked to Lucullus, with his immense wealth and prestige, to rise up as a bulwark against the looming ambitions of warlords like Caesar and Pompey. Lucullus failed to meet their expectations. Instead he withdrew more and more from public life into an existence of sensual pleasure and seclusion. People said Lucullus had lost his ambition. Conventional wisdom presumed he had been corrupted by Greek philosophy and Asian luxury. Few knew that his mind had begun rapidly to fail, for Lucullus and Marcus did everything possible to hide that fact for as long as they could.

By the time of his death, several years after I met him, Lucullus was as helpless as a baby, completely under the care of his brother. A curious rumor attended his demise: one of his beloved cherry trees had died, and Lucullus, denied the delicacy he most desired, had lost the will to live.

Lucullus had faded from the scene, but the people of Rome recalled his glory days and reacted strongly to his death. Great funeral games were held, with gladiatorial contests and reenactments on a massive scale of some of his more famous victories. During the period of public mourning, his gardens were opened to the public. I braved the crowds for the chance to see them again. If anything, the exotic flowers were more beautiful and the foliage more luxuriant than I remembered.

Escaping from the crowd to walk down a secluded pathway, I came upon a gardener on all fours, tending to a rose bush. The slave heard my approach and glanced up at me with his single eye. I smiled, recognizing Motho. I thought he might recognize me in return, but he said nothing, and with hardly a pause he went back to what he was doing.

I walked on, surrounded by the smell of roses.

The Life and Times of Gordianus the Finder: A Partial Chronology

This list places all the short stories and the novels (published so far) of the Roma Sub Rosa series in chronological order, along with certain seminal events, such as births and deaths. Seasons, months, or (where it is possible to know) specific dates of occurrence are given in parentheses. The short stories previously collected in *The House of the Vestals* are followed by a double-dagger (‡); the stories that appear in the present volume are followed by an asterisk (*).

B.C. 110	Gordianus born at Rome
108	Catilina born
106	Cicero born near Arpinum (3 January)
	Bethesda born at Alexandria
100	Julius Caesar born (traditional date)
90	Events of "The Alexandrian Cat"‡

73   "The House of the Vestals"‡ (spring)

"A Gladiator Dies Only Once"* (June and after)

Spartacus slave revolt begins (September)

72   Oppianicus is murdered

Arms of Nemesis (September); the murder of Lucius Licinius at Baiae

71   Final defeat of Spartacus (March)

70   Gordiana (Diana) born to Gordianus and Bethesda at Rome (August)

"Poppy and the Poisoned Cake"*

Virgil born

67   Pompey clears the seas of piracy

64   "The Cherries of Lucullus"* (spring)

Gordianus moves to the Etruscan farm (autumn)

63   *Catilina's Riddle* (story begins 1 June 63, epilogue ends August 58); the consulship of Cicero and the conspiracy of Catilina

60   Titus and Titania (the Twins) born to Eco and Menenia at Rome (spring)

Caesar, Pompey, and Crassus form the First Triumvirate

56   *The Venus Throw* (January to 5 April); the murder of the philosopher Dio

55   Pompey builds the first permanent theater in Rome

52   *A Murder on the Appian Way* (18 January to April); the murder of Clodius and the burning of the Senate House

Aulus born to Diana and Davus at Rome (October)

49   *Rubicon* (January to March); Caesar crosses the
        Rubicon River and civil war begins
        Last Seen in Massilia (late summer to fall);
        Trebonius, under Caesar's command, lays
        siege to Massilia

48   *A Mist of Prophecies* (story begins 9 August);
        Gordianus investigates the death of the
        woman known as Cassandra
        Caesar defeats Pompey at Pharsalus (9 August)
        and pursues him to Egypt
        The Judgment of Caesar (story begins 27
        September); Gordianus travels to Egypt;
        Caesar arrives in Alexandria where he
        confronts the royal siblings Cleopatra and
        Ptolemy

47   Bethesda is born to Diana and Davus at Rome
        Ptolemy Caesar (Caesarion) is born to Cleopatra
        (23 June)

44   Caesar is assassinated at Rome (15 March)

HISTORICAL NOTES

"The Consul's Wife" grew out of two desires: to deal with Sempronia, one of the more remarkable women of her age, and to explore the role of the chariot race at this period of the Roman Republic. No one who saw the movie *Ben-Hur* as a child could ever forget the spectacular chariot race staged (long before the advent of computer-generated images) with live riders and horses and an audience of thousands. *Ben-Hur* left indelible images in my mind; for further research, I turned to *Sport in Greece and Rome* by H. A. Harris (Thames and Hudson/Cornell University Press, 1972), a *veddy* British take on Roman racing and gambling that includes an amusing list of translated Latin names for actual horses.

The *Daily Acts* referred to in the story actually existed, as we know from references to the *Acta Diurna* in Cicero and Petronius; my use of the *Daily Acts* owes a debt to a very funny but painfully dated hard-boiled mystery titled *The Julius Caesar Murder Case* by

Wallace Irwin, published in 1935, in which the intrepid "reporter" Manny (short for Manlius) snoops out trouble along the Tiber.

As for Sempronia, readers may learn more about her in Sallust's *Conspiracy of Catiline*, which gives an intriguing description of her pedigree, character, and motives; not only did she play a small role in that conspiracy, but she was the mother of Decimus Brutus, who with the more famous Junius Brutus was one of the assassins of Caesar. In an early draft of my novel *Catilina's Riddle*, I wrote a lengthy passage describing her, which I later decided to cut; I was glad to be able to return to Sempronia in "The Consul's Wife." "That she was a daughter of Gaius Gracchus is unlikely," writes Erich Gruen in *The Last Generation of the Roman Republic* (University of California Press, 1974), but it is intriguing to speculate that Sempronia might nonetheless have been a descendant of that radical firebrand of the late Republic who was murdered by the ruling class and achieved the status of a populist martyr.

"If a Cyclops Could Vanish in the Blink of an Eye" reflects on the domestic life of Gordianus. Cats were still something of a novelty in Rome at this time, and not universally welcomed. The cultural clash of East and West, as exemplified by the different worldviews of Gordianus and the Egyptian-born Bethesda, will increasingly become a part of the fabric of cosmopolitan Roman life, as the emerging world capital attracts new people and new ideas from the faraway lands drawn into her orbit.

Of all the historical incidents between *Roman Blood* and *Arms of Nemesis*, the most notable is the revolt of Sertorius; "The White Fawn" tells his story. The fabulous tale of the white fawn is given in several sources, including Plutarch's biography of the rebel general. The discontent of those who flocked to Sertorius's side presages the growing discord in Rome, where a series of escalating disruptions will eventually climax in the civil wars that put an end to the republic forever.

In 2000, on a book tour to Portugal, my publisher arranged a private tour of the excavations of a garum manufactory located directly beneath a bank building in downtown Lisbon (ancient Olisipo); that experience inspired me to take Gordianus to such a manufactory, and to uncover "Something Fishy in Pompeii." Readers craving a taste of garum can make their own; consult *A Taste of Ancient Rome* by Ilaria Gozzini Giacosa (University of Chicago Press, 1992), which gives the recipe of Gargilius Martialis, who wrote in the third century A.D.

How Hiero, tyrant of Syracuse, put a puzzle to the inventor Archimedes, who solved it in a bathtub with the cry "Eureka!", is a famous tale from the ancient world. When I came across Cicero's claim (in his *Tusculan Disputations*) to have rediscovered the neglected tomb of Archimedes, I decided there must be a mystery yarn to be made from such material, and so "Archimedes's Tomb" came to be written. The sixteenth idyll of Theocritus, extolling the good government of Hiero's reign, makes an interesting contrast to Cicero's own *Verrine Orations*, which exposed rampant corruption and mismanagement in the Roman-run Sicily of his own time.

Reading Theocritus during my research for "Archimedes's Tomb," I came across the poet's twenty-third idyll, which became the inspiration for "Death by Eros." The details of the spurned lover, the cold-hearted boy, the suicide, the pool, and the statue of Eros are all from Theocritus. In his version, death is a result of divine, not human, vengeance; I turned the poet's moral fable into a murder mystery. "Death by Eros" was originally written for *Yesterday's Blood: An Ellis Peters Memorial Anthology* (Headline, 1998), in which various authors paid homage to the late creator of Brother Cadfael. In that book, I noted that the story's theme "would be familiar to Ellis Peters, who frequently cast lovers (secret and otherwise) among her characters. In her tales, for the most part, love is vindicated and lovers triumph; would that it could have been so for the various lovers in this story."

Having never written at any length about gladiators, I decided to do so with "A Gladiator Dies Only Once." The financial and critical success of the movie *Gladiator* was something of a puzzle to me (inspiring me to post my own review of the film at my Web site), but the timeless fascination of the gladiator cannot be denied. Not all Romans craved the sight of bloodshed in the arena (Cicero found the combats distasteful); nonetheless, the distinctly Roman tradition that linked blood sports with funeral games eventually grew into a cultural mania. Centuries later, these gruesome enterprises continue to puzzle us, prick at our conscience, and tickle our prurient interest.

"Poppy and the Poisoned Cake" was written at the height of the Clinton impeachment scandal; hence its cynical flavor. The details of the crime can be found in Valerius Maximus (5.9.1) and are further explicated in Gruen's *The Last Generation of the Roman Republic* (particularly on page 527). Cicero's quip regarding the piece of cake is recounted by Plutarch; that I have tied it to this particular case is an exercise of artistic license. (Small-world tidbit: The Palla in this story is the same Palla whose property was said to have been stolen by Marcus Caelius; that accusation was one of the counts against Caelius, along with the murder of an Egyptian envoy, in the trial at the center of my novel *The Venus Throw*. The ruling class of Gordianus's Rome was a very tight-knit community, indeed.)

"The Cherries of Lucullus" was inspired, in a roundabout way, by a reader in Germany, Stefan Cramme, who maintains a Web site about fiction set in ancient Rome (www.hist-rom.de). When my editor told me a new paperback edition of *Roman Blood* would be forthcoming, giving me a chance to correct any small errors in the book, I contacted Cramme, whose knowledge of ancient Rome is encyclopedic, and asked him to "do his worst." Cramme informed me of an anachronism, which until then seemed to have slipped past every other reader: in *Roman Blood*, in a moment of erotic reverie, Gordianus commented that Bethesda's lips were "like cherries." Alas, as

Cramme pointed out, most historians agree that cherries did not appear in Rome until they were brought back from the Black Sea region by the returning general Lucullus around 66 B.C.—fourteen years after the action of *Roman Blood*. Since it appeared unlikely that Gordianus could have used cherries as a simile, I amended that reference. In current paperback editions of *Roman Blood*, Bethesda's lips are likened not to cherries but to pomegranates—an echo, perhaps not entirely fortunate, of a line uttered by the wicked Nefretiri (Anne Baxter) to taunt Moses (Charlton Heston) in the campy film classic *The Ten Commandments*.

No historical novelist likes to be found in error, and the problem of cherries at Rome continued to nag at me. I did further research into the diffusion of cherries around the Mediterranean, and discovered that the sources are not entirely unanimous in asserting that cherries were unknown in Rome prior to Lucullus's return from the Black Sea region, and so there is a slight chance that Gordianus's musing was not anachronistic after all; but a more significant result of my research was a growing fascination with Lucullus and his amazing career. (Plutarch's biography makes splendid reading.) Never having touched upon him in the course of the novels, I decided to do so with a short story—and at the same time, to confront head-on that business about cherries and exorcise it from my psyche once and for all. Thus "The Cherries of Lucullus" was conceived. The incident of the gardener Motho is fictional, but the members of Lucullus's circle, including the philosopher Antiochus, Arcesislaus the sculptor, and the poet Aulus Archias, were actual persons, and all the pertinent details of Lucullus's remarkable rise and sad decline are based on fact.